Praise for Steve Frech

'I absolutely LOVED this book … An unputdownable
page turner of a read'

'This book just pulls you right in … I couldn't put it down!'

'One of the best thrillers I've read this year'

'So gripping I just could not stop reading'

'Like riding a rollercoaster … Should be on everyone's
reading list'

'I burned through this'

'I was hooked from page one'

D0721206

STEVE FRECH lives in Los Angeles. In addition to writing, he produces and hosts the *Random Awesomeness Podcast*, an improv-comedy quiz show that has been performed at Upright Citizens Brigade, The Improv, iO West, and Nerdist.

Also by Steve Frech

Nightingale House
Dark Hollows

Deadly Games

STEVE FRECH

ONE PLACE. MANY STORIES

HQ
An imprint of HarperCollins*Publishers* Ltd
1 London Bridge Street
London SE1 9GF

www.harpercollins.co.uk

HarperCollins*Publishers*
1st Floor, Watermarque Building, Ringsend Road
Dublin 4, Ireland

This paperback edition 2021

This edition published in Great Britain by
HQ, an imprint of HarperCollins*Publishers* Ltd 2021

ISBN: 9780008372217

MIX
Paper from
responsible sources
FSC™ C007454

This book is produced from independently certified FSC™ paper
to ensure responsible forest management.

For more information visit: www.harpercollins.co.uk/green

Printed and bound in Great Britain by
CPI Group (UK) Ltd, Croydon CR0 4YY

To my HQ family and especially you, Abigail;
Thank you.

Chapter 1

My phone pings with a text.

I'm not going to answer it. Not even going to look.

When you're being led by a detective down a hall at a police station to be interviewed, it's not the time to respond to what is probably a message from your boss, asking you to come in twenty minutes early for your shift tomorrow.

At the end of the hall, Detective Mendez motions to an open door and I step inside.

The walls are painted cinderblock. The floor is concrete.

In the middle of the room is a metal table with metal chairs on either side. There's a file resting on the corner of the table.

"Again, I'd like to thank you for coming in and talking to me," Detective Mendez says, following me into the room. "Please, have a seat."

He indicates the chair on the other side of the table, away from the file.

"Of course." The confusion in my voice is genuine as I ease myself into the chair.

He comfortably lowers himself into the chair on the other side of the table.

"I'll try to make this as quick as I can. We're just asking some questions, trying to get an overall picture of things."

"Okay." I nod. "Um, what things?"

He leans forward, resting his elbows on the table and lacing his fingers together.

"How well do you know Emily Parker?"

How well do I know Emily Parker?

I know everything about her, the same way I know everything about a lot of people. I know their name, their birthday, their kids' names, where they live, where they work. I know when they get that big promotion. I know how they feel about that cute coworker they haven't told their spouse about. I know when things are bad at home. Hell, I know when people are on anti-biotics. I know all this stuff because they tell it to me; freely, willingly, because everyone wants to be my friend, even though they don't know a thing about me.

They tell me all these things because I'm their bartender.

Of course, with Emily Parker, it's a little more complicated but I sort of knew this was coming.

Katie, my coworker, was interviewed earlier this morning by Detective Mendez and as I pulled into the parking lot of the police station, she texted me the heads-up that they had asked her about Emily. She said she didn't know why they were asking, but that she had kept me out of it; a fact I very much appreciated.

"Mr. Davis?" Detective Mendez asks from the other side of the table.

There are some things about Emily and I that I'd rather not discuss and I know she feels the same way. I need to buy a little more time so I can figure out what's going on and talk to Emily.

Luckily, I have the training to bullshit all day, if need be.

"You can call me Clay."

"Your ID says that your name is Franklin Davis."

"Yeah, but everyone calls me Clay. In my business, you make

2

a lot more in tips with a cool name. I found that out when I worked at one of those corporate chains where you have to wear a nametag and like, buttons with witty sayings, you know? Well, one day, I forgot my nametag, so I had to wear a spare one we had in the office. For one shift, my name was 'Clay', and you wouldn't believe how much more in tips I made that day. So, I decided to stick with it."

"That's really interesting," Detective Mendez says, dryly, while making a note on his pad.

"Thanks."

I can't tell if he's being sarcastic or not. He's got this perfectly neutral, bulldog expression and while bulldogs look kind of dumb, you're pretty sure they could rip your arm off if they felt so inclined.

"Do you often do that?" he asks.

"Do what?"

"Lie to people."

Is he being serious? What is happening, right now?

"It's just a work thing." I shrug.

He makes another note and looks up from his pad.

"So, Mr. Davis ... I'm sorry, Clay," Detective Mendez says, maybe sincerely. "You still haven't answered my question."

"I'm sorry. What was the question?"

"How did you know Emily Parker?"

"Well, she's a regular at my bar. She comes in from time to time. She's one of my best regulars, actually— Wait ... Wait. What do you mean 'how *did* I know Emily Parker'?"

Detective Mendez gets a slight, pained expression and his eyes inadvertently glance at the file resting on the table.

"Mr. Davis, we're just asking some questions and we know that she was at the bar two nights ago," he says, trying to be reassuring.

"No. What did you mean by that?" I can't help the worry that finds its way into my tone. "Has something happened to her?"

3

"Mr. Davis, I'm not sure it's the right time—"

"Please. Tell me, did something happen to her?"

Detective Mendez sighs, reaches over, flips open the file, takes out a photo, and slides it in front of me. And then another. And another.

At first, I can't process what I'm seeing. Then, it becomes clear. The horror sets in and bile climbs up my throat.

This can't be real. It can't be, but it is.

Oh my god.

Cold beads of sweat pop from my forehead. My heart is slamming into my chest.

Detective Mendez leans forward further.

"Mr. Davis ... Clay ... How did you know Emily Parker?"

Let me back this up to that night.

"Goose martini. Filthy. One olive!" Mr. Collins calls over the din of the crowd.

"You got it."

Good. He's in a chipper mood. Things must be going better at home.

Mr. Collins, a retired fifty-something aerospace engineering consultant, has been coming to The Gryphon for years. A filthy Goose martini was his standard drink and I used to start making it the second I saw him walk through the door, but for the past few weeks, he's been drinking cheap scotch, neat. He and his wife have been having problems. He's never told me this, directly, but it's obvious to me. He's been down, quiet, and the times he's come into The Gryphon recently, he goes outside whenever he gets a phone call. He doesn't want anyone to hear him, which is what you do when it's personal. On slow nights, I've watched him through the window while he was on the phone. The body language, the pleading posture, all point to problems at home. This is the kind of stuff you notice when you work behind the bar; the stuff that you as a patron don't realize you're doing, but

4

your bartender sees all of it. And if Mr. Collins is back to his favorite drink, that means he's happy, which means I'm happy, because he'll be tipping big.

I head to the well and start working on his martini.

My partner in crime, Katie Watson, one of the main attractions at The Gryphon, is holding court at the end of the bar. She brings in tons of business and I'm the one to grind out the drinks. Don't get me wrong, I'm a good-looking guy. I've got a thick, sculpted beard, sleeves of tattoos, keep a regular schedule at the gym, and I've got a sharp wit that has earned me my own little knot of admirers, but Katie is straight out of a 1950's pinup calendar, and she's wearing a black leather corset that is fighting a losing battle with her breasts.

I can't keep up with that, not even going to try and that's what makes us a perfect team.

"Coming right up!" Katie shouts to someone and goes for the beer taps behind me. "Clay!" she calls out as she approaches. "Can you make me a Bullet Rye Old Fashioned while you're at the well?"

"Yep."

"Thank you," she says, and slaps my ass as she passes.

I do not recommend doing this at your place of employment, but this is not sexual harassment. I'm not going to call HR. This is bartending. When you bartend with someone, you're going to experience a lot of physical contact with them; a *lot* of physical contact. Your bodies are going to press together and you're gonna bump uglies as you try to get around each other. You have to get physically comfortable with your coworkers very quickly. Katie and I passed that obstacle a long time ago. We've been working together for years and we do it so well, people have nicknamed us "The Dream Team". We've developed such a rhythm that we know when to help each other without asking, we silently agree on who should handle which customers, we know when the other is having a bad night, and out of that working relationship, we've grown into best friends.

The group of guys standing near the well are staring at me with what I can only describe as the equivalent of high-fives.

"You have the best job in the world," one of them says.

"Damn right," I reply.

It is pretty great.

The Gryphon is a block from the ocean in the town of Avalon, which is about halfway between San Francisco and Monterey. I literally found this place by throwing a dart at a map. Not kidding. I had gotten fed up with living and working in Los Angeles. All the bartenders who were waiting to be discovered by a casting agent had done my head in. I pinned a map of the US to my wall, took a couple steps back, and fired. I knew I wanted to stay in California, so I took a general aim in that direction. The nearest town to the point of the dart was Avalon. That was that. I didn't worry about finding a job. I had the experience where I could walk in and get a job at any bar that was hiring, and people drink everywhere. They drink when times are good and when times are bad. Bartending is the only job that is bulletproof.

So, I packed up my stuff, moved to Avalon, and found my current employment: The Gryphon.

This town is a mix of everything, and from the first time I stepped through the door of The Gryphon, I knew I had found something special. Nowhere on the building does it say "The Gryphon". It's too hip for that. Instead, there's this cool neon sign in the shape of a gryphon above the door as you enter. I've been working here for five years and it's by far the best gig I've ever had. It has this cool, library vibe with some subtle hints of steampunk thrown in. It brings in everyone from locals, to surfers, to hipsters, to yuppies, to businessmen, to you name it.

Such is life on the central California coast.

The Gryphon isn't a dive, so I don't have to deal with the bums or the seedy crowd, and it isn't corporate, so I don't have to worry about ridiculous oversight, company mantras, or secret shoppers coming in to make sure I was pushing the specials. The money is really good for how easy the work is. Of course, I don't want to bartend forever, but for now, I'm perfectly happy where I'm at.

I pop the shaker tin onto the cup containing Mr. Collins' martini, raise it above my head, and start to shake it. The rattling ice makes a sound like maracas.

Before I get started on the Old Fashioned, I glance to the slender guy with the shock of wiry red hair, long, spindly nose, and tortoise-shell glasses sitting at the bar, writing in his little notebook.

"You doing okay, Mr. Loomis?" I ask.

He nods without looking up.

Sydney Loomis is a weird dude.

He's been coming to The Gryphon since before I showed up. He walks in, sits in the same chair, orders three gins on the rocks with lemon over the span of a few hours, simply watches everyone and everything, but never says a word, only writes in his notebook, and then leaves. He's incredibly out of place, but he's an institution at The Gryphon. The one night a week that we're closed, he drinks at a bar down the street. He's not a big tipper, but he always tips, and any bartender will tell you those are the people who pay the rent. You always make sure they are happy, and since Mr. Loomis is happy, it's time to start the show.

With my free hand, I begin to build the Old Fashioned. I glance down the bar to my left to make sure a certain someone is watching.

She is.

Emily Parker.

She's in her forties and impossibly sexy. She's got blond, wavy hair, and a body born of yoga and morning jogs on the beach. She's watching me with an appreciative eye as she takes a sip from her almost spent vodka tonic.

I bring the martini down, hit the shaker against the side of the bar, which causes the tin to jump off, and strain the martini into the chilled glass. Then, I grab a cherry and toss it high in the air above the Old Fashioned. I quickly dump the shaker into the sink next to me, snatch an olive, and drop it into the martini, just as the cherry falls into the Old Fashioned with a light *plop*.

The crowd around me applauds and I take a bow.

Katie finishes pouring the beer and joins in the applause by adding a loud "whoop". With her free hand, she slaps my ass, again, and reaches around my waist to grab the Old Fashioned.

"Thank you, Clay!" she says.

"Can you take this martini over to Mr. Collins?" I ask.

"Sure," she says, carefully adding the martini to the drinks she's carrying. "By the way, can we switch 'out-times' tonight?"

"Tonight?"

"Yeah. I want to go home early."

"You want to leave early, but you're not going home," I say with mock disapproval.

"Not really your business, but you owe me for all the times I've traded with you so you could 'leave early but not go home'."

Damn.

I do owe her for multiple occasions in the past where she's traded with me so that I could leave early.

I roll my eyes. "Yeah. Okay. Fine."

"Thanks," she says, kissing my cheek and carrying the drinks away.

Time to deliver some bad news.

Avoiding all the outstretched hands and requests for drinks, I slink down the bar to Emily.

The one person I make certain to avoid is the customer that I've labelled 'The Blonde'. She's been coming in from time to time over the past couple of months, always on her own. Unlike almost everyone else in here, I don't know who she is or what she does. She's never hung out at the bar or tried to strike up a conversation with me. She keeps to herself, which I would totally respect, except for the fact that she's insistent to the point of being rude if she's not served right away, even if the bar is busy. Also, she doesn't tip, and carries herself with a "holier-than-thou" air. One time, she felt that I took too long getting her a Cape Cod and complained to our manager, Alex, about my service. She treats Katie the same way. So, we've had a not-so-pleasant relationship. I still haven't caught her name. Kind of don't care, but unfortunately, I've accidentally locked eyes with her as she uses her elbows to knife her way to the bar.

"Can I get a Stella?" she asks.

"You got it!" I reply and keep moving.

I have no intention of pouring her beer.

Katie can take care of her, but that's only if Katie wants to, which I doubt. If she tries to get Katie's attention, there's enough people for Katie to pretend like she didn't hear her. We bartenders do it all the time to customers we don't care for.

"Doing okay over here?" I ask, pulling up across the bar from Emily.

"Just fine, Mr. Showoff."

"Gotta give them what they want."

"I wasn't complaining," she says, giving me a seductive glance and taking the last sip of her drink.

"Another one?"

She ponders the wet ice in her glass. "Nah. I'll settle up."

She reaches into her sleek, expensive handbag, extracts a couple of twenties, and hands them to me.

I reach for the cash. "Listen, I'm gonna be a little late, tonight. I have to close."

She pulls the cash back. "I thought you were going to be cut first."

"I was, but I kind of owe Katie for our last time … and the time before that."

Emily gets a dreamy, far-away look. "I remember those times."

"Sorry. You know that I would do anything—"

"It's okay," she sighs. "I may just get started without you."

"I promise I won't keep you waiting."

"You'd better not." She hands me the cash.

"I'll be right back," I say with a sly smile.

After closing out her tab at the register, I put the change and receipt into a faux-leather check presenter embossed with The Gryphon logo. Even though there's nothing for her to sign, I slip a pen into the presenter and lay it on the bar in front of her.

"Have a good night."

"I'd better," she replies.

We hold each other's gaze before the surrounding requests for drinks become too much.

I turn to the thirsty crowd and start knocking them down, taking three orders at a time, mentally triaging them to be the most effective with my time. I bury myself "in the weeds" and do what I do best, which is crank out drinks.

Occasionally, I'll steal a glance back towards Emily to catch her watching me, but finally, after a blitz of pouring beers and shaking cocktails, I turn to look and she's gone.

The countdown to last call begins …

The evening settles into a steady hum.

Katie takes advantage of the lull and begins clearing the bar top of empty pints and highballs. She reaches for the check presenter left by Emily on the bar.

"No, no, no! I got that one. That's for me!" I call out, quickly moving towards her.

She picks up the check presenter and turns to me.

"You two are ridiculous. You know that, right?"

"I have no idea what you mean," I reply as though I'm offended.

"Cut the crap, Clay. Yes, you do."

Of course, I do. Others may have their suspicions, but Katie is the only one who knows for sure about Emily and I.

"Okay. Fine. You think we're ridiculous?" I ask.

She nods, emphatically.

"Two words, Katie: Nick McDermitt."

Her cheeks flush with anger.

Nick McDermitt is an ex-ballplayer for the Giants. He and his wife used to occasionally stop by The Gryphon until the night Mrs. McDermitt found Katie and her husband in the parking lot being a little too flirty. In fact, they were being waaaaaay too flirty. After that, we never saw the McDermitts again.

Our manager, Alex, who's in the office right now, had a talk with Katie. He wasn't going to fire her. She brings in too much business for that, but it was a bad look for the bar. Since then, there has been an informal "Please Don't Bang the Spouses of Our Customers" policy.

Katie presses the check presenter into my chest.

"Just be careful, okay?"

"If by 'careful', you mean 'no nookie in the parking lot', I think I can do that."

She groans and walks away, remembering to toss up a middle finger at me over her shoulder.

I laugh and open the check presenter.

Emily has left all the change, which comes out to about a fifty-dollar tip on a thirty-five-dollar tab. I toss the cash into the tip jar to split with Katie. The receipt is what I'm after, and I'm not disappointed.

Written on the receipt with the pen I provided is a message: "Seaside Motel. Room 37. Don't keep me waiting. You promised."

Tucking the slip of paper into my wallet, I glance up to see Katie shaking her head at me in disgust.

I make the sign of the cross and press my hands together, as if begging for forgiveness.

She gives me one last shake of her head and goes back to cleaning bottles.

It's five past midnight. I'm wiping down the bar while Katie enters her credit card tips into the register. We've stopped serving and

11

the few remaining customers are finishing up their drinks. The music has been turned off and the lights are turned up, which is the universal sign for everyone to get out.

Alex emerges from the office.

"Okay, who is leaving first?"

Katie raises her hand. "That would be me."

Alex pops open Katie's register and runs her sales report.

They disappear into the office to do her checkout. A few minutes later, she reappears, holding her check presenter and counting her credit card tips. She tips out Tommy, our barback, who is mopping the floor, and comes to sit at the bar.

"You want to hand me the tip bucket?" she asks, settling onto a barstool.

Instead of handing it to her, I extract the cash from the bucket and lay the bills on the bar in front of her.

"Keep it. It's yours."

"Seriously?"

"Yeah. I still owe you." I tip the bucket over in my hand. A mass of coins slides into my palm and I deposit it into my pocket. "I'll keep the change."

I really do owe her and I'll still get my credit card tips for tonight. Besides, I love taking the change. I keep it in a jar on my dresser. Every month or so, I'll cash it in. It's usually a couple hundred bucks and I treat it like that ten-dollar bill you find in your jacket pocket at the beginning of autumn. I'll go out for a steak dinner or take a day trip to Napa.

"Thanks," she says, placing the bills in her personal check presenter, which is already stuffed with slips of paper.

"How many numbers you stack?" I ask.

We each have our own check presenter where we keep our change, credit card receipts, cash, order pad. A bartender never wants to leave their check presenter behind. It's also where we keep the phone numbers customers give us. Katie and I have our own little rivalry. We call it "Stacking Numbers". At the end of the night, we'll see who got more phone numbers. It's always Katie, to the point that I have a "ten-phone-number" handicap.

"You don't want to know," she replies, confidently.

"I would like to know who you're having dirty sex time with tonight."

She tuts her tongue at me and takes my hand. "Oh, Clay. Are you jealous?"

"Hey, don't worry about me. I'm having my fun."

"Yeah," she says, sadly. "But it's not with me, is it?"

I snatch my hand away. "I hate you."

"No, you don't." She laughs and gives me a knowing wink.

"Then get out of here before I do."

She hops off the stool and heads for the door. "Good night, Tommy!"

"Good night, Katie!" he replies, bent over the mop.

"Good night, Clay!"

"Good night, Worst Person in the World!"

She stops in the door, turns, and blows me a kiss. I grudgingly return the gesture. She "catches" it, slaps it on her backside, and heads out into the street.

"You two are a walking lawsuit."

I spin around to see Alex standing at the end of the bar.

"You ready?" he asks.

"Yeah."

"Let's go," he says, popping my drawer and running the sales report.

I grab the drawer and follow him into the office.

Alex sits at his computer, working on the inventory while I count my drawer.

I quickly make sure that the amount in the drawer is the same as when I started, minus my sales and credit card tips.

"I'm dropping four-hundred-twelve dollars and sixty-two cents and my credit card tips are two-seventy-four-eighty," I announce and hold the drawer out to Alex.

"Give me a sec," he says, slowly pecking away on the keyboard.

I keep the drawer right where it is, hovering near his face, and don't say a word.

Unable to ignore it any longer, he looks at me. "You got somewhere to be?"

"Maybe. And she doesn't like to be kept waiting."

He snatches the drawer. "I don't want to know."

He double checks my figures and counts the money.

"Perfect, as always," he says, signing my drop slip. "Get out of here and do whatever it is you need to do."

I pop out of my chair and head for the door. I know I shouldn't, but I can't resist getting one last dig before I go.

"I'll tell her you said 'hi.'"

He jams his fingers into his ears. "La-la-la-la-can't-hear-you-la-la-la-don't-want-to-know-la-la-la."

"Have a good night!" I shout as I exit the office.

A couple minutes later, I'm driving past the gazebo in the town square, which is festooned with lights, as I head towards to the ocean. I'm already anticipating the sex that is mere minutes away.

Emily and I have been seeing each other for months and it hasn't lost any of its shine. It's fun, thrilling, and a challenge in its own way. It's almost entirely physical. That's not to say that I don't care about her. I do, but we've laid our cards on the table and "love" was not one of them. We are fine with it.

I didn't even know that she was married the first time it happened. She conveniently forgot to mention it. She came into the bar by herself, we flirted all night, and ended up in bed together. It was fun and I thought it was a casual, one-night stand.

Then, a few nights later, she came into The Gryphon with her

14

husband. They were a total physical mismatch. She was stunning, sensual. He was a short, thin, balding man. He was also arrogant, demanding, and eager to show her off. To put it another way, he was that stereotypical short, incredibly insecure guy with a massive chip on his shoulder, but as a hedge fund manager, he possessed the one asset that levelled the playing field: money. For Emily's part, she was bored.

I was speechless.

She and I kept exchanging glances while he would speak too loudly about his business deals in an attempt to impress those around him, many of whom were also millionaires and didn't care for his grandstanding.

At one point, he theatrically announced that he was stepping outside to take a phone call about a "billion-dollar project". After our shared glances, I took the opportunity to approach her.

"So, who exactly is that?" I asked.

"My husband," she casually remarked.

"You didn't tell me you were married."

"You didn't ask." She smiled. "Don't worry. You're not in danger of breaking up a happy family or anything. There's no kids. We're only married in a legal sense."

"Isn't that kind of the only sense that matters?"

"Do you regret the other night?"

My hesitation was all the answer she needed.

"Good," she said with a look that intimated we were just getting started.

I liked her little game. I liked her confidence. I liked her.

Just then, her husband re-entered the bar with a swagger and a sense of self-congratulation that was almost comical. He ordered a round of shots for the bar in celebration of the deal he had just closed. I was pretty sure he was lying but he paid the exorbitant tab and insisted that Katie and I join in by taking a shot. We were more than happy to oblige. Emily and I locked eyes as we took our shot.

In that moment, I knew that what I had thought was a one-night stand was far from over.

When they closed out their tab, I thanked them, saying I hoped they would be back soon, all the while keeping my eyes on her.

A week later, she did come back, sans husband.

"No date, tonight?" I asked as she settled into the bar, surprised at how happy I was to see her.

"Nope."

"That's too bad."

"Isn't it? I'm so distraught. I'm going to be so lonely."

"Tragic." I nodded. "Well, I suppose I can keep you company if you don't mind me working for a bit."

She gave me a hungry look from head to toe. "Not at all."

She and I continued our parries and jabs of innuendo all night.

When I got off work, we went back to her place. Her husband was in San Francisco at some conference, so we had sex on his prized pool table. I was in a little bit of a dry spell, but from our two encounters, it was obvious that she had been starved for a long time.

Ever since then, we had seized every opportunity offered to us.

I turn right onto Kensington, which runs along the beach, and will take me right to the Seaside Motel. If I had kept going straight instead of turning, I would have eventually reached the Parker house.

When we first started sleeping together, that's exactly what I would have done, but not anymore. We've stopped meeting there. We had been on a mission to break in every room in the house while her husband was away. It was fantastic. We'd have sex, and afterwards I'd walk naked out of their bedroom onto the massive balcony, which was cantilevered out over the sea, and marvel at the view. Then, I'd go back inside and we'd have sex in another room. I would spend the night. We'd fall asleep around eight in the morning. I'd wake up and leave from her place to go to work in the afternoon with a flushed glow and receive looks of scorn from Katie and Alex. Alex knew I was seeing someone but he didn't know who. Katie figured it out because she had seen us flirting at the bar multiple times.

Emily isn't a fan of being a trophy wife. In fact, she hates it and she's most definitely not a fan of her husband. She's talked about leaving him, but she loves the perks and she's not in a hurry to part with them. Eventually, she began swinging from paranoid about being caught to "devil-may-care". Sometimes, she would be overly worried about someone finding out and cancel plans at the last minute. Other times, she would rail about how much she didn't care and we'd take ridiculous risks, like the time during one of my shift breaks when we had sex on the hood of a car on a side street next to The Gryphon. Then there were the times when we'd just go back to her place.

But we were sloppy and almost got caught at her house.

After that, she decided that we would only meet up at motels, and not good ones, either. In my opinion, I think it's lame but after a world of fine Egyptian cotton sheets, marble floors, and a private wine cellar, she finds it a turn-on to meet at these "seedy" establishments. Whatever. I'm not going to say no to getting the chance to see her.

Which is why I'm already fantasizing about what I'll find in room 37 as I pull into the Seaside Motel parking lot. It's an L-shaped, single-story structure forever stuck in the 1960s, but it's not without its charm. They've embraced the retro look and there's a stunning view of the ocean across the road. Avalon is full of places like this.

I park in one of the numerous open spots. The air is heavy

with the taste of salt, churned up by the low tide. I notice that there's another gray Honda Civic just like mine occupying one of the spaces near the office. I don't see her car, which is not a surprise. Like I said, since we were almost caught, she's become much more paranoid. She always pays cash at the bar. She also bought a burner phone for us to text each other. She finds Uber and Lyft drivers that will accept cash to drive her to our hookups. There's always a handful of them outside The Gryphon. They don't want to split the fare with the rideshare company. They also don't want to pay the taxes and their riders don't want anything showing up on their credit card statements for their spouses to find. Emily also discovered that motels like the Seaside often don't need to see your ID or make a record of your stay if you offer to pay double their nightly rate in cash. She's become very good at making sure that her husband's assistant won't find something that will raise any red flags on her credit cards, which her husband pays, and that he won't see anything in her bank accounts, which he controls.

I stroll down the row of numbered doors. Next to each is a large window. Some have the curtains drawn and are illuminated by the soft, flickering glow of a television but at this hour, most of them are dark.

I arrive at number 37.

The lights are on inside.

On the other side of this door, I'm going to find her on the bed, naked, lying on her side, head propped up in her hand. She'll ask something like "What took you so long?". That'll be the extent of our conversation. I'm already anticipating her hungry touch, her skill, and reveling in the abandon that comes from two people who are comfortable with the fact that they are using each other for physical pleasure.

I push on the door, but it doesn't budge. She normally leaves it open a fraction of an inch so that she doesn't have to get up to let me in, but there's a problem; the deadbolt is engaged.

What the hell?

I check the number on the door.

Yeah, this is room 37.

I lightly knock.

"Emily?"

There's no answer.

Maybe she fell asleep.

I knock again. No response.

I take out my phone, dial her burner phone, and press my ear to the door. There's the sound of a cellphone ringing inside. If she fell asleep, I'm hoping the call will wake her up, even though the knocking should have.

The call goes to the generic, automated voicemail.

I glance around. The Seaside Motel is quiet. There's only the soft buzz of the lamps in the parking lot and the crashing of waves from across the road.

I'm about to knock again when my phone pings with a text message.

I don't want to do this tonight.

Damnit.

Sorry I'm late, I text back. *But it doesn't have to ruin our evening.*

I hit send.

I'm too tired, is her reply.

My thumbs fly across the screen. *Okay, but can you please open the door?*

There's a long pause and then my phone pings again.

No. Leave me alone.

Great. She's having one of *those* nights, but even on nights that she's suddenly canceled plans in the past, we'd at least talk for a little bit.

It's no good trying to get her to reconsider. She's made up her mind.

So, that's tonight down the drain. It's a little weird but I'm not gonna waste any more time with this. If it's not happening, it's not happening.

Good night, I text.

She doesn't answer.

Once inside my apartment, I head straight for the bathroom. I hop in the shower, scrub down, towel off, and climb into bed, not a little frustrated.

She'll be back at the bar in a week or two, and we'll pick up where we left off.

Still, that was odd.

She's run hot and cold but that felt different.

Oh, well.

As I drift off to sleep, I think about what was behind that door, waiting for me ...

Sitting across from Detective Mendez, staring at these photos, now, I know.

Even though there is a Post-it Note covering a section of the image, I can see Emily's face.

Mechanically and in utter shock, I reach towards the photo.

"Mr. Davis, I'm sorry but you can't—"

I remove the Post-it.

There's Emily, just as I had envisioned her, lying naked on the bed, but her throat has been cut by an angry slash across her windpipe. Her lifeless eyes stare up at the ceiling. The mattress is soaked in blood.

"Mr. Davis!"

The photo is snatched away but the image is seared into my brain.

"I'm— I'm sorry. I didn't mean to—" I stammer. "I wasn't thinking."

"It's my fault," Detective Mendez says, replacing the photo into the folder. "I shouldn't have shown you that."

While he collects himself, I stare at the other photos which show the rest of the room; there's her clothes placed neatly on a chair, her purse, keys, and cellphone on the table.

I'm able to choke down the bile in my throat, but my hands continue to shake. The beads of sweat that popped on my forehead have run down into my eyes. In all of this, there's this strange thought in my head amidst the chaos that something was wrong about the photos; something other than the woman I was sleeping with lying naked on the bed with her throat cut. Something was missing.

"Mr. Davis? ... Clay?" Detective Mendez asks.

Of course, I'm going to tell him. I'm going to tell him everything; the affair, the sneaking around, the motels, all of it but with everything that's happened in the past thirty seconds, I've forgotten how to speak.

Wait. I know what was missing in the photo: Emily's burner phone.

I check the photos again, to be sure. There's no sign of it.

Which means whoever killed her took it and ...

I suddenly remember the text I received as I was walking down the hall into this room.

My brain on autopilot, I reach into my pocket for my phone.

"Clay?"

"I'm sorry, Detective. I just need to check something ..."

Detective Mendez may as well be on the other side of the world, and it's a good thing that my expression is already at "maximum bewildered" because this text message, sent from Emily's burner phone, has taken what was a surreal situation and turned it into a nightmare.

Keep your mouth shut or I'll tell them about the blood in your car, MY SWEET LITTLE CUPCAKE.

This can't be happening.

Another realization causes my stomach to plummet into my shoes: last night, as I stood outside the door of number 37 at the

21

Seaside Motel, it wasn't Emily that I was texting. It was this guy. He knows who I am. He knows my number ... and he knows about "my sweet little cupcake".

That's impossible! It was a joke!

"Clay? Are you all right?"

My mind snaps into horrible focus.

Whoever this is can easily make the cops think I killed Emily. I didn't, but how can I explain that to Detective Mendez? Yes, we were having an affair. Yes, I was at the Seaside Motel and yes, my fingerprints are on the door, but I didn't kill her. And if I show him this text, and there is blood in my car, how do I explain that? Even if there's not, he's going to ask what "my sweet little cupcake" means, and if I tell him, that's it. I'll be locked up in a cell and whoever did this to Emily goes free.

"Mr. Davis?"

Some sort of survival instinct is triggered. The chaos happening in my head is swept away and I see my situation, clearly. If I try to tell him everything and show him the text, they'll think I did it. I'll be locked up. No one will ever believe me and this guy, whoever he is, walks away.

I can't believe I'm about to do this, but I see no other option.

I have to lie.

I blink my eyes and shake my head in an attempt to concentrate.

"I'm sorry, Detective Mendez. I just—I can't believe it."

"It's all right," Detective Mendez says, picking up the rest of the photos and putting them back in the file folder. "I know it's a shock but I need you to tell me: how did you know Emily Parker?"

"She, um, she was a regular at the bar."

"That's how you met?"

"Yeah ..."

All I can do is keep the panic at bay. This guy, whoever he is,

22

knows who I am. He knows things about me and Emily that no one could possibly know.

"When was the last time you saw her?"

"Um … two nights ago when she came in."

"Did you talk to her?"

"Yes. I served her some drinks."

"How many drinks?"

"A couple of vodka tonics."

"How many?"

"Like, maybe four."

"Did she seem strange to you?"

"No."

"Did she say if she was meeting anyone?"

"No."

He nods and makes a note on his pad of paper. "Who texted you?"

"It was a work thing."

He nods again, not looking up at me.

I'm keeping my trembling hands under the table so he can't see them. I don't know if he believes me. Is he like this all the time, or is this an act to get me to break?

"So, you two were … friendly?"

"I'm a bartender. I'm friendly with everyone. It's my job."

Something about his question causes my mind to click.

What can I get you?

It's the old bartender question. I know it sounds like I'm being subservient to you when I ask, but your answer, what you ask for, your body language, your tone, tells me everything I need to know. Are you happy? Sad? Do you have money? Do you want someone to talk to or do you want to be left alone? You tell me everything about yourself and I'm going to use that to get what I want, which is the biggest tip. But now, looking at Detective Mendez, I think, "What can I get you?" What is it that you want that I can give you that will get me what I want, which is out of this room?

His demeanor is infuriating. He's not intense. He's not digging too deep. He just wants some answers. He seems like kind of a loner, someone without many social skills; a Sydney Loomis-type. I need to be casual with him. Make him forget about his social awkwardness.

"Did she ever come into your bar with anyone?" he asks.

There. Right there is my "out".

I try to relax or at least appear to relax because relaxation is not possible under the circumstances, and treat the table between us like it's the bar. I slip into my bartending persona, which makes me feel gross, but I have to get out of this room.

"Yeah," I say with a slight roll of the eyes. "Her husband. Have you seen that guy?"

The change in him is instant. He loosens up.

"Yes," he says, mirroring my eyeroll. His lips tighten into something almost like a smile.

My tactic worked. Now, we're just two guys talking.

"He's a piece of work."

"Mmm-hmm," he says, making another note. "How did they seem to you?"

I shift uncomfortably in my seat.

"It's okay," he says. "I'm only asking for your opinion."

"They were … not great."

"Really?"

"Well, yeah, but nothing like that," I quickly add, pointing to the file. I may have overplayed this. I wanted to get on Detective Mendez's good side to loosen him up so I can get out of here, but I don't want to insinuate some other innocent person is guilty of Emily's murder.

"I see," he says, taking more notes. He's much more at ease. "But she came in by herself two nights ago?"

"Yes."

"And where did you go after you got off work?"

"Home."

"Can anyone vouch for you?"

"Bachelor for life," I reply with a shrug and a sheepish grin.

He makes a note. "Okay. That's all I've got for now." He takes something from his pocket and slides it across the table. "Here's my card. If you think of anything else, please tell me."

There are a million things I could tell him, right now, a million things I want to tell him because I want him to catch whoever did this to Emily, but if her blood is in my car, he will never believe me. No one will.

"Okay." I deposit the card in my pocket and try not to rise too quickly from my chair. I have to get to Katie. I need to know what they asked her. Why did Detective Mendez show me those photos? There's no way he showed them to Katie because she would have said something. So, why me?

Detective Mendez stands. "And let me know if you plan to go out of town any time soon, okay?"

"Sure."

"Thank you, Mr. Davis," he says, extending his hand. "Oh, I'm sorry. I mean 'Clay.'"

"No problem," I reply, shaking his hand. He's got a grip.

I being walking towards the door.

"I'm sorry, Clay. One last question."

Well, there it is.

He's done it. He's spotted a crack in my story. He's been playing me. I don't know what this question is, but I'm sure it's going to pin me to the wall and slap handcuffs on my wrists.

"Yeah?"

"Your bar; The Gryphon. Is it any good?"

Seriously?

"… yeah."

"What makes it good?"

"Me."

He laughs, proving it was the perfect response.

"What's your favorite drink to make?" he asks.

Bartenders hate this question. It's like someone asking you what's your favorite sales report to compile. There are drinks that we know we make well, but that's different than what's our favorite drink to make. I always give the smart-ass answer of "bottles of Bud Lite", but this is the one time that I'm relieved someone is asking me this question. This guy wants a friend.

"I make a mean margarita."

"Really? Well, I may just have to come by and see if you're telling the truth."

The way he says that last part about telling the truth, I'm back to not knowing if he's messing with me, but I've already committed.

"The first one's on me."

He smiles. "Well, all right. Thanks for coming in and, remember; if you think of anything, don't hesitate to call me. I mean that."

"Will do, and I mean it about the margarita, too."

He nods and I head out the door.

I'm staring at my Civic like it's radioactive. My initial urge was to search the inside of the car right then and there, but it would look really suspicious right in the middle of the police station parking lot. I do a quick scan through the windows. I don't see anything, but it could only be a drop or two somewhere. Or there might not be any blood at all.

I didn't see anything when I drove over here but I wasn't really looking for—

My phone pings again.

It's another text from Emily's burner phone. Up until a few minutes ago, I would have expected it to have been a flirtatious message about how she couldn't wait until she saw me again and I would try to convince her to meet up with me as soon as possible.

I'll never receive another message from her like that again.

Instead, this one reads:

26

447 Sweetgrass Road. Evergreen Terrace Apartments. #208. Inside the apartment you'll find something that will help you. It's blue. You'll know it when you see it. The key to the apartment is under the doormat.

Once more, I glance to the packed park across the street and the countless cafés and restaurant patios that stretch into the distance.

He's here. He has to be, right? He had to have been watching me as I walked into the station. That's how he knew when to send that first message. How else—

Another text message arrives and answers my question.

You look nervous. Don't be nervous. It's time to play.

Chapter 2

"What are you doing? What are you doing? What are you doing?" I panic-mumble for about the seventieth time.

What else can I do? My head is still spinning. I can't have this guy tell the cops about "my sweet little cupcake" or the blood in my car. I have to buy time until I can figure out what to do, and the only way to do that is to play his game, for now. This might be stupid but I don't have any options at this point.

From my vantage point, parked across the street, Evergreen Terrace Apartments doesn't look to be anything special; just another faceless courtyard building of units whose best feature is that it's perched on the edge of Avalon, and you can sort of see the ocean from here. The banner out front announces that they have a vacancy. The bunches of balloons, tied to the railings leading up to the front door, bob and bounce off of each other in the sun-soaked breeze.

The glass doors lead to the lobby, which is nothing more than a room with some older couches. Set into the side wall are the mailboxes for the apartments. Another set of glass doors leads me to the open courtyard. The leasing office is to the left. There's a small pool that takes up most of the courtyard, where two kids are splashing while their mothers sit in patio chairs, talking. They notice me. I smile at them, trying to play it cool, but I'm worried they can tell that I'm barely holding myself together.

After crossing the courtyard, I take the stairs up to the second level.

Number 208 is in the corner. The red doormat on the floor proclaims "Welcome!". I glance around. The only signs of life are the kids and moms at the pool. I quickly reach down and flip up a corner of the doormat. Sure enough, there's a gleaming, metal key. I snatch it up, slide it into the deadbolt, and twist. The bolt slides back and I push open the door.

I'm expecting a million things: a torture room, someone pointing a gun in my face, or even the police. The one thing I'm not expecting is exactly what I get: a boring apartment. From the front door, I can see almost the whole interior. The furnishings are spartan. There's a couch and a loveseat in the living room in front of a television. In the kitchen, there's a table and chairs. Past the kitchen is a short hallway, leading to a bedroom.

"Hello?" I call out before setting foot in the apartment, which is, of course, a stupid thing to do if the killer is waiting for me, somewhere inside. But I can already feel it. No one's been here in a while.

A quick search of the apartment confirms my suspicions.

There's a king-sized bed in the bedroom. The closets are empty. In the small bathroom, there's some toiletries and two tooth-brushes in a cup next to the sink. Two towels hang off the rack. I head back to the kitchen, which is almost bare. There are a couple of plates in the cabinets and utensils in a drawer. The fridge is empty. So is the pantry.

I don't see anything that could "help me", much less anything that is blue.

In the living room, I check under the cushions of the couch and behind the television. Nothing. At least nothing that looks like something I would "know it when I see it".

What is this guy talking about?

I open all the cabinets and drawers in the kitchen. I check the undersides of the shelves in the pantry to see if there is something written or taped to them, like a piece of paper, telling me what to do next.

Back in the bedroom, I pull the sheets off the bed. Nothing. There's nothing on the walls, either. It's the most basic apartment imaginable. Revisiting the bathroom, I check under the sink, in the tub, and the medicine cabinet behind the mirror. I even check the toilet tank. There's nothing here.

After my fruitless search, I find myself back in the living room.

Frustrated, I send a text to Emily's burner phone: *What am I looking for?*

I hit send and wait … and wait …

Are you there? I type and hit send.

The tumbling nerves in my stomach solidify into a knot, which grows into a sense of dread that courses though my limbs.

I make another search of the apartment as I wait for a response that I'm certain isn't coming.

"This is a waste of time," I say aloud as I rifle through all the cabinets and drawers in the kitchen, again. I can't shake the feeling that I've made a terrible mistake in coming here.

Another search of the closet in the bedroom yields nothing.

I'm left standing in the bedroom, scrutinizing the bare walls.

Goddamnit!

I take out my phone and text.

What am I looking for?!!

I hit send and wait.

The cursor blinks at me.

My dread turns to anger.

This guy is messing with me.

There's nothing here and there's probably nothing in my car. I had just believed him when he said he put blood in it, and his knowledge of "my sweet little cupcake" caused me to panic and lie to Detective Mendez, when I should have come clean.

30

I know how to fix this.

There's an easy way to prove this guy is full of shit, and when I do, I'm going right to Detective Mendez. I don't care how this guy knows about "my sweet little cupcake". It was a joke. Detective Mendez will understand.

Let's settle this.

Stepping out of the lobby and into the Avalon sunshine, I stride purposefully across the street towards my Civic.

There's no blood in my car. Once I prove it, I'm going to tell Detective Mendez about the affair. It doesn't make me a killer. Yes, I was at the Seaside Motel, but I didn't kill her. I'll show him the texts. No, I don't know who they're from and no, I don't know where the phone is now, and yes, I lied before, but he'll understand. I'll tell him about "my little cupcake", which will be difficult, but I've got to do it. This guy said he put Emily's blood in my car. I'll show Detective Mendez and he'll see that there's no blood in it. Sure, he'll be skeptical at first and it'll take a lot of explaining, but he'll believe me. He'll understand why I lied and I'll admit that it was a terrible mistake.

I unlock the car doors and open all of them. I begin meticulously inspecting every inch of the interior. My car is pretty tidy and any blood is going to stand out against the cloth seats. When I don't find anything, I'm going straight to Detective Mendez.

There are no signs of blood on the dashboard. No signs of blood on the seats. There are no signs of blood on the floor, either, only some wayward nickels, two pens I swiped from The Gryphon. These spots right here? They're from a while back when I spilled a little bit of energy drink.

Each passing moment of non-discovery adds to my confidence.

I pick myself up from inspecting the floor of the back seat, go to the driver's side, and pull the handle to pop the trunk.

I'm already rehearsing what I'm going to say to Detective Mendez.

31

"First off, Detective, I want to apologize. I lied to you but I hope you understand. You see, Emily Parker and I were having an affair, but I didn't kill her. It was someone else who is now using our relationship to set me up. They said to keep quiet or else they would tell you about the blood in my car, but as you can see—"

I lift the lid of the trunk.

My lungs seize up.

There's a moment of shock and revulsion. Then, I slam the lid closed but continue staring at the trunk.

I can't go back to Detective Mendez. Not now. Not ever.

The inside of the trunk of my car is covered in blood.

Chapter 3

My knocking on the door goes unanswered for two seconds, so I knock again.

"Katie? Katie, it's me." I'm trying to keep my voice somewhere between making sure she can hear me and not alerting the neighbors.

I rap on the door, again.

"C'mon, Katie. Open the door."

She's home. I know she is. This is the only night of the week that The Gryphon is closed and there's a car parked in the spot outside her apartment.

"Katie, please, op—"

The door flies open. Katie is staring at me with wide, furious eyes and flaring nostrils.

"What the hell are you doing?" she asks, breathlessly.

"I have to talk to you. Can I come in?"

"It is *really* not a good time."

"Listen, I have to know: what did the police ask you about Emily and me?"

"Clay," she says, quickly glancing over her shoulder. "This is not the—"

"Please. It's important."

"They asked me about the other night at the bar and I said that I didn't talk to her and that you were the one taking care of her."

"Did you tell them that we were … you know?"

"Sleeping together? No. I didn't. Now, can we talk about this later?"

"Did they show you the photos?"

"What photos? What are you talking about?"

"Katie, Emily Parker's dead."

She freezes, her mouth hanging open.

"Someone killed her at the motel where we were going to meet, and when I spoke to the police today, I didn't tell them about us."

Katie finally finds her voice. "You have to go back, right now, and tell them."

"I can't. Something's happened and I can't."

"What do you mean you can't? Clay—"

"Katie, please listen to me. I know I screwed up, I do, but if the police ask to speak to you again, I need you to do something for me."

She begins to shake her head. "Clay, stop."

"Please, *please*, don't tell them or anybody else about Emily and me."

"Shut up, now!"

"Katie, please listen to me; I had nothing to do with this. I swear to you I didn't, but something happened, and I need some time to figure it out. All I'm asking is that you don't tell anyone about me and Emily."

"Clay, stop!" she hisses through clenched teeth.

"Katie? Everything okay?" a voice asks from the inside of her darkened apartment.

For the first time, I notice what Katie is wearing: a long T-shirt and apparently nothing else. Her hair is disheveled and her cheeks are flushed. Also, that's not her car in her parking spot.

Over her shoulder, a man appears from the doorway to the

bedroom. He has sharp facial features, a chiseled, hairy chest, and he's wearing jeans he hasn't bothered to button.

Katie closes her eyes and hangs her head in resignation. "Everything's fine. I'll be back in a second."

The man and I lock eyes.

Oh, this is sooo bad.

"Hello, Mr. McDermitt," I say in a quiet mixture of panic and mortification.

"Clay," he responds. He's obviously not my biggest fan at the moment.

I wanted to talk to Katie to keep anyone else from finding out about Emily and I. Instead, I've added one more person.

He turns and goes back into the bedroom.

"Seriously?" I ask Katie.

"I told you it was a bad time."

"That his car in your spot?"

"Yes. Mine's in the shop. Nick's been giving me rides to and from work. That's one of the reasons I wanted to switch out-times the other night. He gave me a ride to the station this morning and we came back here."

"And what does Mrs. McDermitt think about this?"

Katie crosses her arms.

"I wouldn't know because they split last month and are you really going to try to lecture me on this particular subject at the moment?"

I take a breath. "I'm sorry. I'm being an asshole."

She takes it down a notch as well.

"You want to tell me what happened?" she asks.

If I tell her about the text messages and the blood in my car, she's going to call the police, and I wouldn't blame her.

"I can't tell you right now."

"Clay—"

"I can't but I need you to know that I didn't kill her, okay? You know I could never do that, right?"

"Of course I do." She sighs. "But you know something, don't you?"

"Not me, but someone does."

"Who?"

"I don't know."

"Then, I don't understand. Why don't you go to the police?"

"Because I can't."

"Why?"

"Because I *can't*."

She shakes her head, unhappy with my answer but knows it's all she's going to get. "Fine … But tell me; are you okay?"

I'm not sure how to answer, but decide to be honest. "I don't know, but, Katie, please promise that you won't tell anyone about Emily and me."

She tilts her face towards the ground.

"Katie?"

She looks up at me with eyes that are filled not only with worry, but with hurt. "Clay, if they ask me, I'm not going to lie to the police … and I can't believe you would ask me to do that now, when she's dead."

"Please, Katie, it's really—"

"I'm not going to lie to the cops," she says quietly, but forcefully.

She's right. I can't ask one of my best friends to risk getting herself in a lot of trouble for me. I rapidly come up with a middle ground.

"I apologize. It was wrong of me to ask you to lie to the cops."

She won't make eye contact.

"Katie, please look at me."

She reluctantly does.

"You believe me when I tell you I didn't kill Emily, right?"

"Yes, of course, I believe you."

"Okay. How about this, if they ask you about us, don't lie, but please promise me that you won't say anything unless they ask. Is that fair?"

It's a really fine hair to split, but I'm hoping our friendship wins me the benefit of the doubt.

She considers it. "... okay."

"Yeah?"

She shrugs. "Okay."

"Thank you."

"So, what are you going to do?"

"I can't tell you that."

"Why not?"

"Because I don't want you knowing something else that you wouldn't want to lie about."

There's a long, awkward pause as we've hit a wall where I won't say anymore and she won't promise anything else.

"I'll, uh, I'll let you get back to ... that," I say with a wave of my hand towards the bedroom door.

Katie scoffs in disbelief.

"See you at work, tomorrow," she replies and closes the door in my face.

My apartment has never felt so small. So claustrophobic.

I pull the shades on every window but can't shake the feeling that there are eyes watching me.

Dinner consists of some reheated leftovers and a beer, but I hardly touch either one as I obsess over watching the news on television and checking the news on my phone. There's nothing about Emily's murder, but it's only a matter of time. A million-aire's wife found naked in bed at a seedy motel with her throat cut? It's a true-crime podcaster's dream.

Midnight hits and I'm still wide awake, trying to imagine what a conversation with Detective Mendez would look like if I tried to come clean now.

I could possibly explain away one thing or maybe two, but there are so many things that I would have to explain. Even if I try to plead that I cared for Emily, it would make me sound crazy, especially when you threw in the blood in my trunk and "my sweet little cupcake".

The ship where I tell everything to Detective Mendez has sailed.

I go to the bathroom and take a shower. I open the small window to the blind alley behind my apartment building to let out the steam.

While standing under the stinging hot water and trying to think my way through this, I realize that even the text messages don't really help me. How can I prove it's her phone? I mean, it's a burner phone that no one else knew about. Also, where is it? If I admit that I was at the motel that night, wouldn't Detective Mendez assume I took it, and maybe I'm sending the messages to myself to try to lamely throw him off the scent?

There's no way around it.

This guy has me in a corner and there's no way out.

I climb into bed and hit the lights, but sleep is an impossibility.

Lying in bed, phone in hand, I scroll through the text messages. For the first time in my life, I'm having a panic attack. I can't breathe. My chest hurts and my stomach is boiling. I'm lying here, stewing in my bed, going around in circles, and have no clue as to what I should do next. I want to vent to someone, but who? No way I talk to Detective Mendez. I tried to talk to Katie and that made it worse. There's no one to—

No. There is someone to talk to.

I quickly begin typing into my phone. The letters appear under my last text to Emily's burner phone.

What was that at the apartment?

Send.

I stare at the cursor and start typing again.

Why did you want me to go there?

Send.

I pause ... and then begin furiously typing.

Why did you kill her?

Send.

Why are you doing this?

Send.

What do you want?

Send.

WHO ARE YOU?!!

Send.

Even though I'm lying in bed, I'm out of breath and gripping the phone so tightly, I feel like it's going to break. Under the string of messages, the blinking cursor patiently waits for some more unhinged typing.

Minutes pass.

Finally, my phone goes into sleep mode, darkening the room.

Exhaustion crashes over me. I put the phone on the bedside table, pull the sheets up to my chin, and roll onto my side. My body is drained but my mind is still spinning out of control.

My eyes start to close. I just want to sleep, to escape for a little—

Ping.

I'm instantly alert. I roll over, grab the phone, and unlock the home screen.

There's one new message from Emily's burner phone.

It's a single emoji reply ...

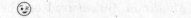

Chapter 4

So, it's no surprise that I didn't get a whole lot of sleep last night.

I don't know how long I stared at my phone, but eventually, I started to fall asleep and dropped it on my face, hitting my nose and bringing tears to my eyes.

Don't laugh. You've done it, too, and I'm not in the mood.

I didn't reply to the pyscho's text and I'm not going to. It would only give him the chance to further mess with my head.

I slept in fits and starts. Every time I woke up, I was certain I had been asleep for hours, only to check my phone and discover that it had been a few minutes. Then, I would check the news. Around four in the morning, the dam broke.

There it was.

Murder in Avalon! read one headline. *Wife of Hedge Fund Manager Found Dead* read another, which kind of pissed me off; that their best description of Emily was the "wife of hedge fund manager". That's really the best they could do? And on it went. Each article was accompanied by photos of Emily's smiling face and the exterior of the Seaside Motel. Thankfully, the details of her murder were sparse. She had been discovered by a cleaning lady in the early hours of yesterday morning. There were some mentions of her throat being cut, but nothing about her being found naked on the bed.

Needless to say, I was up and out of bed in minutes. I chugged coffee and watched the local morning news, which didn't have anything on the murder, yet. The next few hours were spent scrolling through the news but there were no updates. By noon, I realized that I was driving myself crazy. I had to get away from it, just for a bit, and did everything I could to get my mind on something, anything else. I cleaned my apartment. I tried to go for a jog but was nearly run over by a car because I wasn't paying attention. Then, I went to the gym, only to half-ass a few machines, and walk out.

I'm just going through the motions.

It's all I can do.

Four o'clock. Time to open The Gryphon.

I've done this so many times, it's become mundane. I could do it in my sleep, but now it's surreal. Everything looks the same as those hundreds of other times, but feels different, like everyone is watching me. Every window, every alley, every parked car that I can't see the inside of holds a pair of spying eyes.

The blinking white figure of a stickman tells me it's safe to cross the street, but I hesitate.

The Blonde is on the other side of the crosswalk, but she doesn't start crossing. She's waiting. What is she doing? Is she waiting for The Gryphon to open? She's never done that before.

No. It looks like she's waiting for me.

I cross the street and try to avoid eye contact as I step onto the curb to walk past her.

"Clay?" she asks.

I pretend I don't hear her as I reach the door, extracting my key ring.

"Clay Davis?"

"We open in an hour," I reply, fumbling with the key.

"Actually, I wanted to talk to you."

"Look, I'm sorry that I didn't get your Stella the other night. I was busy and—"

"No. That's not what I wanted to talk to you about."

She's obviously not going away, so let's get whatever this is over with.

"Okay … What did you want to talk to me about?"

"Emily Parker."

On second thought, let's not even start this.

"Absolutely not." I hasten my efforts to open the door.

"Please. Just a few questions."

"'Just a few questions'? I'm sorry. Who are you?" I ask.

"No, I'm sorry. I totally messed this up," she says, reaching into her pocket and holding out her card. "My name is Genevieve Winters. I'm with the *San Francisco Herald*."

Of course, she's a reporter. Of course she is. I don't even reach for the card.

"Not interested."

"I saw how you two acted towards one another at the bar," she says.

Get away! Get away from her! my mind screams, which only adds to the trouble with the key. Talking to a reporter isn't going to help me figure out who killed Emily. It can only get me into more trouble.

"I have nothing to say."

I'm trying desperately to open the door, but my hands are shaking so bad, that when I attempt one last time to get the key in the lock, it slides off to the side and I stab the glass, thankfully not hard enough to break it. That's it. She's got me.

I finally look up.

She's staring at me like a ravenous cat eyeing a one-legged mouse.

"How well did you know her?" she asks.

"I said I'm not talking to—"

"Were you sleeping with her?"

There's no use trying to hide the fact that she's rattled me. I give up with the keys and give her my full attention.

"What makes you ask that?"

"Like I said, I saw you two together. You seemed pretty … friendly."

"I'm a bartender. 'Friendly' is kind of my job."

"I've also heard some things."

"Have you?"

She nods.

That question pops into my head; the question that changed the dynamic with Detective Mendez: What can I get you? What is it that I can get you that will get me what I want, and what I want to know is where she heard anything?

I take her card and stuff it into my hip pocket.

"Tell me where you heard that."

"If I tell you, will you answer some questions for me?"

I make a small show like I'm thinking it over. "Sure."

She smiles triumphantly, confident that she has a story.

"I've been asking around. People said you two were friendly. Some people were suspicious that she was having an affair. Even the police know about it."

I scoff. "The fact that she was found naked in a dive motel wasn't enough to tip them off that she was having an affair? You are some reporter."

"How did you know she was found naked?" Genevieve asks.

This is exactly why I didn't want to start talking to her.

She waits.

"Are you gonna answer my question or—?"

"Nope," I reply, finally sliding the key into the lock.

"'Nope'? What do you mean, 'nope'?"

"I'm not going to answer your questions."

Her initial shock quickly gives way to anger. "We had a deal."

"Yeah. I know."

I've gotten what I needed and it's clear that I know more than she does.

"Are—are you serious?"

"Yep," I say, opening the door.

She's royally pissed and not without justification, but I don't feel sorry for her.

She gives me a furious stare. "You open in an hour?"

"That's what the sign says."

"Well, maybe I'll come back, have a drink, and talk to some of your customers to see what they might know."

"I'm afraid I can't let you harass them like that. If you come back, I'll call the cops."

"Fine," she fires back, not missing a beat. "Maybe I'll just have a drink. It's a free country."

"Yeah but, see, it's not a free bar." I step inside the door.

"You need to talk to me! I can get your story out th—"

"There's a TGI Friday's up the road. It strikes me as a little more of your kind of place."

I close the door and lock it.

There's a brief staring contest through the glass before she turns and leaves.

Once she's out of sight, I sprint to the bathroom and vomit.

This is the longest damn shift of my life.

Katie and I have barely said two words to each other. I want to ask her for more details about her talk with Detective Mendez yesterday, but there's no time for talk and she doesn't seem very receptive. We're still putting on our little show for the customers, but the ass-slaps are half-assed, the innuendo is weak, and I'm on a short fuse, which is obvious to all.

Things that I normally let slide are setting me off.

A group of office bros order a round of drinks but only one at a time, which is a massive headache. I make one drink, bring it to them, then they order another drink. If you're in a group, order your drinks all at once. Good bartenders can work on three or four drinks at a time. They're going one by one.

"Come on, guys," I sigh after their fifth drink order. "Let's act like we've been to a bar, before." That stops them in their tracks. Katie shoots me a look.

Later on, a man studying the bottles in the display asks, "What's the cheapest thing you've got here?"

"You," I reply.

He blinks like I just slapped him in the face, which I sort of metaphorically did. He walks back to his table, has a quick word with his friends, and they collect their things and leave.

To top it all off, I'm catching snippets of customers talking about Emily's murder. It's not much. Not everyone knew her, but there's enough that I try to discreetly eavesdrop on the conversation, only to find that, like Genevieve, I know more about what happened than they do.

An hour later, a young-looking girl orders a Long Island. I ask for her ID and she hands me this utter monstrosity of a fake. There's no hologram. The picture is dark and obviously photoshopped. And here's the secret to spotting a fake ID: a blind person can do it. It's not how an ID looks, but how it feels. Is it flimsy or hard? When you handle hundreds of IDs a night, you know what a real one feels like in your hand. This thing is as hard as a rock. Avalon is a wealthy town, so we get our fair share of rich kids who have spent a lot of money on fake IDs and I've seen some damn good ones, but this is laughable. Normally, I'd hand the ID back, and wish her good luck someplace else, but tonight ain't that night.

"Are you kidding me?"

"What?"

"What is this?" I ask, holding the ID.

Her eyes go wide. "It's, uh … It's my ID."

"Okay, I don't know how much money you paid for this, little girl, but you should ask for a refund."

45

She wilts but for some stupid reason keeps pushing it. "It's … It's real."

I sigh. "The image is shopped and too dark. It's hard as a rock and there's no hologram."

"I—I left it in the wash."

"Now I'm worried that you don't understand how a washing machine works."

"Okay … okay. I'm sorry," she says, holding out her hand. "I'll take it back."

I nonchalantly toss the ID into the trash behind the bar and nod at the door.

"Get out."

Stunned, she turns and quickly leaves.

Wonderful. I've turned into the asshole bartender I've always hated.

"Clay?"

Alex is staring at me from the end of the bar. He's been watching me and obviously doesn't like what he sees.

"Can I talk to you for a second?"

I walk over. "What's up?"

"You okay?"

"I'm fine."

"You don't seem fine. You want to take a break? I know it's been a crazy forty-eight hours."

"No. It's okay. I don't need a break." It's getting late in the evening and the last thing I want to do is stop working because I'll start thinking.

"All right," Alex says, "but if you could do everyone a favor and stop being a jerk, that would be great."

"She was trying to use a fake ID."

"I get that, but she's not the only person you've been a jerk to this evening, is she?"

My shoulders drop. There's nothing to say in my defense.

"Sorry. I'm just on edge."

"Listen, I know that Mrs. Parker was one of your regulars and these past few days have been kind of crazy and if you need a break to calm down, that's fine. Got it?"

"Yeah, I got it."

As I turn back to the bar, I catch a glimpse of a lonely figure sitting at a high-top table against the wall across the room.

Genevieve Winters.

She's sipping a cocktail by herself, eyes locked on me. In front of her on the table is a notepad.

There's a knot of businessmen two tables over, sizing her up, deciding who's going to make a move.

How did she get in here without me seeing her?!

Once our eyes meet, she casually glances down and starts writing in her notepad.

"Alex! Alex, hold on."

Alex halts his retreat to the office.

"What's up?"

"See that woman sitting over at table twenty-four?"

He glances over and definitely sees her.

"What about her?"

"We have to kick her out."

"What are you talking about? She's been here before."

"She's a reporter. She was waiting for me when I opened up and started harassing me. She said that she was going to ask customers about Mrs. Parker's murder. She's gotta go."

He takes another look.

"She's not talking to anyone right now."

"But she might."

"We're not kicking her out. She's minding her own business."

"But—"

"Clay, we're not kicking out someone for calmly having a drink at a table, especially if they're a reporter. I wouldn't want her writing about it."

"She's a reporter, not a Yelp reviewer."

"Whatever. If you're not going to take a break, then you need to calm down, stop being a jerk, and do your job, okay?"

With that, he turns and goes back to the office.

Through the sea of people, Genevieve has been watching my discussion with Alex. She can tell from my expression that she won and gives me a light wave with her fingers.

I fight the urge to wave one finger at her and get back to work.

The hours drag on.

Alex's little admonishment worked for a time, but the simmering frustration is building into a flame and it's fanned every time I look over and see Genevieve watching me. She's been here for six hours. It feels like twelve. Every drink order is tedious. Every special instruction for a martini or a Manhattan is a chore. Every question is inane.

"What do you have on tap?" a customer asks while looking directly at the beer taps.

"What can you make?" a girl asks, which is like asking an accountant what they can "math".

Business picks up steam. Katie and Tommy are pulling my dead weight. I botch one drink order after another. People are simply yelling their orders at me before I acknowledge them.

"Can I get a beer?"

"Yeah. Hold on."

"Can I get a Jack and Coke?"

I grit my teeth. "One sec."

"Hey, man! We want to do a round of shots!"

"I'll get to you in a minute," I mutter through a clenched jaw.

"Buddy, we've been waiting here forever."

Okay. To hell with this. To hell with Alex. To hell with Katie. To hell with The Gryphon.

"Can I get one of those margaritas you were telling me about?" someone asks behind me.

And to hell with whoever this clown is.

I turn from the beer I'm pouring and look back over my shoulder. "Yeah. Can you hold on for one damn sec—"

Detective Mendez sticks out from the crowd like a sore thumb. He's short, stocky, alone, and smiling at me like we're long-time friends.

My heart takes the stairs to my throat.

"S-sure ..." I manage to sputter. "Be right there."

I finish the beer, drop it off, take a breath, and then start his margarita while keeping a side-eye on him as he surveys bar and the crowd.

I take my time. This will be—no, this has to be—the greatest margarita I've ever made.

I salt the rim of a glass, then fill it and a shaker with ice. Using the most expensive tequila we've got, I pour a shot into the shaker ... better make it a double. This would normally be a sixty-dollar drink, but it's on the house. Alex and the inventory will have to suffer. I add the Cointreau and our own special margarita mix, squeeze a few lime wedges in there, give it a vigorous couple of shakes, and strain it over the ice in the salted glass. After popping a lime wedge on the rim, I set it on the bar in front of him.

"There you have it," I say. "The Clay Special."

He regards it with that infuriating neutral expression, but thanks to Genevieve, I know that he knows or at least suspects that Emily was having an affair.

"You weren't kidding," he says with a gesture to the crowd. "This place is great."

"Wait until you try the margarita." I smile. It's unnerving how quickly I've slipped back into my bartender persona.

He brings the straw to his lips and takes a sip. He leans back and his eyes light up.

"Whoa! That packs a punch." He takes a second sip. "But it's really smooth," he adds before going in for a third sip.

"The trick is to really shake it. It makes it ice-cold and knocks down the heat of the alcohol but not the flavor of the tequila."

He raises the glass. "Mr. Davis, you are an artist."

I execute a humble bow as he takes another healthy pull on the straw, and sets the drink on the bar.

"This is the perfect end to the work day," he says.

"How's that going?" It's not the most subtle transition I've ever made, but I need to get him talking, and fast. At any moment, I'm expecting Genevieve to come crashing over.

He considers the straw sticking out of the margarita. "I probably shouldn't say anything."

Yeah, he probably shouldn't, but I can tell he really wants to. If he didn't, he would have looked me in the eye. That's something you notice on this side of the bar. As I've said before; you know more about what someone wants from their body language rather than the words they use.

"I completely understand." I nod, sympathetically. "A lot of people here have been talking about it, though."

"Really? What are they saying?"

I shrug, trying to play it cool.

"Just rumors about her ... personal life."

He leans in. "What kind of rumors?"

I slyly look to the left and right, making sure no one will hear our conversation. "You know, like maybe she was having some fun with someone on the side."

He's enjoying this. We're conspirators, again, just like back at the station.

"Well ... that might be true," he says.

"Yeah? What makes you say that?"

He takes another long sip of his margarita, which is now almost finished. "Well, we were looking at her accounts yesterday for anything suspicious and found out that she was renting an apartment, just outside of Avalon."

An apartment? She never told me about ... Oh, shit ... Shit ... SHIT!

"We were at the apartment this afternoon," he continues.

"We found her fingerprints and the fingerprints of one other person. Looks like they were using it as a little bootypad." His eyes go wide and he covers his mouth in embarrassment, but can't resist a short laugh. "Okay, I definitely shouldn't have said that." He laughs, again. "Whoa! Clay! What did you put in this margarita?"

I'm laughing with him but I want to scream.

I know the apartment. Of course I do. I was there, yesterday, putting my fingerprints all over everything. Through my nervous laughter, all I see is that damn winky-face emoji.

Detective Mendez catches his breath and wipes his eyes. "That's our little secret, okay?"

"Of course."

He polishes off the margarita and sets the glass down on the bar. "Mmmmmm. That is delicious. You do know your trade, Mr. Davis."

"Thank you," I say and want to add, "but if it's all the same, I want to curl up in a ball and die".

They're not closer to catching the psycho who killed Emily. They're closer to catching *me*.

He stands up and steps away from the bar. "Well, I should go. Wouldn't be a good look for a detective to get pulled over for a DUI, but thank you for the drink." He extends his hand.

"My pleasure," I say, shaking it, because of course, Detective Mendez is the kind of guy who thinks I pay my rent in hand-shakes.

Someone moves behind me.

Detective Mendez glances past me to my left. "Ah, Ms. Watson."

I turn in time to see Katie stop dead in her tracks, almost dropping the drinks she's carrying.

"Oh … hi, Detective Mendez."

"We're still on for another discussion at the station tomorrow, right?"

"… of course," she says, trying not to look at me.

"Great. You two have a good night," Detective Mendez says, turns and walks out the door.

I stare at the door, unable to move. Now my heart is taking the elevator to my feet.

He knows that Emily was having an affair and he's already asked Katie for another interview. It has to be because of the apartment and the rumors. He's going to ask Katie, and Katie isn't going to lie.

"Clay?" Katie asks from a million miles away. "Clay, I was going to tell you but he called me this morning bef—"

"It's okay," I reply, mechanically.

In the span of two seconds, I've already forgotten her and Detective Mendez and the blood in my car and the fact that I've been set up by a murderer. I've forgotten all of it because moments after Detective Mendez walks out the door, someone else walks in.

Henry Parker; the husband of the late Emily Parker.

And he's walking right towards me like he has something to say.

Chapter 5

He's wearing jeans and a button-down blazer.

I quickly shoot a glance to my left. Genevieve's head is up, watching us, completely ignoring the middle-aged business guy who's trying to talk to her.

STOP! TURN AROUND AND WALK OUT THE DOOR, PLEASE! I mentally plead to Mr. Parker.

Unable to read my mind, he continues towards me, stopping directly across the bar from where I'm standing. He sizes me up like he's looking at an unwashed child.

My response is instant, automatic, ingrained, and under the circumstances, ridiculous. "Good evening, sir. What can I get you?"

"I understand that you knew my wife," he says, quietly.

"Sir," I say, lowering my voice to match his. "I'm sorry but this is not the time—"

"Shut up and listen to me."

I'm too stunned to respond.

"I know. I know everything about you and Emily." He pauses, and snorts in derision. "Do you do that often? Hmm? Screw other men's wives? Does that make you feel important? Like you've actually done something with your shitty, wasted life?"

"Sir, I'm going to have to ask you to leave."

"No. You listen to me," he insists.

There's a couple sitting at the bar two seats down from where we're standing. I don't think they can hear what we're saying, but they've definitely noticed the tension and they're trying to hide the fact that they're watching us.

Sooner rather than later, and by that, I mean a few seconds from now, people are going to start recognizing him like Genevieve has.

"Sir," I repeat with emphasis. "I'm not going to ask you again—"

"'My sweet little cupcake,'" he hisses, barely above a whisper.

My knees buckle momentarily, but I'm able to stay upright.

He continues to pin me to the spot with an intense stare.

"I know the trouble you're in … That we're *both* in … And as much as I hate to admit it, Mr. Davis, we have to work together, all right?"

We have officially crossed into *The Twilight Zone*.

The trouble that we're "both" in? What does that even mean?

"I … I have no idea what you're talking about."

"No, not yet. That's why I need to talk to you. You need to know what's going on. It's the only way you and I get through this."

"'You and I'? Is there a 'you and I', here?" I've gotten good at telling when people are lying and he's not. He's tense, earnest, and maintaining eye contact.

"I need your help with something," he says, reaching for his inside breast pocket. "We have to figure out what this means so we—"

"Stop, stop, stop," I insist.

He blinks at me with his hand just inside his blazer. This is a guy who is not used to being contradicted.

"Not here," I say.

Another quick look over the crowd reveals that Genevieve is

54

out of her chair, notebook in hand, poised like she's about to charge us.

"But I need to talk to you."

"Okay, but not here. Too many people are going to see us and it's only going to make things worse. We have to meet somewhere private."

He considers and comes to a conclusion. "All right. Once you get done with work, come to the house." A disgusted expression crawls across his face. "You know where the house is, right? You've been there?"

I lightly nod. "Yeah. It might not be until around midnight, though."

"Fine. Midnight."

He turns, walks straight to the door, and out into the night.

There's movement out of the corner of my eye. Here comes Genevieve.

She stands at the bar, and looks from the door to me, frantically trying to make a decision; stay here or follow Mr. Parker.

"Okay. Kick me out if you want, what just happened?" she asks breathlessly. "What was that about?"

"I'm sorry. I don't know what you mean."

"Oh, come on. Mr. Parker. The guy who was just here, talking to you. What did he say?"

"Was that Mr. Parker?" I ask, feigning ignorance.

"Cut the crap. What did you two talk about? Why did he leave so quickly?"

"He asked if we had root beer. I told him 'no', and he wasn't happy."

She glares at me, turns, and hurriedly fights her way to the door, rudely shoving people out of her way.

Good.

She's figured I'm not going anywhere for a while, so she's going after Mr. Parker, who I assume is going back to his house to wait for me, but she doesn't know that.

I need to get out of here before she comes back.

I find Katie on the other side of the bar. Thankfully, she missed my brief interaction with Mr. Parker and Genevieve.

"Katie, I need a favor."

"What is it?"

"I need you to close for me tonight."

She tilts her head in disapproval at me. "Clay, I know that you stayed for me the other night, but Nick's picking me up tonight, and I don't want to make him wait."

"I know, but it's *really* important."

"Is it about …?"

"I can't tell you, not when you're going to talk to the police tomorrow."

"I told you; I'm not going to lie."

"No, and I don't want you to, but I might be able to clear this up."

She wavers.

"Katie, if you close for me tonight, I promise, I will take all of your closing shifts for the next month and you and Mr. McDermitt can have all the dirty sex time you want."

Business slows to a crawl. Katie accepted my offer and I'm able to cash out a little before eleven. After checking out and running my report, I give my credit card tips to Katie because, hopefully, she really is saving my ass.

We wish each other a perfunctory "good night" and I hurriedly walk out the door.

Instead of going straight to the Parker house, I park down the street from The Gryphon, amongst the Lyft and Uber drivers, and watch the door, praying that my hunch is right.

About an hour later, my patience is finally rewarded.

There.

A green Hyundai parks in The Gryphon parking lot. Out jumps Genevieve Winters. She hurries to the door since the bar is about to close and goes inside.

I twist the key in the ignition.

She must have followed Mr. Parker, waited for a while, decided that he had just packed it in for the evening, and come back to the bar to harass me a little more.

Too bad. I hope Katie tells her that I left an hour ago.

I pull a u-turn and drive off towards the cliffs.

Chapter 6

Driving past the deserted public beach down the road from the Parker house, I'm reminded of the last time I was on this road.

It was the day that we were almost caught.

Mr. Parker was supposed to be in San Diego that afternoon, so Emily and I had the house to ourselves. We had just finished having sex in the upstairs bedroom. I had gotten out of bed and went out to the balcony overlooking the sea. I stood there, naked, feeling the sun on parts of my body that normally never felt the sun, and looked out over the water. Down to my left was the infinity pool and patio. Directly below, the ocean churned against the rocks.

"How do you get this?" I thought. "Is it only possible to attain this if you're willing to sell your soul? How do you get here?"

My musings were interrupted by Emily's cries from the bedroom.

"Shit! Shit! Shit!"

She had received a text from her husband that the meeting had been canceled and he had flown back, landed at Monterey Regional Airport, and was on his way home. Of course, she and I had been having sex when the text arrived an hour ago, and hadn't seen it.

"You have to go!" she screamed. "You have to get out of here!"

She wouldn't even let me put on my clothes. I scooped them up in my arms, ran down the stairs and out the front door. Jumping into my car, I threw my clothes onto the passenger seat, and peeled off onto the sea road. It was the first and only time I've driven totally naked.

I thought that she was being ridiculous, but to her credit, as soon as the Parker house disappeared in my rearview mirror, I passed Mr. Parker in his Bentley coming the other way. Had I had taken the time to even put my pants on, he would have seen me pulling out of the drive and that would have been game over.

That's what kicked off Emily and I visiting some of Avalon's seedier motels.

There's no one on the road tonight. I have the winding asphalt ribbon perched on the sea cliff to myself.

The Parker house is the only speck of light on the horizon. It's one of those massive, structurally minimalist monstrosities composed of white rectangles stacked on top of one another, with large windows that allow anyone outside to see almost everything going on inside.

Tonight, however, that one speck of light I could see in the distance is the motion-sensor light that illuminates the half-circle drive.

I pull off the sea road and up to the steps to the house. The open-plan ground floor is dimly illuminated by the lights of the infinity pool in the back. They shine through the blue water and dance and ebb across the walls and ceiling.

I walk up the steps to the front door, but stop when I see that it is slightly open.

"Mr. Parker?" I call out through the small crack.

There is only the faint sound of the ocean crashing against the rocks.

I press the doorbell. The chimes sound but after a few moments, there's no answer.

I push and the large, heavy door swings noiselessly inwards. Quietly, I step inside and close it behind me.

The reflection of the infinity pool gives the illusion of movement to the walls and ceiling. It's disorienting and it takes my eyes a second or two to adjust and focus on the shapes in front of me.

There are tables, chairs, couches, the marble floor, and the fireplace, just as I remember them. In one of the chairs is the silhouette of Mr. Parker, facing out the massive window towards the infinity pool and the ocean, beyond.

"Mr. Parker?"

He doesn't move.

"Listen; I want to apologize," I say, stepping towards him. "You're right. Your wife and I were having an affair, but I didn't—"

I'm close enough that I begin to reach out to him, but my foot slides out from under me, and I crash to the floor.

I try to pull myself up, but my hand slips through something slick and warm.

I bring my hand closer to my face. It's covered in a thick liquid that looks almost black in the dimness.

Blood.

I scramble backwards from Mr. Parker, until I'm out of the pool that surrounds him and stand. My hands and clothing are now covered in blood. I look at Mr. Parker.

He's sitting in the chair, arms hanging by his side. His throat is slashed open and his lifeless eyes are staring straight ahead.

I start to hyperventilate. I run my hands through my hair, streaking blood across my scalp, which makes the hyperventilation worse.

I'm going to pass out. My ears are ringing ... wait ...

No. That's not ringing.

Those are police sirens.

60

My mind snaps back into focus.

They're going to find me here. They're going to find me here, covered in Mr. Parker's blood next to his body with my car in the driveway, the trunk of which is covered in Emily Parker's blood. And tomorrow, Katie is going to tell them that I was sleeping with Emily.

"No, no, no, no, no, no, no," I mutter, stumbling around the room. The sirens are growing louder. Faint blue and red lights begin dancing across the walls.

I return to Mr. Parker's body.

Only a few hours ago, this guy was talking to me at the bar. He was asking for my help with something, something that he said would help me understand the trouble we were *both* in.

He was reaching for the inside pocket of his blazer.

I step closer, careful not to slip again on the blood around his feet, and shove my hand into the breast pocket of his blazer. My fingers close on something; a piece of paper. I quickly pull it from his pocket.

There's the screeching of tires as the cop cars skid to a halt outside in the drive.

Stuffing the piece of paper in my back pocket, I race to the stairs, taking them two at a time as they gently curve to the upper floor.

I have no idea where I'm going. My only impulse is to get away.

I come out into the massive, open bedroom just as the front door downstairs is kicked in, accompanied by cries of "Police!", and the sounds of squeaking shoes on the marble floor.

There's nowhere to hide up here. There's the walk-in closet but that'll be the first place they check. The bathroom is no better.

"I got footprints!" someone yells from downstairs.

I look down at my feet. My bloody shoes have left tracks, like something out of a cartoon.

There's only one option.

I dash to the glass sliding door, throw it open, and run to the railing. The backyard is dimly illuminated by the glow from the infinity pool. Below me is nothing but darkness, but I can hear the waves slamming into the rocks. I'm not sure how far down it is. More importantly, I don't know how deep the water is.

Flashlight beams from the stairwell begin bouncing off the ceiling of the bedroom.

This can't be happening. *This can't be happening!*

I grab the railing and throw my feet over. I stand there, and for a brief moment wonder, "How did I get here?"

… and then jump.

Exhausted, I haul myself out of the surf and onto the public beach down the shore from the Parker house.

I collapse onto my back in the sand, take deep breaths, and rub my stinging eyes.

I have to keep moving, but I need a minute. That's all I want. Just one minute.

I roll onto my side and push myself up. A breeze slides off the ocean and washes over me, pressing my cold, wet clothes against my skin.

In the distance, I can see the Parker house. Even from here, the chaos is evident. The lights from the fleet of cop cars strobe off the white walls of the house.

I hold my breath and listen …

Okay, now I really need to keep moving because that is the sound of a helicopter.

But before I do that, I have to see.

As carefully as I can manage, I reach into my pocket and pull out the wet, blood-soaked paper.

I delicately unfold it so it doesn't rip.

The air rushes from my lungs like I've been kicked in the chest. My shoulders sag.

What the hell is this?! How was this supposed to help me?! Is this a joke?!

I'm fighting the urge to scream.

I read it again, and again, and again. It doesn't take long because it's only one, handwritten word, and that word is …

PERKiest

Chapter 7

I have no idea what time it is as I walk back into Avalon.

It has to be somewhere around three, but I can't check my phone because it's dead. I prayed that it would work after letting it dry out, but no amount of pleading or "power button" mashing could coax it back to life. After the hundredth attempt, I finally gave up.

I've stayed far away from the main roads. Occasionally, I'd hear the sound of another wailing cop car, racing to join the circus at the Parker house. In the distance, I could even see the helicopter hovering in the night sky, searching the coast.

The phone is the least of my problems.

The police have my car, the trunk of which is covered in Emily's blood. They've found the car at the home she shared with her husband, who was sitting in the living room with his throat cut only hours after he was seen talking to me. They have my bloody handprints on the floor where I slipped and the railing where I jumped. It won't take them long to match them to the fingerprints in the apartment that I had no idea Emily and I were using as a "bootypad" and to the fingerprints on the door of number 37 at the Seaside Motel.

It's only a matter of time before they find me.

The question is, how long? How long can I hide?

I stop and ask myself, "Why?"

What can I do? I know I didn't kill Emily or her husband, but there's no way anyone would believe me and no way that I can prove it. I don't even have the killer's text messages anymore to create even a hint of doubt.

There's no way around it; I'm one-hundred-percent screwed.

But, right now, more than anything, I just want to sleep. I want to close my eyes for a little bit. The urge to lie down on the side of the road is overwhelming. Asphalt never looked so soft.

But I keep going. One foot in front of the other.

Thankfully, the ocean rinsed the blood from my hair and hands. It took care of most of the blood on my clothes and since I'm wearing my black shirt and pants from work, you can barely see what's left. You can't even tell it's blood … There's something I never thought I'd be happy to say.

Still, I need fresh clothes. The sun will be up in a few hours and I can't look like this. I could wait until a store opens and buy some clothes but I don't want to use my credit or debit card. They've already got to be looking for me.

Thirty-three dollars in sea-soaked bills is all I've got to work with. I need clothes and cash and there's only one place I can go that has both.

I'm praying that they're not already there.

Well, my current run of luck is intact because they're already here.

From two blocks away, I spot the police cruiser parked on the street a few doors down from my apartment.

My adrenalin spikes, overriding my exhaustion.

I duck behind a parked car and wait.

Thankfully, the lights on the cop car don't suddenly blink to life. The siren doesn't kick on. Whoever is sitting in the car didn't see me.

I turn and go up one block to the apartment complex that's

directly behind my own apartment building. I carefully hop the fence into the courtyard, and work around to the back of the complex, where there's a small gate to the alley for the residents to take their trash to the dumpster.

Quietly I push open the swinging gate, step into the alley and walk over to the dumpster, trying to stay in the shadows to keep from being seen.

I quickly go to the small window that leads to my bathroom. I place my hands on the panel of frosted glass, and push up. It slides open. I remove the screen, grab the window frame, and pull myself up. After wriggling through the small space, I land with a heavy thud on the bathroom floor.

It takes a lot to keep from loudly cursing as I think I just screwed up my shoulder but I can't worry about that right now. I've seen enough police procedurals on television to know they have to have a warrant to come inside my apartment.

Even though all the blinds are drawn, I stay low, out of view of the windows. In the bedroom, I take my gym bag out of the closet, and dump the contents onto the floor. Then, I go to the dresser, and start stuffing the bag with clothes. I also change out of my damp black shirt and shove it into the bag, as well. They probably have more than enough on me already, but I don't want to leave the damp shirt, which may have traces of Mr. Parker's blood, to give them anything else. Also, I don't want to waste time changing my pants, so they're staying on for the moment. Just a dry, thick shirt to keep me warm.

Now, for the money.

My change jar is sitting on the dresser. There has to be about two hundred bucks in there. The problem is that it weighs a ton. I heft it down off the dresser and slide it into the already over-stuffed bag.

I carry it into the bathroom, where I put some toiletries into the bag's side pocket and zip it closed.

It takes both hands to lift the bag onto the windowsill. I slide it through but hold on to the handles. If I let go, two hundred dollars' worth of change is going to smack into the pavement below and you can be damn sure that's going to wake someone up. My shoulder throbs as the weight of the bag tries to pull me through. Leaning out the window, I ease the bag onto the cement. Now, the problem is that two-thirds of my body is dangling out the window, head-first and I can't pull myself back in.

Since I've left myself no other options, I slide the rest of the way through the window and try to get my hands out to cushion the blow. I'm partially successful, and by partially successful, I mean that I think I just screwed my wrist to match my shoulder, but I'm intact enough to keep going.

I pick myself up, close the window, replace the screen, step out of the alley, and walk in the direction of the ocean.

Surf's Up! Liquor is a twenty-four-hour convenience store a block from the shore.

It's taken me almost an hour to get here, due to the added weight of the jar but I'm going to take care of that right now because Surf's Up! Liquor has exactly what I need: a CoinStar.

The clerk on the other side of the counter barely gives me a second glance as I walk in with my bulging gym bag. He's too busy with the two homeless guys in front of him at the register, paying for two cans of Steel Reserve with nickels and pennies.

I go over to the CoinStar machine, take out the jar, and begin pouring the change onto the metal tray. It crashes with a sound like a loud, metallic waterfall. After punching the button to accept the fee, I lift the tray and start feeding the coins into the slot.

The homeless guys at the counter stop talking. I can feel their eyes burning into the back of my neck and I awkwardly turn.

"... Good morning," I say.

They continue to stare amidst the deafening sound of the machine sorting the coins.

One of the homeless guys scratches the back of his neck. "Say, uh, listen, friend. I hope you don't mind me asking, but where are you setting up shop that you're pulling in so much?"

"… Um … I've been saving up my pennies for a while."

"Oh," he says and goes back to his partner to count out the rest of their change to buy their beer.

I'm just glad that they were looking at me and not the muted television behind the counter, which has an early morning local news broadcast, showing aerial shots of the mass of police cars outside the Parker house.

Thirty pounds lighter and two hundred and thirty-six dollars richer, I walk out of Surf's Up! Liquor. I also bought a candy bar and an energy drink to keep me going until I can get to a place where I can rest, but I need to get there soon.

I mentally go through all the motels Mrs. Parker and I visited, remembering her tip that if you pay extra, some places don't ask for an ID. The nearest is the Starry Night Inn, an establishment that makes the Seaside Motel look like The Ritz.

The sun is beginning to rise as I cross the cracked, uneven parking lot of the Starry Night Inn.

Just like the Seaside Motel, it's another one-story building whose only selling point is the view of the ocean.

On the other side of the screen door to the "check-in" office is a man in his late fifties, wearing a stained tank top undershirt, and asleep at the desk.

"Umm … excuse me?" I say, stepping into the office.

He snorts awake, looks at me, and then looks around like he has no idea where he is or how he got there before coming to his senses. He exhales, and the smell of stale liquor emanating from his mouth nearly knocks me over.

"Time is it?" he asks.

"It's, uh, it's about seven thirty," I answer, reading the clock on the wall behind him.

He groans and sits up. "Welcome to the Starry Night Inn. What can I do for you?"

"I'd like a room, please."

"How many nights?"

"I'll start with one."

"Okay. That'll be fifty-six ninety-nine."

"Great." I pull out my wallet.

"And I'll need to see ID."

"I'm sorry. I lost it," I reply, holding my wallet open so he can see the cash inside.

Nothing has changed about the rooms at the Starry Night Inn since I was last here with Emily. I forget which room we were in before, but room eighteen looks exactly the same.

The wallpaper is a dull, seafoam green that's peeling in the corners. The carpet may have been blue decades ago, but now it's a faded gray.

Once the door is closed and locked behind me, I flip on the light switch. Nothing happens. I flick it a few more times but the room remains dark. Thankfully, the bedside lamp works and while it does provide a little illumination, it does nothing to cheer the place up, and the bathroom ... Let's just say that it matches the rest of the room.

Sleep is racing towards me. I don't even have the energy to take a shower. I double-check that the deadbolt is engaged, peek out of the blinds one time to the quiet parking lot, and then let the blinds fall back into place.

I shuffle over to the bed and collapse on top of the covers.

I don't know what happens next. I can't think about that. I'll figure it out later. I just need a few hours of sl—

I roll over on the hard mattress.

Emily is awake. We smile at one another.

Sure, the Starry Night Inn is a seedy dive, but that's what makes it fun. Our little secret. The thrill of almost getting caught. The physical abandon.

From the devious look in her eyes, I can tell she's thinking the same thing as I am. Her lips pull her smile tighter, revealing her perfect, gleaming teeth.

We hungrily take each other in.

I slide closer to her, reaching my hand towards her face.

That's when her throat splits open and blood begins pouring across the sheets towards me.

I bolt upright and frantically wipe the warm, slick blood from my body, but it's only my own sweat, which has drenched the bed.

How long have I been asleep?

The cheap clock next to the bed says that it's eleven-thirty at night. A look out the window confirms it. I had been exhausted, stressed, running on adrenalin, and my body simply crashed. So, it's no surprise that I've been asleep for sixteen hours.

Honestly, I feel like I could go back to sleep, right now, but I don't want to have any more dreams about Emily. I want to remember the fun, flirtatious Emily. I don't want to keep seeing the Emily I saw in the crime scene photos. That's not her or at least that's not how I want to remember her.

However, it is time for that overdue shower, and I head for the bathroom. I wish I had some flip-flops to protect my feet from whatever the cleaning crew has missed. Afterwards, I dry off with the sandpaper the Starry Night Inn has deemed a "towel".

If I want to stay out of a jail cell, I have to change my appearance as much as possible, but all I can do right now is shave off my beard.

I open my duffel bag to get my razor, and as soon as I pull the zipper, I'm greeted by a smell that lets me know I've done something incredibly stupid. I put my damp, blood-stained shirt in with the clean clothes I took from my apartment. Now, all the clothes are damp and after all those hours stuffed in the bag, there's a whiff of mildew.

Damnit.

I pull out the clothes and lay them out all over the room in an attempt to air them out. The last thing out of the bag is the offending shirt.

I need a plan, but a plan requires a goal, so I have to ask myself, what is it that I want? I could simply try to get away. I could run, but I won't get very far. I don't have a car and only a little bit of money, and besides, that's not what I want.

I want to find out who this guy is. It's the only way to prove I didn't do it, but more than that, I want him to pay for what he did to Emily.

So, how do I go about doing that?

There's no way I can go to the cops. They have got to be searching for me. I can't contact the killer. Why would I? What good would that do?

I have to focus on the immediate future.

The one thing I'm going to need before too long is some more money. I have some cash but any pennies, nickels, and dimes will help. I search the hip pockets of my work pants, which I haven't taken off in two days. Sadly, thanks to my mildew error, they're the only pants I have that don't smell. They're not in great shape after a shift at work, being covered in blood, and then a dip in the ocean but they'll do. There are no coins in the left pocket, but in the bottom of the right hip pocket, my fingers brush something.

I pull it out and hold it to the light.

It's a business card.

Its glossy surface is cracked and feels brittle due to being soaked in salt water but the phone number is still legible; the phone number for Genevieve Winters.

Chapter 8

The sun's coming up and I haven't gone back to sleep. I've been working on the plan. It's risky and I'm going to have to venture out into the world, but there's no other way to do this.

Upon opening the door, I'm greeted by a gray Avalon morning. A fine mist hangs in the air and there's a blanket of gunpowder clouds overhead.

It's still early and there are no signs of life in the Starry Night Inn parking lot or from any of the rooms. Across the street, the ocean is a calm, melancholy reflection of the sky.

As I near the screen door that leads to the check-in office, there's the sound of voices on a television, but as I reach for the handle, there's movement and the television abruptly shuts off. I step into the office to see the same man sitting behind the counter. He's wearing the same clothes as yesterday, but for the most part, so am I. Still, he could do with a shower.

"Good morning," I say, trying to ignore his body odor.

"Good morning," he mumbles. His bloodshot eyes are more alert than yesterday and he's noticed that the beard is gone. "Checking out?"

"No. Actually, I wanted to do one more night, if that's okay."

Instead of answering right away, he scratches his belly in thought.

"And it would be great if we could keep the same arrangement as before," I add.

There's only enough money for one more night and a little left over to execute my plan.

"That'd be fine." He burps.

"Thank you, sir," I say, taking the cash from my wallet and placing it on the counter.

He stares at it, as though he's afraid to touch it.

"Everything okay?" I ask.

"Yeah," he says, finally picking up the short stack of bills. "Yeah. Everything's fine. Enjoy the rest of your stay."

There's an awkward pause where he won't look me in the eye.

"I will," I reply and go back out the door to the parking lot.

I'm not sure what his problem was but it might be best to avoid the office for the duration of my stay at the Starry Night Inn.

Being a seaside town popular with tourists, Avalon is littered with shops that sell everything to cater to their needs: cheap T-shirts, towels, sunglasses, toiletries, alcohol, etc. Along Route 1, which runs next to the shore, there are at least two or three on every block. They're plentiful, but I need one that sells burner phones.

As Avalon awakes from its slumber, I keep my head down, trying to avoid eye contact with the handful of people walking the streets. It's strange to feel the cool air on my face and neck, now that my beard is gone.

The first general store I come across is about a block and a half from the Starry Night Inn. They don't have burner phones, but what they do have out front is a display of newspapers. The headlines are surreal:

Millionaire Husband of Murdered Wife Found Dead
Multiple Homicides Strike Avalon
Wealthy Avalon Resident Murdered

Each headline is accompanied by images of Emily and Henry Parker from happier times next to photos of the police chaos at their home.

I quickly resume walking.

Everyone is looking at me. At least that's what it feels like; as if there's a big target on my back or a blinking sign over my head that says, "Here he is! Here he is!" but I don't know if the papers even mention me.

Another two blocks yields more general stores that don't sell burner phones. The good news is that the closer I get to the heart of downtown Avalon, the odds of finding a store that sells them goes up, but so do my chances of being spotted.

Finally, there's a store that sells them. It also has the added bonus of self-checkout. Any opportunity to limit my interactions with people is an opportunity I'm going to take.

The woman behind the counter barely looks up from her phone and continues to pop her gum as I walk in and head to the small electronics section. It's filled with cheaply made, over-priced headphones, car chargers, and a handful of generic Bluetooth speakers. It's the kind of stuff you'd only buy on vacation after realizing you've left yours at home.

There's a limited selection of disposable cellphones. I select a mid-range model with plenty of minutes. It's not that I'm being cheap. I need it to be reliable but I also need to stretch the little money I have left as far as I can. After selecting a phone, I quickly browse the aisles and pick out a pair of sunglasses and a blue ball cap that simply reads, 'AVALON'.

At the self-checkout kiosk, I put my items on the small metal shelf next to the scanner. On my left is a display filled with candy and granola bars. I grab a few of each, along with an energy drink from the small cooler with the sliding glass door, and add them to my purchases. There's also a display of newspapers. Once again, I'm paralyzed by the screaming headlines.

Okay. I have to do it. I have to see how bad this is.

I grab one and run the sticker with the barcode across the scanner, along with the rest of my items.

Once completed, I start feeding the cash into the slot, where the notes are gobbled up with a mechanical *whir*. The machine spits out my last $20 bill three times, almost causing me to panic, before I smooth it and feed it back through. Finally, it accepts the last bill with a *ka-chunk* and vomits my change into the tray.

I scoop up the change, dump it in my pocket, grab the flimsy plastic bag full of my new gear, and walk towards the door.

"Have a nice day," the woman behind the counter says, still not looking up from her phone.

"Thanks. You too," I toss over my shoulder as I hurry through the door.

Once outside, I immediately pop into a side alley, pull the tags off the hat and sunglasses, and put them on. I take the phone out of the box and hit the power button. It's got three-quarters of a charge. I also wolf down the two granola bars and chug the energy drink. It's surprising how quickly I start to feel better with something in my stomach. This is the new breakfast of champions.

Step One of "the plan" is complete. Now, I need to get back to the motel. I'll read the paper there. I don't want to be out here any longer than I have to and risk someone recognizing me.

I step out of the alley and start walking back in the direction of the Starry Night Inn. There are more people on the streets and more cars on the road. Every one of them is fueling my paranoia.

As I pass the patio of a coffee shop filled with people sipping lattes and espressos, I glance up to the multiple televisions mounted above. One of them is tuned to the local news.

"And stunning developments out of the seaside town of Avalon this morning regarding the brutal murders of Emily and Henry Parker. The two were found dead within days of each other. Authorities say that they are investigating ..."

I slow down and try to listen as much as I can, but I can't stop. I can't risk standing there if they flash a photo of me on the screen, even if I don't have my beard anymore.

Once I pass out of range of the television's volume, I lengthen my stride. The Starry Night Inn is three blocks away and this paper is burning a hole under my arm. I still keep my head down but peer suspiciously over the lenses of my sunglasses, paradoxically trying to avoid attention while studying people to see if they recognize me.

There's still a block and a half to go, but I have to know how bad this is.

I step into the doorway of a building, pull the paper out from under my arm, and flip it open.

... oh shit.

It's right here, just below the fold.

My face.

It's the profile picture from my Facebook page. I'm smiling into the camera. It was taken at The Gryphon last year. Under it, in bold print, is my name. I frantically scan the article. My eyes race past phrases like "Seaside Motel", "brutally murdered", "multi-million-dollar home", and find the words "authorities are searching for Franklin (Clay) Davis, a local bartender who is wanted for questioning ..."

I stop reading.

Not because of what I just read, which would be reason enough, but no. I stopped because of what I'm hearing.

There they are, again.

Sirens.

I've been so freaked out by the article, they hadn't registered. I join everyone else on the street who is craning their heads to the right to see the line of four cop cars, speeding in our direction.

I should run, but I can't.

My legs won't move. My mouth hangs open. My pulse races. By the time I regain control of my body, it's too late and besides, there's nowhere to go.

The sirens are screaming, deafening, as the cop cars barrel towards me.

They're going to come to a screeching halt in the street right next to me. The cops are going to jump out, aim their guns at my head, and tell me to get on the ground.

It's over.

The newspaper slides from my hand, lands on the sidewalk … and is blasted by the rush of air as the cop cars go flying past.

Everyone, including me, watches as they race ahead. Their brake lights flare and their tires scream as they turn into the parking lot of the Starry Night Inn.

The guy in the office. That's why he was acting so weird earlier. He must have been watching the news when I came in and recognized me.

Pulling my hat lower, I jam my hands into my pockets, and walk in the opposite direction.

I have to move up my plan.

And, now, it has to work.

Chapter 9

"Listen, whoever you are, you can just go right ahead and fu—"

"No, Genevieve. I swear to you. This is really Clay Dav—"

The line goes dead.

"Damnit!" I spit, ripping the phone from my ear.

Okay. Calm down. I can't attract any attention.

Listen, I've never done this before and I'm pretty sure you haven't either, so let me tell you the type of thought processes you'll have should you ever be the subject of a manhunt.

I need to call Genevieve but where do I go to make a phone call? Do I go to a public place and try to blend in with the crowd but risk having more people to spot me or overhear what I'm saying? Do I go someplace a little more private where I might not be seen but if I am seen, I'll stick out like a sore thumb? I'm even questioning my hat and sunglasses. Are they helping me blend in, or do they make me stand out?

In the end, I split the difference and go to one of the less-crowded public beaches. There are some people, but not too many. I find a corner, close to the rocks, and call Genevieve.

I can't ask Katie for help. There's not much she could do and

I'm sure the cops are keeping an eye on her place. Alex? No way. We respect each other professionally, but I wouldn't trust him not to call the cops if I tried to talk to him.

Genevieve is the only person I can ask to help me find Emily's killer, and as you just heard, it did not go well.

I hit redial and put the phone back to my ear.

It begins to ring.

I can almost see her at the other end, trying to decide if she should answer it.

Thankfully, she does.

"Listen, whoever you are, you're wasting your time and, more importantly, mine. So why don't you—?"

"Did you go to TGI Friday's like I suggested?"

There's a long pause.

"Mr. Davis?"

"God, please, call me 'Clay'."

Her voice immediately assumes a journalistic tone. "Where are you?"

"I can't tell you that."

"I can hear waves. Are you at the beach?"

I am really not good at this.

"… okay, yes, I am, but—"

"Stay right there. Tell me what beach and I'll come to you."

"No. I can't stay out here."

"What do you mean?"

"I need a place to hide. I'll come to you."

"Ummmmm. No."

"No? What do you m—?"

"You killed two people. Why would I let you into my place?"

"I didn't kill them."

She laughs. "You were having an affair with Emily Parker who was found murdered in a hotel room while she was

79

presumably waiting for you. Then, her husband is killed in the same way hours after he spoke to you with your bloody fingerprints everywhere and your car out front of their home with her blood in it. You're telling me you didn't kill them?"

"I know this looks bad."

"Bad? I've been a reporter for a while and I can tell you that this is way beyond 'looks bad'."

"I think I can prove it."

There's another long pause.

"How can you prove it?"

"That's why I need to come to you."

"Just tell me."

"No. I can't do it like that and besides, I need a place to hide and you want a story."

A quick scan of my surroundings shows at least three people are reading newspapers that have my face on them while they drink their morning coffee.

"Genevieve, I really need to get out of sight."

She sighs. "Two people's throats have been cut and everything says you did it."

"I know, but I really think I can prove that I didn't do it."

"Yeah, and wouldn't you say anything, like you could prove you didn't do it, to get me to let you into my place, where you'd kill me and just hide out?"

"You can take whatever precautions you want. Anything you can think of, and I'll do it."

"… Anything?"

"Yes."

Now comes the longest pause yet.

"Genevieve? You still th—?"

"Avalon East Apartments. You know it?"

"Yeah." It's one of the most expensive apartment buildings in Avalon.

"I'm in apartment 302."

"I'll be there in ten minutes."

"Be here in one hour."

"Genevieve, I need to get off the streets right now."

"One hour."

The line goes dead.

Chapter 10

Now I know why Genevieve insisted on the hour delay; she needed time to purchase the duct tape that is currently binding my wrists to the arms of this chair, my feet to the legs, and the strap around my head that's covering my eyes.

That was the first thing to go on.

When she opened the door to her apartment, she was holding the roll of tape in one hand, and a cannister of mace at the ready in the other.

"You shaved," she said.

"Yep."

"Changing your appearance?"

"Yes."

"Not something an innocent person usually does."

"Can I come in?" I asked, glancing up and down the hallway, worried that a friendly neighbor might poke their head out to say "hello".

"Turn around."

"Can I come in first?"

"No."

"Please, I need to—"

"The longer you wait to do what I tell you, the longer you're going to be standing in the hall for everyone to see."

"Okay, okay, okay," I muttered, turning my back to her.

"Keep your hands at your side."

"I got it. Just hurry up."

There was the sticky, ripping sound as she tore off a strip and wrapped it around my head, placing it over my eyes. She pulled it tight and pressed it against the back of my head.

"Now, I want you to slowly walk backwards into the room, and keep your hands at your side."

I did as I was told, anxious to get out of the hallway.

Once I was inside the apartment, she closed the door.

"Keep walking backwards very slowly, and keep your hands where they are."

After a few steps, the back of my legs bumped up against something.

"Stop. There's a chair behind you. Sit down, put your hands on the armrests, and keep them there."

I slowly sat back and eased myself into the chair, keeping my arms on the armrests.

"Can I take off the blindfold, now?"

"No."

"Why not?"

"Because if you do anything stupid, I'll be out the door, running down the hall screaming before you can get the blindfold off."

"It sort of sounds like you've done this before."

"Shut up."

"Okay."

I heard her approach.

She stopped right next to me and there was another sticky, ripping sound.

"Keep your arms on the armrests and don't move."

83

A strip of tape wrapped around my left wrist, tightly binding it to the armrest. She repeated the process with my right wrist.

"Is this really necessary?" I ask.

"Yes."

Fine. If this is what it takes, I have to go along with it.

She even wrapped tape around my ankles, securing them to the base of the chair, rendering me completely immobile, which brings me to my current situation.

"Okay," she says with an air of finality and I hear her drop the tape onto what I assume is a table, since I can't see anything. "Start talking."

"Can you at least take the tape off of my eyes, please?"

"Why?"

I don't want to tell her that I'm extraordinarily claustrophobic and the sensation of being unable to move or see is starting to freak me out. "Look, I can't move. At least let me see."

There's a silence as she considers, then her footsteps approach, again. She goes around behind me. Her fingernails dig at the edges of the tape and she yanks, hard. My hair is pulled in a circle as the tape comes clear with a loud *rrrrrrip*.

I blink my eyes and wonder how much of my eyebrows are left.

Her apartment is a small studio, but because of the building and the neighborhood, I'm sure she's paying three times what I am for half the space of my apartment. Prints of modern art hang on the walls. There's an opening to a small kitchen space. The bathroom is off the hallway, just inside the front door.

Genevieve walks around and sits in front of me on the corner of the bed.

We stare at one another.

"… hi," I say.

"Did you kill Emily Parker?" she asks, skipping the pleasantries and jumping right in.

"No."

"Did you kill Henry Parker?"

"No."

"Do you know who killed them?"

"No."

"Then how are you going to prove to me that you didn't do it?"

"That's going to take some explaining."

She gets up, goes over to the table, picks up her small, spiral notebook and a pen, and sits back down on the bed.

"Do you mind if I take notes?"

I look down at my wrists. "How exactly would I stop you?"

She shrugs. "Fair point."

Genevieve clicks the pen and allows it to hover over the paper. "So, what do you want to tell me?"

"Everything."

For the next half-hour, I tell her mostly that: how the affair started, how we almost got caught, the hotels, the rideshare drivers, the burner phone, the night at the Seaside Motel, the text messages, Detective Mendez, the apartment, the blood in my car, the smiley-face emoji text, and finally, the night at the Parker house. She listens intently while scribbling notes in her notebook, and occasionally asking questions that I do my best to answer.

When I'm done, she studies me.

"You still haven't told me everything," she says.

"I know."

"Why?"

"Because I was saving the best for last."

"All right, so tell me; what does 'my sweet little cupcake' mean?"

I take a deep breath.

Once again, allow me to back this up a bit ...

I am spent.

It was our second time this afternoon, and most likely our last, since I've got to be at work in a little while.

A naked Emily steps back into the bedroom from the bathroom and walks towards the bed. The sound of the ocean crashing against the rocks reaches us through the open balcony door.

She stops next to the bed and gazes down at me.

"Something on your mind?" I ask.

"Just wondering how long we can keep doing this."

"Funny, I was thinking the same thing, but I have to go to work."

"No, you idiot." She laughs, crawling back into bed. "I mean 'us'."

"You getting bored with me, already?"

"No," she says, cuddling up to my side and resting her head on my chest. "But I will. Then, I'll leave you."

This is how we joke. We're both assertive, competitive people, so there's an edge to it, but it's harmless.

"Oh, you will, will you?"

"Probably," she says, tracing a finger around the outline of the tattoo that spreads from my shoulder to my chest.

I shake my head. "We can't have that."

"We can't?"

"Nope."

"And what are you going to do to stop me?"

"Well ..." I sigh. "I guess I'd just have to kill you."

She raises her head off my chest to look at me. "Seriously?"

"Yep."

"And how would you do that?"

I shrug. "I'd simply cut your throat, my sweet little cupcake."

She crinkles her nose. "Ugh. Don't call me that."

I laugh.

"What's so funny?"

"I just told you I'm going to cut your throat, and you're more upset that I called you 'my sweet little cupcake'."

"It's weird."

I shake my head. "You have issues."

86

"You're the one who said you're going to cut my throat. I'd say you're the one with more pressing issues."

"Probably. I guess I can't let you get bored with me."

"And how are you going to do that?" She smiles.

I smile back. "Let me show you."

Genevieve has stopped taking notes. In fact, it looks like the pen is about to fall from her hand.

"I was joking," I say, breaking the silence.

She doesn't move. She doesn't blink.

"Genevieve?"

It takes another second for her to snap out of it.

"Okay. Let me get this straight: you were having an affair. You were at the hotel where she was murdered, but you say you didn't kill her. You also say you were never in the apartment before, even though your fingerprints are all over it. Her blood was in your car. You were at the house where her husband was killed only hours after talking to you. Your bloody fingerprints and shoeprints are all over, but you say didn't kill him either. And now, you're telling me that you *jokingly* threatened to murder her in the exact way that she happened to be murdered, and you expect me to believe anything you say?"

"Now you know why I lied to the cops."

"Yeah. I would lie, too, if it was that obvious that I had done it."

"It was a joke!"

"Sure." She laughs.

I notice a small, black furry head poke out from under the bed to look at me. It quickly retreats out of sight.

"Who is that?" I ask.

"My cat, Snoozy," she says, still regarding me with a sense of amusement. "Okay. Fine. How?"

"How what?"

"You said you can prove you didn't do it. How can you prove it?"

"I *think* I can prove it."

"All right. Let's hear it."

I take another breath. "The killer still has her burner phone. At least, I *hope* he still does. I texted him the other night and he answered. I want to text him and see if he'll answer, again."

"What would that prove?"

"That he's out there and I'm in here. I'm going to try to get him to say he killed both Emily and Henry Parker and that will be your proof."

"How do I know you're not working with whoever you're texting?"

I nod to my bound wrists and ankles. "You think this is working with the killer? That I would put myself in this much danger with the police while all my co-killer partner has to do is text? What could I possibly be getting out of this?"

"I'm just spit-balling every possibility. So, why come to me?"

"Because you're the only person who can help me catch this guy," I answer, trying to convey my sincerity.

She studies me and lets out a light laugh. "Okay, let's give it a shot."

"Good. Cut my hands free and I'll text him."

She stands up and steps over to me. "Where's the phone?"

"In my pocket."

She reaches in, grabs the phone, and walks back to the bed.

"What are you doing?" I ask.

"I'm going to text him."

"No. Cut me loose, give me the phone, and I'll do it."

"Not a chance," she says, pressing the buttons. I've been a little distracted, and haven't set up a PIN lock, so it goes right to the home screen. "What's the number?"

I'm still not sure about this and don't answer.

She rolls her eyes. "You can tell me what to text. He's not going to know that I'm the one typing it."

"Fine," I say and give her the number. I've memorized Emily's burner phone number because it was the only contact that I hadn't assigned a name to in my old phone.

"Okay, what do you want me to text?" she asks as she finishes typing in the number.

"Tell him that I'm alive and that we still get to play."

"... what?"

"He was watching me as I came out of the police station after they questioned me. He said I looked nervous, that I shouldn't be nervous, and that it was time to play."

"Wow," she says with an appreciative whistle. "That's messed up." She begins typing. "And ... send." She dramatically taps the key and drops the phone onto the bed. She then pulls out her own phone and starts tapping.

"Now, what are you doing?" I ask.

"Setting a timer."

"What for?"

"Five minutes. You've got five minutes for this so-called 'psycho' to answer. If he doesn't, I'm calling the cops."

"Wait. You don't believe me?"

"Are you kidding me? Of course I don't. You really think with the ridiculous amount of evidence that points to you and your own little story about 'my sweet little cupcake' that I'm going to believe someone else killed the Parkers? Come on. Give me a break."

"But it's true!" I insist, straining against the tape.

"Then he'll answer and you have nothing to worry about." She smiles, sarcastically.

It's quickly dawning on me how flimsy my plan was.

"Listen, Genevieve, you've got to give him more time than that."

"Ummmmm, no I don't."

My mind is reeling, trying to come up with any excuse to get her to extend the deadline.

"Haven't you ever taken some time, like more than five minutes, to answer a text?"

"Oh, sure, but that was stuff like what I wanted for dinner. Not texting a psycho about the multiple murders they've committed. If this guy is real, then I'm sure he'll see this text as very important."

"What if he doesn't know the message is from me? You didn't give him my name and it's not from my phone."

"You think there was someone else that he was playing this game with? And, besides, did anyone else other than you have the number to Emily Parker's burner phone?"

"... no."

"Well, there you go." She checks the timer on her phone. "Don't worry. You've got three minutes and thirty-eight seconds. Plenty of time."

"Genevieve, if you turn me in, you'll lose your story."

She laughs. "You really don't get it, do you? This is a win-win for me. If by some miracle, this mysterious killer writes back, you'll be vindicated, and we can work together to find out who it is. If not, I get to put myself in the center of the story by turning you over to the police. You pretty much just gave me an exclusive interview and I'll be the resourceful reporter who saw past the charade of a clever, cunning killer. You know they have a name for you?"

"Who does?"

"The police. They're calling you the Bloody Bartender ... Two minutes, ten seconds left, by the way."

I can't worry about my new nickname, right now.

"Genevieve, you have to give him more time," I plead. "What happens if you call the cops and then thirty seconds later, he texts back?"

"I still get to be at the center of the story and I still have your exclusive interview. You gave me the whole story before the cops. I'll have to be part of the investigation." Her face lights up. "I hadn't even thought of that. I mean, it's even better, because then

I get to work with the cops. It opens up a whole new dynamic for the story, but come on, you and I both know that's not going to happen." She points the lens of the camera on her phone at me and snaps a photo before I have a chance to say anything. "That is going to get me a Pulitzer when the article runs ... One minute, aaaaaand seven seconds."

I've come all this way. I jumped from a balcony into the ocean to escape the cops, I've changed my appearance, and it's going to end because I stupidly tried to trust a reporter and idiotically allowed myself to be taped to a chair.

"Genevieve, please, listen to me—"

"I did listen to you," she says, with a nod towards the notebook. "I've been more than fair, and honestly, it's not just the story. I knew Emily Parker. Not well, but I knew her enough and she didn't deserve that. No one does. So, catching the guy who did this to her is going to be a nice little cherry on top."

"Genevieve, I want to catch this guy, too! Why do you think I took a chance on you?! I could have tried to run! I could have gotten out of Avalon but I didn't! I came to you because I want to catch this guy for the same reasons you do!"

The fierceness in my voice surprises her.

She examines me for a moment. It looks as though there is a sliver of doubt, but she shakes her head. "I don't know what you planned to do to me, but let's face it, I won. You really have been incredible. Your story is great but no one was going to believe it. And now ..." She looks down at her phone and holds up a finger. "Three ... two ... one."

The timer on her phone begins to chime.

"Genevieve—"

She silences the alarm and pulls up the keypad. She taps nine, then one, pauses for dramatic effect, and hits one again, before putting it on speaker phone.

The purr of the other end ringing comes through. It rings again ... again ... and again ... There's a click.

"Nine, one, one. What is the nature of your emergency?"

"Hi, this is—"

The burner phone pings.

Genevieve stops.

Both of us are perfectly still.

She checks the burner phone and looks back up at me, her face ashen.

"Hello?" the 911 operator asks through the speaker phone. "Is someone there?"

"Oh my gosh! I'm so sorry," Genevieve says towards the phone, her eyes locked on mine. "I'm so soooo sorry. I meant to unlock my phone but I accidentally hit the emergency call button. I'm so sorry!"

"Ma'am, are you sure that everything is okay?"

"Yes, yes. Everything is fine. It was a mistake. I'm sorry." Her tone is strikingly convincing even though her expression doesn't match.

"Are you sure?"

"Yeah. I'm really sorry. Everything is fine," she says, her wide eyes still on me.

"Okay. You have a good day," the operator says.

"You too."

The operator hangs up. Genevieve does the same.

She keeps staring at me in the silence.

Then, she takes the burner phone, stands, and goes to her purse on the table. She reaches in and pulls out a small folding knife. She opens it to reveal a gleaming, small-but-lethal-looking blade. She walks over, drops the burner phone into my lap, and leans in close. I instinctively recoil from the blade. In two easy movements, she cuts the tape, freeing my wrists, and goes back to sit on the corner of the bed.

I pick up the phone from my lap and read the text message from Emily's burner phone.

Well, well. I guess like me, you're more than what people give you credit for but I'm afraid you weren't supposed to get away from the house. Know that I have newfound respect for you, but we can't play anymore. I'll have fun thinking of a new way to get rid of you. I'm so bored with cutting people's throats.

Chapter 11

I don't recognize this guy staring back at me from Genevieve's bathroom mirror.

I've never thought of myself as vain, but apparently, I'm ridiculously vain. In addition to my beard being gone, my hair has now left the building. It's piled sadly in the sink below me and it's messing with my brain. I gave myself a buzzcut with the cheap electric clippers Genevieve purchased. She also got me these business-casual clothes that I'm wearing. Yes, changing my appearance was a necessity, but without my beard and hair, I feel like my face is too narrow, too drawn, and my jawline is not as defined as I remember the last time I saw it. I keep turning my head, taking in my face from every angle. This is going to take some getting used to.

"I'm still trying to understand this. She never mentioned the apartment?" Genevieve asks from the living room/bedroom, which in the small apartment is only a few feet away outside the bathroom door.

"No. Never," I answer, buttoning up the shirt and cuffs. The long sleeves cover my tattoos. One last look in the mirror confirms that this is a different guy.

"That doesn't make any sense."

I scoop the hair out of the sink as best I can and deposit it in the trash. "I'm telling you, she never mentioned it." I turn on the faucet, which washes the remaining stray strands down the drain.

"Then why would she rent it if you two weren't going to … you know … use it?"

I step out of the bathroom to join her. "I have no idea."

Sitting at the small table, Genevieve takes in my new look with a slight grimace.

"What?" I ask.

"When this is all over, you should grow the beard back."

"Thanks for that little pick-me-up," I answer, sitting on the corner of the bed.

Genevieve takes my work pants, which are draped on the chair next to her.

"What do you want to do with these?" she asks.

"That's up to you."

"Why?"

"Pretty sure that there are traces of Henry Parker's blood on them. If we throw them away, we'll be destroying evidence."

"And why are you leaving it up to me?"

"Because I want you to trust me. I say get rid of them, but it's your call."

I thought it was a cool gesture on my part, but Genevieve rolls her eyes.

"Oh, please. I 'aided and abetted' you when I didn't turn you in and now I'm helping you change your appearance so you won't get caught. I've already cast my lot."

"Okay. So, what's it gonna be?"

She inspects the pants as though she might see the faint traces of blood and shakes her head. "Let's get rid of them. Either you killed them or you didn't. The pants don't matter at this point."

"You still think I might have killed them? Who do you think was texting you while I was taped to that chair?"

"You might be working with him."

95

"Genevieve—"

"Listen, until we get this guy, I'm always going to treat it as a possibility."

"Fine." I sigh, flopping back on the bed. "Get rid of the pants."

"Did you get everything out of them that you needed?" she asks, searching the hip pockets.

"Yeah, I did. So, for a moment, let's set aside the fact that you still think I may have killed them or that I might be a part of some murdering tag team, and get back to figuring out why she'd take the chance of renting that apartment. Her husband would see it in her accounts. That's why she paid for everything in cash. She was afraid—"

"What is this?" she asks.

I sit up. "What is what?"

She's got her hand inside one of the back pockets and pulls out one blood-stained, folded piece of paper.

My eyes light up. "That's it! That's the note he tried to give me at The Gryphon! I pulled it out of his jacket at the house. I forgot I had it."

After being splattered in blood and soaked in the ocean, the paper is brittle. It cracks and crinkles as she carefully unfolds it.

"'Perkiest'?" she asks, staring at it.

"Yeah, and here!"

I grab my wallet off of the table next to her and find the note that Emily wrote me on the register paper, letting me know that I could find her in room 37 of the Seaside Motel. It's a little worse for wear after being in the ocean, but it was somewhat protected and is still clearly legible. I hand it to Genevieve.

"That's the note Emi—Mrs. Parker wrote me the night she was killed. This proves my story."

Genevieve shakes her head. "It doesn't prove anything. It's only your word."

"Oh, come on! I'm telling you; she wrote that note and he

wrote that one and tried to give it to me. He said it was the only way to get out of the trouble that we were both—"

"Wait ... wait ..." She holds the paper open to me. "You're saying he wrote this?"

"Yeah."

"And she wrote this?"

"Yes ... Why?"

She intently studies the two pieces of paper.

"Genevieve?"

Her head shoots up to look at the art deco clock on the wall. "What time is it?"

Before I can even answer, she grabs her phone, unlocks the screen and begins tapping away. After one last tap, she holds it to her ear.

"Hi. Do you have any vacancies? ... Oh, that's perfect. What floor is the unit on?"

"Genevieve, what are you—?" I whisper, completely confounded. She cuts me off with her finger.

"... and what time do you close?"

Chapter 12

"I'm having second thoughts about this."

Actually, I'm having the eighty-eighth and eighty-ninth thoughts about this as we get closer and closer to Evergreen Terrace Apartments.

"They have one vacancy and they close in forty-five minutes."

"They'll be looking for me!"

"They'll be looking for Clay Davis, and you're not Clay Davis anymore. You're Thomas Richards. And besides, they won't be looking for you here. It would be crazy for you to show up."

"Yes! Thank you! My point, exactly!"

"Listen," Genevieve says from the driver's seat. "If there was any other way to do this, we would. We could go through the city's property records but that would take weeks, which we don't have."

"And you're willing to risk this just to see a copy of the lease?"

"We have to. We need to know who owns the building, which will be on the lease. Once we have the owner of the building, my editor at the *Herald* will be able to find the actual copy of the lease in the city records in a few hours."

"And what exactly are we after?"

"I want to see her name on it."

We turn the corner onto Sawgrass Road, inching closer to what I'm convinced is an absolutely terrible idea.

"Fine. Then go in there and act like you're looking for an apartment for yourself," I offer, desperate for any excuse to back out of what I tentatively agreed to back at her apartment. "There's no need for me to go in there."

"Nope. There's no way that they would offer a three-bedroom apartment to a single woman. We don't want them to question for a second whether or not we can afford it. That's why you, a young, successful businessman, and I are recently engaged and looking for a place to start our new lives."

"That is the dumbest plan I've ever heard."

Genevieve yanks the wheel to the right, bringing us to the curb, and stops.

"Great! Then give me your plan. You said you wanted to get this guy, right? Prove it. Tell me how *you're* going to do that? Give me a better idea, because if you don't have one, I need you to get your head straight and help me, because if you screw this up, we will be caught."

Cars woosh by as I stare out the windshield, unable to look at her, because I don't have an alternative.

I wish I could have come up with one, because all of my doubts about Genevieve's plan come surging back as we pull into the parking lot of Evergreen Terrace Apartments. The balloons tied to the handrails leading up to the entrance bob in the breeze.

Genevieve pulls into a spot, kills the engine, and takes a breath. "Okay, let's go."

She hops out.

I stay rooted in my seat. My eyes are fixed on the cop car that's parked at the far end of the lot, away from the entrance. Two policemen are leaning against the car, wrapped in conversation.

Genevieve takes two steps towards the entrance before she

stops, realizing that her faux-fiancé isn't at her side. He's still sitting in the car like he can't figure out the childproof locks.

"Thomas?" she says. "Come on."

That's my name for this little fact-finding mission. She's Karen White. She chose those names because she thinks they sound plausible and yet easy to forget.

My eyes stay glued to the cops as I get out of the car.

She's seen them, too.

And they've noticed us.

She smiles and takes my hand.

"It'll be okay, sweetie," she says, and appears to kiss me on the cheek, but keeps her lips close to my ear and quietly whispers, "You've got to loosen up. No one is going to recognize you unless you keep acting like this, okay? Let's go."

She pulls back and gives me a smile that might look "loving" from afar, but up close, the pleading intensity and the tension in her jaw are plain to see.

I do my best to smile, but my nervousness makes it appear as if I'm baring my teeth at her.

"Oh god, let's get you out of here," she says through her forced pleasant expression.

She takes my hand and leads me to the front doors.

The lobby is just as I remember it from two days ago. Genevieve takes it in as if she's judging it with a practiced eye.

"Well, this is fun," she says in a cheerful tone.

I'm looking around, trying to figure out if she's referring to something in particular when her elbow connects with my side.

"Don't you think?" she asks, quietly.

"Yeah. It's great," I say, a bit too loudly, and obviously not up to Genevieve's stage-acting standards.

We walk through the glass doors into the courtyard and over to the door of the leasing office. There, we find a woman in her mid-fifties, sitting behind one of two desks. The other desk is empty. She's dressed vaguely like a flight attendant. Behind her

100

is a corkboard with some generic motivational posters and charts that are indecipherable to me. The only thing I do recognize is a photo of a brand-new, gleaming, KIA Sorento that's thumb-tacked to the board.

Genevieve lightly knocks on the door. "Hello?"

The woman looks up.

"Can I help you?" she asks with a wan smile.

"Hi," Genevieve says, in a bubbly tone. "I called a little bit ago. We understand that you have a three-bedroom available?"

The woman's smile goes nuclear. "We certainly do!" She stands, walks around the desk, and excitedly extends her hand. "I'm Tracey Sommers."

"I'm Karen White," Genevieve says, shaking her hand. "And this is my fiancé, Thomas Richards."

"Oh, 'fiancé'? Well, congratulations!" Tracey proclaims.

"Thanks," I reply.

Genevieve happily squeezes my arm.

"When's the big day?" Tracey asks.

"SeptOctembober."

I said 'September'. Genevieve said 'October'.

We stare at one another.

Tracey is understandably confused.

Genevieve quickly recovers. "We're still going back and forth on the date. I keep saying October. He insists on September."

I shrug. "I think October is going to be too cold for an outdoor wedding."

"And I think it'll be just fine," Genevieve lovingly counters.

There's an uncomfortable pause. Karen and Thomas have just had their first fight.

"Well, I'm sure whichever you choose will be lovely," Tracey chimes in to break the silence.

"Yes, it will," Genevieve agrees.

"You're interested in the three-bedroom?" Tracey asks, rapidly switching gears.

101

"Yes. You have one available, correct?" Genevieve asks.

Tracey eagerly nods. "We do, but only the one. It's our last unit. So, we should probably get up there."

We follow a very motivated Tracey across the courtyard, around the pool, and up the stairs to a corner unit on the top floor, the door of which is slightly ajar.

"I'm sorry," Genevieve says, sympathetically as we try to keep up. "I know it's late in the day and you're probably ready to go home, but we appreciate you showing us the apartment. We'll be very quick."

Tracey lightly laughs. "Oh, I'm sorry if I'm moving a little fast, but it's not because it's late."

"Oh?"

"Well, it's sort of that."

Tracey pushes open the door.

There's a young couple standing in the living room. The dad's got a Baby Bjorn resting against his chest with an infant snuggled inside. They look at us in confusion, as does the woman who is showing them the apartment. She's dressed almost exactly like Tracey.

Tracey walks in with that nuclear-powered smile plastered on her face.

"Helloooo."

The woman showing the couple plus baby launches pure fire from her eyes at Tracey, but then puts on a smile to match hers.

"Tracey. Hi. I thought you knew I was showing the unit to the Carlsons right now."

Tracey waves her hand. "I know, Sarah, I know, and I do apologize, but it was getting late and I was hoping that you wouldn't mind if I showed this lovely engaged couple the apartment really quick before we closed shop for the night."

Sarah keeps that smile, but mentally, she's envisioning all the violent crimes she could commit against Tracey.

"Well, sure," Sarah says. "It's not how we *normally* do things, but we're almost done here."

"Oh, wonderful." Tracey claps.

These women loathe each other and I have no idea why.

"Right this way, please," Tracey says, motioning for us to go down the short hallway to the master bedroom.

As we pass, Tracey glances at Sarah and all pretense is dropped. The hatred between them is palpable, but only for a second. Then, it's back to sparkling teeth and bright lipstick.

Sarah turns back to the Carlsons. "So, uh, sorry for that rather *rude* interruption. There's only supposed to be one party showing the unit at a time, but as you can plainly see, the place is in demand."

Tracey grumbles something as she leads us into the master bedroom, but when she turns and faces us. Her nuclear smile is back.

"So, we'll do the tour a little backwards, and let's be honest; this is the most important room in the place, right? Ha ha! Now, as you can see, it's incredibly spacious. You can easily fit that California King bed that I'm sure is on your wedding registry," she says with a sly wink, and then motions to the wall. "Over here is the walk-in closet."

Genevieve and I go to check it out.

"This is wonderful," Genevieve announces, a little too enthusiastically.

I mean, sure, it's a closet and there's space for two steps, which counts as walking but—

"And over here you have your own balcony with an exceptional view!"

Tracey is standing by the sliding glass door.

Genevieve and I walk across the room and step onto the balcony.

The "exceptional view" is of the street down below and the parking lot, where the cops are still leaning against their car. One of the cops looks up at us. We lock eyes.

I quickly duck back inside, suddenly unable to breathe.

Did he recognize me? I think he recognized me.

"It's great," I say.

"Oh, I'm so glad you like it," Tracey says loudly enough that it carries down the hall.

I have no idea what's going on, but I glance to Genevieve and she gets this look like she's just been hit by a bolt of lightning.

"It really is wonderful," she says and grabs my arm. "Don't you think, sweetheart?"

"… yep." Clearly, I'm supposed to say this.

Genevieve turns to Tracey. "We'll take it."

Tracey blinks. "You will?"

"We will?" I ask.

It takes everything I've got to keep from wincing as Genevieve's nails sink into my arm.

"Yes, we'll take it," she says.

Tracey looks back and forth between us, conflicted.

"Listen," she says. "I want nothing more than to get you folks into this apartment, but don't you think that you and your fiancé might want to discuss it first?"

For a moment, I wonder who she's referring to, and then I remember that I am said fiancé.

"We did," Genevieve says, looking towards me, and tightening her grip on my arm. "You remember, sweetie. On the drive over? You said that if I liked it, we'd take it?"

Her nails sink deeper into my arm. She's got hands like beartraps.

"I sure do remember," I reply.

Tracey is still unsure and looks back towards the open door.

"Is there a problem?" Genevieve asks.

"No," Tracey says quietly, trying to keep that million-watt smile on an even keel. "It's just—" Her smile falters. She hurriedly goes over and begins to close the door, while loudly proclaiming, "And see, if you close the door, it's really quiet. So, if you have company and they won't leave, you can go to bed and not hear them." She closes the door and quickly walks back over to us. All of her showmanship is gone.

"Okay. I need to know, right now: are you serious about taking this place?"

"Tracey, we are so goddamn serious," Genevieve replies. "We want it before those people out there get it."

"And I want you to have it." She looks at us, back at the door, and then huffs in frustration. "Okay. I'll lay all my cards on the table; I work on commission, so, yes, I want you to have it, and the property management company has a little competition going on. It's come down to me and that monster out there. The winner gets a brand-new KIA Sorento. Sarah's an insufferable wretch, but if I say it's yours and you screw me over, it's going to be bad for me. So, I need to know that this is for real."

Genevieve looks at her, dead in the eye, and says, "Tracey, we want this apartment."

Tracey glances at me.

Genevieve's beartrap hands tighten on my arm. I think her nails just hit bone.

"We want this apartment," I squeak.

Tracey sizes us up, nods, goes to the door, triumphantly throws it open, and announces at full blast, "Then let's go sign the paperwork!"

"Have a good night, Sarah," Tracey says, oozing condescension.

Sarah collects her things from her desk and walks to the door of the leasing office, heading out to the courtyard. "Good night, Tracey," she says, matching her tone. She looks at Genevieve and I, sitting across the desk from Tracey. "And congratulations to you both."

"Thanks," Genevieve answers, fully playing the game.

Once Sarah leaves, Tracey sits back in her chair with a wide, contented smile.

"I love you, guys," she says, and leans forward. "Ah! You couldn't have arrived at a better time!"

Genevieve takes my hand. "Well, we've been looking for a while, and with the wedding coming up, we decided that today was the day."

"For you and me both!" Tracey exclaims. She swivels her chair around, kisses the tips of her fingers, and touches the picture of the KIA Sorento mounted to the corkboard. She completes the rotation, coming full-circle. "Let's do this!" she exclaims and begins opening drawers, pulling out various packets of paperwork, and laying them on the desktop. "We'll have to do background checks, credit checks, and income verification. It's all standard stuff. It usually takes forty-eight hours and then we'll have you sign."

She plops a copy of the lease on the desktop.

"Do you folks have your IDs with you?" she asks.

Genevieve drops my hand. "We do," she says. "But there's something we'd like to do first."

"Yes?"

"We'd like to have a friend of ours take a look at the lease."

There's a long pause, accentuated by Tracey's furrowed brow.

"Well ... it's ... it's a standard lease."

Genevieve gets a pained expression. "Yeah. We had a little problem with one of the last places we rented. We signed right away because they told us it was a 'standard lease', and it turned out that there was all this fine print and we ended up getting royally screwed over, didn't we, Thomas?"

She looks at me.

Oh, yeah. I'm Thomas.

"It was a mess," I fake confirm.

"It was our fault," Genevieve continues. "We had been dating for a year, and were so anxious to move in together, that we ended up getting taken for a ride." She starts laughing. "I mean, we were total idiots. Right, Thomas?"

I nod. Her performance is Oscar-worthy.

"So, we've got this friend, his name is Marcus, and he works in real estate law. We told him what we were doing today and asked him if he would take a look at the lease, tonight, if we brought him a copy. So, what I'd like to do is take that and let him have a glance. Once he gives it the all-clear, we'll be back tomorrow with IDs and paystubs, and we'll seal the deal."

The confusion on Tracey's face is undeniable. "Oh … I'm … I'm not sure I can do that."

"Tracey, Tracey, Tracey," Genevieve soothes. "You don't have to worry. That KIA is yours. We're taking the apartment. This is just us covering our asses."

She's still not convinced. "It's a little odd …"

"I understand," Genevieve replies sympathetically and has an idea. "How about we prove that we're not going anywhere? Hmm? Get out your phone," Genevieve says while pulling out her own phone.

Tracey obliges, but appears just as lost as I feel.

"Call this number," Genevieve says, and proceeds to read out a phone number that makes no sense to me.

Tracey follows along. Once Genevieve is done, Tracey dials.

The phone in my pocket begins to buzz. I take it out.

"See?" Genevieve says. "That's Thomas's cell number. Now, you know where to find us. If anyone comes in tomorrow, you tell them that unit is taken."

It doesn't completely win her over, but it does set her mind somewhat at ease.

There's a knock on the door.

"Mrs. Sommers?" a male voice asks.

Every muscle in my body goes rigid. I know that voice. Oh god. I know that voice, but I can't turn around. If I do, I'll be looking directly at Detective Mendez.

"We're almost done in the unit," he says.

"Okay. Thank you," Tracey says, annoyed at the interruption.

Genevieve's hand grips my wrist. I keep my face locked straight ahead.

"Sorry to interrupt, you folks," Detective Mendez says.

Genevieve turns slightly. "That's quite all right," she warmly replies.

"Have a good night, ma'am. Good night, sir."

Genevieve gives me a glance.

I sure as hell can't turn around but I have to reply somehow. The best I can manage is a slight nod while still facing forward and say, "Good night."

There's an agonizing silence.

"Good night," Tracey says in a not-so-subtle tone that suggests he go away.

I hear Detective Mendez turn and walk back into the courtyard as the door to the leasing office slowly swings shut.

Why did he hesitate?

"Sorry about that," Tracey says. "Now, I want to make sure I understand this …"

Her voice trails off in my head. All I can think of is Detective Mendez and the cop who saw me on the balcony. He had to have told Detective Mendez. That's why Detective Mendez chose that specific moment to come to the leasing office. And Detective Mendez hesitated, right? There was a moment. I'm not crazy. He had to know something was off. He recognized my voice. He had to and right now, he's calling for backup. In a few seconds, this place is going to be swarming with cops.

We have to go.

We have to get out of here. We have to get out of here before he comes back down.

Without thinking, I stand up.

"Honey?" Genevieve asks.

I grab the lease from Tracey's desk and go for the door.

"Thomas?" Genevieve asks, a sliver of panic in her tone.

What's wrong with this damn door?

Tracey stands. "Mr. Richards, now just a moment!"

Why won't this door open?!

Genevieve is also out of her chair. "What are you doing?" she asks, dispensing with our cover story.

What is wrong with this doo— oh, because I was pushing when I needed to pull.

Clutching the lease to my chest, I open the door and walk briskly out into the courtyard. Detective Mendez is heading back up the stairs to the apartment.

"Sir!" Tracey calls out as she emerges from the office behind Genevieve.

Detective Mendez stops on the stairs.

The split second before he looks back at the courtyard, I turn and go towards the door to the lobby.

"Cla—!" Genevieve hisses but catches herself.

No. NO! Please tell me Detective Mendez didn't just hear her almost call me "Clay".

I reach the door, quickly stride through the lobby, and shove open the doors leading to the parking lot. The cops we saw earlier are still there, hanging out. I try to slow my pace.

Genevieve exits the building and pulls even with me.

"What are you doing?!" she says, keeping her voice low.

"That was Detective Mendez. He's in charge of the case. He was the one who questioned me. He had to be on to us."

"No, he wasn't. Goddamnit, we had it. You're freaking out."

"I'm not freaking out. He would have had us if we stayed."

"Christ," she whispers. "Get in the car."

We reach the car just as the two cops look our way. Genevieve waves. They wave back.

I slide into the passenger seat, still holding on tightly to the lease. She gets into the driver's seat and starts the car. She backs out, goes to the exit, and pulls into traffic.

I twist in my seat to look back towards the apartments.

Genevieve erupts. "You just screwed us!"

Chapter 13

"Seriously, what the hell was that?!" Genevieve blasts from the driver's seat as Evergreen Terrace Apartments fades into the distance through the rear windshield.

"Sorry. I sort of panicked, but we got the lease."

"Yeah, and you totally screwed us!"

"What are you talking ab— WATCH THE ROAD!"

Genevieve deftly swerves around a rusty, lumbering, Volkswagen van.

"I got it! I got it!" she says, settling back into the lane but we're still moving way too fast.

"What do you mean 'I totally screwed us'? That was Detective Mendez! You said they wouldn't be looking for us there."

"They weren't! At least not until your little freak out, which just brought us a lot of attention."

"It's not that bad," I lamely counter, but replaying what just happened in my head, yes, it was that bad. If they really had been on to us, we never would have made it out of the parking lot.

"I guarantee you, the first thing that lady did was tell the cops, 'Hey. That really weird guy and that woman ran out with a copy of a lease.' If they show her a picture of you, even with the beard and hair, she'll recognize you. Then, they'll run my plates, and then, we're totally screwed," she says, pulling onto a busy road.

"We've got the lease."

"We have to get out of my apartment …" She suddenly strikes the steering wheel with the palm of her hand. "DAMNIT!"

I'm going to shut up now. As I sit back, wondering how bad this is going to be, my phone pings with a text. Genevieve hears it too. I retrieve the phone from my pocket and check the messages.

"… shit …" I whisper.

"What is it?" Genevieve asks.

I hold the phone up so that she can glance at the text message from Emily's burner phone as she drives.

I knew you'd come back to the apartment! I just phoned in an anonymous tip that I thought I saw you there, but I wasn't expecting you to have company. Who's your friend?

Genevieve slams on the brakes.

My seatbelt catches me as I'm thrown forward and the car comes to screeching halt.

Instantly, there's a chorus of screaming tires and blaring horns from the cars around us.

Genevieve unclips her seatbelt, throws open her door, and gets out.

"Where are you going?!" I yell and throw open my own door but when I try to step out, I'm unceremoniously pulled back down as I've forgotten my seatbelt. I wrestle myself free and get out of the car.

The line of cars stuck behind us is growing. They slowly maneuver around, blaring their horns and rolling down their windows to yell profanities at Genevieve as she stares down each one, and motions them to keep going.

"Genevieve! What are you doing?!"

"Making sure we're not being followed!" she yells over the horns while still peering intently into each car as it passes.

"I thought we weren't supposed to be drawing attention to ourselves!"

She stops and glares at me. "A little late for that, don't you think?!"

I give up.

Genevieve waits a few more seconds and then heads back to the car. "Okay. Let's go."

"Sure. Great," I say, getting back in.

We slap our seatbelts on and Genevieve starts the car. As she reaches for the gear shift, my phone pings again. We stop and she stares at me while I pull up the new text.

Your friend is really clever. I like her. She looked right at me.

Genevieve snatches the phone from my hand and reads the text. She angrily mashes the screen, speaking through clenched teeth as she types.

"Fuck ... you ... you ... sick ... *fuck!*"

She jabs the send button, throws the phone back into my lap, and hits the steering wheel, again.

The cars continue to blare their horns as they are forced to maneuver around us.

"Well ... I'm sure that really showed him," I say.

She grabs the gear shift and throws it into "drive".

"We have to get out of my apartment," she reiterates and stomps on the gas.

The car lurches forward.

Genevieve whips the car into her spot in the parking lot and kills the engine.

"We're going to grab only the things we need," she says, jumping out.

I get out and almost trip on the curb as I try to keep up. "I still don't und—"

She throws open the door to the lobby and continues talking without looking back at me. "I've worked with cops before and the first thing they'll do is mark the license plate of everyone who comes and goes from that apartment complex, which wouldn't be a big deal unless we give them a reason to actually check our license plate."

"Oh, come on," I say, following her down the corridor with the lease in my hand. "You really think they caught your plates?"

"You bet your ass they did. Your little freak out and that asshole's 'anonymous' tip has put them right on to us."

There's a "ding" from her hip pocket.

She stops so abruptly that I nearly crash into her. She pulls out her phone and checks the screen.

"Shit!"

She resumes sprinting down the hall and into the stairwell.

"Genevieve?" I call out as I race after her.

Damn, she's fast. I ran track in high school and I can barely keep up as our footsteps echo up the stairwell. She throws open the door on the third landing. I'm still struggling to stay close as she flies down the hallway.

She rounds the corner and pulls up at the door of her apartment.

"Genevieve, what happened?" I ask, trying to catch my breath.

"My editor just texted me," she says, struggling with the keys. "Cops called the paper, asking where I was."

"Are you serious?"

She stops and looks up at me in disbelief. "No, you idiot. This is the funniest joke in the world." She turns back to the door and slides the key into the lock.

She pushes open the door, runs inside. I catch a faint glimpse of her cat as it darts under the bed. Genevieve grabs her suitcase from the closet, throws it onto the bed, and opens it. The first thing she tosses inside are her notebook and laptop, followed by a handful of clothes, and then the handwritten notes from Mr. and Mrs. Parker.

"You want me to help?" I ask.

113

"No." She points. "Go and stand by the window. Watch the parking lot for the cops."

I cross the room and peel back the curtain a few inches, trying to stay out of view.

The cop car is already here. Two officers step out and begin walking to the front door of the building. They had to have been right behind us.

"They're here," I say, stepping back from the window.

She stops packing and looks up. "Are you kidding me?"

I angrily turn to her. "Yep. Funniest joke in the world."

She frantically looks around.

"Bathroom. Now!" she snaps.

I don't question. I simply go into the small bathroom. I hear her snap the suitcase closed and slide it under the bed before joining me in the bathroom.

"Get behind the door, crouch down, and do not move!" she says.

I do as she says. I step behind the door, crouch down, and pull the door behind me. Through the crack by the hinge, I watch as Genevieve opens the shower door and turns the knobs. The water begins hissing from the showerhead. Genevieve quickly undresses, tosses her clothes on the floor, and steps into the shower.

"HAHHH! Cold!" she gasps and adjusts the knobs. Steam begins to rise from the shower. She then bows her head, letting the water soak into her hair.

I can't take this anymore.

"You're not seriously taking a shower, right n—?"

There's a knock at the door.

"Avalon PD," a voice in the hallway announces. "Ms. Winters?"

We both freeze.

There's another knock.

"Ms. Winters?"

"… Yes?" she calls out.

"Avalon PD. Open up, please."

114

"I'm in the shower! Just a sec!"

She quickly squirts some shampoo into her hand and frantically lathers up her hair. Then, she steps out of the shower and wraps herself in a towel, leaving the water running. As she passes the door, she glances down at me through the crack and raises a finger to her lips.

I press myself closer to the wall and curl into the tightest ball possible.

From my hiding spot, I hear the door open over the sound of the shower.

"Sorry," Genevieve says. "I was in the shower."

"May we come in?" a male voice asks.

"Can I ask what this is about?"

"Were you at Evergreen Terrace Apartments this afternoon?"

"I was there earlier this morning."

"By yourself?"

"Yes."

"What were you doing there?" a woman's voice asks.

"Well, like every other journalist in Avalon, I was going after this Parker double homicide story."

"So, what were you doing at the apartment building?" the male voice asks.

"Trying to find out more about the apartment Emily Parker was renting."

"How did you know about the apartment?" the woman asks.

I can picture the smirk on Genevieve's face as she responds, "Because someone on your force is a friend of mine."

"So, you weren't there half an hour ago with a guy, trying to see the lease?"

"No. I told you, I was there this morning. And what guy? What lease? What are you talking about?"

There's a long pause. I've been holding my breath and my lungs are begging for some of the misty, humid air that has quickly filled the small bathroom.

115

"May we come in and have a look around?" the woman asks.

"Sure. Let me turn off the shower. I didn't know this was going to be an extended interview."

Genevieve, what are you doing?! Don't let them in the room! I almost scream but instead try to curl myself into an even smaller ball behind the door.

Genevieve steps into the bathroom. Through the crack, I can see that she's still dripping wet and her hair lathered in shampoo. She reaches into the shower and turns off the water.

As she does, the woman officer pokes her head in.

She's less than a foot away from me through the door. All she has to do is look down to her left and she'll see me through the crack, but the air is thick and obscured by the steam. Still, all she has to do is step inside, look around the door, and there I'll be; World's Worst Hide and Seek Champion of 2021. She's about to do just that when Genevieve turns back and makes a move to go out the door but is startled to see the officer standing there. She clutches her towel and shuffles to go around her.

"Excuse me," Genevieve says.

The officer steps back, allows her to pass, and then follows her into the room.

I don't know if she planned it that way or if I'm extremely lucky, but Genevieve just flawlessly stopped the officer from finding me.

I stay absolutely still and listen to the sound of the closet door opening and closing as the police conduct their search.

"You want to tell me just what it is exactly that you're looking for?" Genevieve asks.

"You said that you were at Evergreen Terrace Apartments this morning?" the male officer asks.

"Yes. I already told you that. You are correct."

"You were alone?"

"Yes. I told you that, too."

One of the officer's radios squawks with a loud, fuzzy, unintelligible voice.

"And you were trying to see the lease?"

"No. Like I told you thirty seconds ago, I don't know anything about the lease. I was simply trying to find out more about the apartment."

Even I'm confused as to what Genevieve is trying to do.

"What were you hoping to find out about the apartment?" the woman asks.

Genevieve sighs. "Listen, officers, I've been more than accommodating, but that's all I'm going to say. I have a dinner that I'm trying to get to and I'd like to finish showering. So, unless there's anything else?"

One of the radios squawks again.

"You'll be in Avalon a while?" the man asks.

"Seeing as how I live here and you're standing in my apartment, I'd say that's a pretty safe bet."

"But you work for the *Herald*, which is in San Francisco."

"Yes. Correct, again."

"So, why do you live here, in Avalon?"

There's a tension-filled pause before Genevieve speaks. "Will there be anything else, officer?"

"Not at the moment, but we may have some more questions for you later."

Genevieve sighs, again, and there's the sound of rustling.

"Well, here's my card, and if you have any good tips about the case, don't hesitate to call. My paper would be very appreciative."

I can only imagine the death stares the officers are giving Genevieve.

"Okay … Thank you, Ms. Winters," the female says. "Enjoy your dinner."

There's a shuffling of feet and the sound of the front door opening to the hallway.

The footsteps pass from the apartment into the corridor.

"Good evening, officers."

The door closes. I remain perfectly still.

Genevieve bursts into the bathroom and motions with her hand. "Come on, come on, come on."

I slide out from behind the door.

"That was amazing!" I excitedly whisper.

She rips the towel off, steps back into the shower, and begins vigorously rinsing the shampoo from her hair.

"It's not going to take them long to figure out I was lying. Get over to the window. Try to look out and tell me when they're gone, but do not touch the curtain!"

"Got it."

I go back into the living room/bedroom and over to the window. I press myself against the wall so I can see out of the small space without touching the curtain.

"The cop car is still there," I say over my shoulder.

The shower cuts off and Genevieve appears from the bathroom wrapped in a towel while drying her hair with another.

"Damnit. If they're sitting on us—"

There's movement down below.

"Wait … There they are."

The pair of officers walk to their car, engrossed in conversation. The man gets in the passenger side. The woman opens the driver's side door and pulls out the radio.

"What's happening?" Genevieve asks as she throws the towel back into the bathroom and hastily begins pulling on her clothes.

"The lady's on the radio. Guy's in the car."

Genevieve continues getting dressed. "We need to move before they put a tail on us."

In the parking lot below, the woman officer gets in the car. The lights on the cop car flash and the engine revs to life.

"They're leaving."

"Keep watching. Make sure," she says, pulling the suitcase from under the bed and throwing it back on top of the mattress.

The cop car slowly rolls forward and navigates out of the lot. Genevieve snaps the suitcase closed behind me.

The cop car pulls into the street and drives off.

"Gone," I announce, turning back to the room.

Genevieve, her hair still wet and her clothes disheveled, grabs the suitcase off the bed.

"Let's go."

Genevieve pokes her head out of the side door and scans the parking lot while I wait behind her, her suitcase in hand.

"Now!" she says and steps hurriedly through the door.

Moving at a brisk pace, just below a run, we reach her car. She slides into the driver's seat while I open the back. As we've planned, I climb in, put her suitcase on the floor, and lay across the back-seat, out of view.

"It might be too much," she explained as we left the room, "but I don't want them to be waiting for us down the road and see you."

I didn't argue, so now I'm sprawled across the seat, knees bent, feet up against the door.

Genevieve starts the car and puts it in reverse. She's fighting the urge to floor it out of the parking lot. She's largely successful, but manages to take a speedbump a little too hard and I'm momentarily lifted off the seat and crash back down.

"Sorry, sorry, sorry."

"I'm fine. Keep going."

There's another light bounce as we exit the parking lot. She turns right and I'm thrown to the side. My head smacks the door.

"Sorry!"

"Stop apologizing and just drive," I reply, even though my vision blurs for a second.

I hold my breath and watch her. She's my only indication of what's happening around us. After a few minutes, she visibly relaxes and her grip on the steering wheel lessens.

"Okay. I think we're clear."

I begin to sit up.

"What are you doing?" she asks.

"You said we're clear."

"I said I think we're clear. Just stay down for now. Let me think."

I lay back on the seat and bite my lip.

Suddenly, Genevieve pulls out her cellphone and dials.

"What are you doing, now?" I ask.

"Buying us some time ... Greg, it's me," she says into the phone. "Yes, I'm aware. Now, shut up and listen ..."

Welcome to the party, Greg, whoever you are.

We're parked in the far corner of the Walmart parking lot, just outside of Avalon. I've been promoted to the front seat, because now it would be suspicious if someone walking by saw me lying across the back seat.

Genevieve is consulting her notebook while typing on her phone. I've tried to ask what the plan is but each and every answer she's offered has been "shut up".

It's been an hour of watching her type away and I can't sit quietly anymore.

"So, what are you—?"

"If it's about the plan, I've already said 'shut up.'"

"No. I was going to ask what you're writing."

"I'm writing the story."

"Are you serious?!"

She continues typing, unfazed. "It's best to get everything down as quickly as possible after it happened and after everything that just happened, you're damn right, I'm serious."

That smirk. That intensity in her eyes. She's loving this.

I push it aside because there's one question that's been eating away at me since we escaped her apartment and now, I have to know.

"What would have happened?"

"What are you talking about?" she asks, not looking up from her phone.

"When you let the cops in the room. What would have happened if they had found me? What would you have done?"

She shrugs. "Let them take you."

"Unbelievable," I snort.

"If you had been caught, I could still work on the case. I could still track down the killer."

"No, you couldn't."

"Why not?"

"Because you would have been arrested for helping me."

She stops and looks out the windshield at the passing cars, but only for a moment. "Well, that didn't happen, so let's not dwell on it," she replies and goes back to typing.

I can't think of anything to say and resume fuming while staring out the window.

Moments later, her phone pings. She reads the message and then scans the parking lot. She stops when she sees the blue Ford Fusion coming towards us.

"Here we go," she says.

The Fusion makes its way in our direction. As it approaches, the rental car sticker in the corner of the windshield comes into view. There's a skinny guy in sunglasses behind the wheel, who parks in the space next to us.

Genevieve opens her door. "Grab my suitcase and get in the front seat of that car."

She gets out before there's a chance to protest or ask for some more clarification. I follow her instructions because I guess that's what I do now. I pull her suitcase from the back and step out of the car.

The skinny guy exits the Fusion. Without a word, Genevieve hands him the keys to her car and the lease to the apartment. In return, he hands her the keys to the rental. He only gives me a cursory glance as he gets in Genevieve's car, starts the engine, pulls out of the space, and drives away.

"Get in the car, Clay," Genevieve says from the driver's seat of our new ride.

I snap out of it and throw the suitcase into the back seat. I open the passenger door and climb in, but first, I have to move a cash-stuffed envelope that's sitting on the seat.

Genevieve takes the envelope, thumbs through the cash, and hands it back to me.

"Put that in my suitcase, will you?"

"... sure."

I twist around, open her suitcase, and toss the envelope inside. My tasks completed, I sit back and look at her, still trying to comprehend everything and coming up empty.

"Who was that?"

"Greg," she replies, sliding the key in the ignition. "My editor at the *Herald*. I called him after you said you wanted to talk."

"Does he know what's going on?"

"Nope."

She puts it into gear.

"He didn't ask?"

"He knows better."

Genevieve takes her foot off the brake and we roll out of the parking lot.

Chapter 14

"You're sure that this place takes cash and doesn't ask for ID?" Genevieve asks, removing some of the money from the envelope and transferring it to the wallet in her purse.

"Yeah. Positive."

"Classy."

The Gold Coast Suites Motel is nowhere near the coast. It's one of the hotels further out from the center of Avalon. I vaguely remember it from a late-night tryst with Emily months ago. Since then, the memory of it has blended in with all the other motels. I only remember it because of the misnomer.

Genevieve chews her lip as we stare across the asphalt parking lot at the check-in office.

"What are you thinking?" I ask.

"There's no way you're going in there."

"And what if the cops have told people to be on the lookout for you, too?"

She thinks it over. "I'll know. Whoever is in there behind the counter, I'll know as soon as I walk through the door if they recognize me."

"And then what? You'll come running out and we high-tail it out of here?"

"Something like that." She makes a decision. "Okay, here's what we're going to do. Get out your phone."

I take out the burner phone and hold it at the ready. She gets out her phone, as well.

She dials and the burner phone begins to vibrate in my hand.

"Answer it," she says.

I hit "answer".

She puts her phone on speaker and drops it into her purse.

"I do this all the time with my editor when I'm interviewing someone. Do not hang up your phone. You can listen to what's going on so you'll know if there's any trouble. If there is, I'll come running, hop in the car, and we get out of here, understand?"

"You do this with your editor?" I ask.

"Yeah. Essentially, I'm butt-dialing you."

We study the check-in office a little longer and she takes a deep breath.

"Okay. I'll be right back." She opens the door and quickly adds, "Hopefully."

She gets out and begins walking towards the office.

I slide across, awkwardly maneuvering over the gear shift, drop into the driver's seat, and start the car.

A couple of yards away, she stops and looks around as if she's worried that she's forgotten something. Her eyes briefly rest on me. I see her lips move and her voice comes through the phone.

"Can you hear me?" she asks.

It's not as clear as if she were holding the phone to her ear, but it's audible enough. I give her a thumbs up.

"Good," she responds. "Now, get your head down."

I slouch down and she resumes her stride towards the check-in office. The scraping of her footsteps emanates from the phone, as do the jingling bells attached to the door as she opens it.

"Good evening," a woman says in a cigarette-scarred voice.

Through the glass door of the check-in office, I can just barely see the owner of the voice: a husky, gray-haired woman, standing behind the counter.

"Hi. I'd like a room, please."

"Two of you?"

"Yep."

"All right. The nightly rate is seventy-two, eighty-five."

"Great."

There's static and pops as Genevieve rummages around in her purse, containing her phone.

"And I'll need to see some ID and a credit card for the deposit."

The rummaging stops.

"Oh … I was hoping I could pay cash."

"You can, when you check out, but I need a credit card for the deposit and some ID."

I clutch the phone, waiting for Genevieve's response.

"Listen," she says, lowering her voice to the point where I have to hold the phone against my ear to listen. "I'm with someone who I … well, I really shouldn't be with."

"Genevieve, what are you doing?" I say out loud.

"What was that?" the woman behind the counter asks.

My hand reflexively flies to my mouth.

"I'm sorry," Genevieve awkwardly laughs. "I was listening to a podcast on my phone when I walked in here and I think it's still on."

There's the sound of her digging through her purse, again. "There. That should shut the stupid thing up. So, like I was saying," she continues. "I'm kind of here with someone I shouldn't be … Someone my husband would very definitely not approve of."

"… Okay."

"And I don't want him to get an alert about some unusual activity on the credit card or have it pop up on my banking statement. Know what I mean?"

There's a long pause.

Well, here we go, I think, my hand easing towards the gearshift.

"I'm sorry," Genevieve says through the phone. "What did you say the rate was? One hundred fifty dollars? Cash?"

I put the car in "drive".

"Sure," the lady says. "But I still need to see some ID."

My foot begins to ease off the brake pedal, on its way to the gas.

"I'm sorry," Genevieve says. "What did you say the rate was? Two hundred dollars?"

The room at The Gold Coast Suites Motel prove that there is no legal definition of the word "suite". It's a bare box with carpeting, a table, two chairs, a dresser upon which sits a television, and one queen bed.

I'm currently occupying the bed, flipping through the local stations to see if there's any more info about me or Genevieve, who is on the phone with Greg, the editor, and taking notes in her notebook.

"Yes ... yeah ... It's called 'Casper Holdings' ... You got that? ... Okay ... Where are they located? ... Sacramento? ... Okay ... Yeah ... How long do you think it will take? ... No ... No, that's great ... Call me as soon as you've got something ... Okay ... Okay ... Thanks, Greg. And please don't forget to feed Snoozy for me. Give it a day or two to make sure they're not watching my apartment, then it should be fine ... Thanks." She hangs up.

"So, how'd it go?" I ask.

"He's hoping to have something by tomorrow morning."

"What are we supposed to do until then?"

"Rest."

Genevieve takes a shower and gets ready for bed.

She steps out of the bathroom wearing a T-shirt and pajama pants.

I've already showered and have gone back to watching the

news. As she approaches the bed, I take a pillow and an extra blanket and begin to lay them out on the floor.

"What are you doing?" she asks.

"Getting ready to go to sleep."

"Why are you sleeping on the floor?"

"Well—I … um … because …" I stammer, glancing back at the bed.

She rolls her eyes. "Look, we need to stay as sharp as we can, so you need to sleep and you're not going to get that sleeping on the floor." She holds up three fingers in a scout's honor salute. "I promise I won't jump you if you promise not to jump me."

I sheepishly get back into bed. Genevieve goes around to the other side and climbs in as well. She hits the lamp on the bedside table, plunging the room into shadows. She lays down on her side, her back to me, while I stare up at the ceiling.

"I'm sorry for freaking out back at the apartment," I say, unable to stay silent.

"Don't worry about it. It's over. We got what we needed."

The only sound is that of passing cars outside. I can't close my eyes. There's something else on my mind and Genevieve senses it.

"What?" she asks.

"I … I keep thinking about what you said."

"When?"

"When I asked you what you would have done if the cops found me in your apartment. That you would have given me up … I can't help but think that if it comes down to it, if we're truly trapped and there's no other way out, you'll give me up to save your own skin … and I know you saved my ass today, but I don't know if I can really trust you, because I can't help but think you'll have no problem giving me up if it's in your best interest."

For what feels like an eternity, she's absolutely still, but then rolls over to face me. Even in the darkness, her comforting expression shines through. "Clay, listen to me, because I need you to understand this. If it comes to that, if there's no way out … that is exactly what I will do."

She smiles and rolls back over on her side.

I stare at the back of her head.

What do you say to that? I have no idea, so I say the only thing that comes to mind. "Oh … okay … Good night."

She doesn't respond.

Chapter 15

Genevieve snags her keys and purse from the table by the window.

"All right. I'm just getting us some food and other essentials. The less we have to leave this room until we hear from Greg, the better. Do you have a favorite deodorant or anything? Preference of toothbrush firmness?"

"Uh, not really." I can't remember the last time I thought about toothbrush firmness.

"I should be gone two hours, tops. Until then, stay away from the window and try to think of any way we can find out more about the Parkers. And most importantly; don't go outside. I don't care if the motel is on fire. Got it?"

"Thanks for the advice."

"If anything happens, call me."

She does one last check, making sure she's got everything, nods, and opens the door, but stops when she sees that she's left her notebook on the table. She quickly grabs it. "I'll be back as soon as I can."

Before I can ask why she's taking the notebook, she's already closed the door behind her.

Just outside the door in the parking lot, I hear the Fusion start and drive away.

Now that she's gone, it's way too quiet in this room; way too quiet and way too cramped.

The best thing for me to do would be to get some more sleep. Having half of the bed last night was certainly better than having the whole floor, but I was awoken every hour or so by Genevieve's snoring. I stretch out on the bed and rest my head on the pillow, but my eyes have no interest in staying closed. I turn on the television. Flipping through the news on television doesn't bring any updates about the murders, only national and international stories. Normally, I like to stay up to date with what's going on in the world, but I can't focus. I give up and start surfing through gameshows and soap operas. They're trash, I know, but I'm hoping that I can escape into the drama of the love child Amy had with her husband's evil twin because she didn't realize her real husband was in a coma. It succeeds in holding my interest for only a minute or two, but then I'm right back to thinking about my situation.

The television goes off and I think about what Genevieve asked; Is there some way we can find out more about the Parkers?

Nothing comes to mind.

Emily and I never talked much about her marriage, other than the fact that she was unhappy. She liked the life, but there was no love. Once or twice, when she had been in one of her devil-may-care moods, she had said she was thinking of leaving him and we joked about how he couldn't get it up, but we never talked about him or their marriage in-depth. She and I were having fun. I cared about her, and that was all I needed to know. There was never much discussion about his business, either. She didn't seem to know much about it. It's possible that she did and simply didn't want to discuss it with me. I guess I was an escape for her; a way of forgetting him, just for a little while.

So, who would want to kill them? And why would they go to such lengths to frame me for it?

None of this makes sense. It's like I'm staring at a jigsaw puzzle but all the pieces are from different puzzles, there are no edges, and the lid to the box with the completed picture is nowhere to be found.

Pacing the floor usually helps me think, but the room is too small. I can only take a few steps before turning back. It's like I'm pacing in a prison cell … That is a terrible analogy.

When is Genevieve getting back? It feels like she's been gone for hours, but a quick check of the time informs me that she's only been gone for forty-one minutes.

Claustrophobia is setting in. The sweating starts, as do the shallow breaths.

Maybe the view out of the window will make this place feel bigger. I'm about to draw back the curtain, but recall Genevieve's warning.

Can't move. Can't look out the window. Can't watch television. Can't sleep. Can't think.

With a frustrated grunt, I drop into one of the chairs at the table and press the palms of my hands against my eyes.

Ping.

Great. It's probably Genevieve asking me my shoe size.

I walk over and grab the burner phone from the nightstand and open the text messages.

I'm glad you have found a friend. You're going to need all the help you can get.

All of my frustration becomes laser focused on the phone as I carry it back to the table. I'm composing snarky replies in my head, but that's exactly what he wants, so I set it on the table in front of me and sit in the chair.

Minutes pass.

Ping.

Leave it alone. Do not answer it.

My resistance lasts for about thirty seconds before I pick up the phone.

You can read it, I tell myself, *but don't answer.*

131

Her last words were about you. Do you want to know what they were?

I shouldn't have picked up the phone.

Put it down, Clay.

There. That's it. Good. Now, just grip the armrests of the chair tightly and stare at the carpet until Genevieve gets back.

Ping.

I can only tap the toe of my foot against the carpet for so long before the frustration wins out.

I grab the phone.

The life was running out of her neck, all over the bed, and she wanted me to tell you something. Want to know what it was?

Get away from the damn phone, Clay.

I put the phone back on the table and start pacing again, but the room is still too small. It's impossible to get away from it. I should turn the phone off, but what if Genevieve tries to get hold of me.

Ping.

He's not going to stop. He's going to keep texting. He's going to keep torturing me.

I grab the phone.

It was something she really wanted you to know.

I begin typing.

Fine, asshole. What did she say?

I push send and wait.

Ping.

She said, "Tell Clay that this is all his fault."

I want to hurl the phone against the wall. Instead, I type.

Fuck you.

😂 *Don't worry, Clay. She didn't say that. I just missed talking to you. I'm really enjoying this and I'm genuinely glad you found a friend. It's going to make this so much more interesting.*

Laugh it up, asshole. We're on to you, I respond.

On to me? Are you and your friend playing detective? I assume she's Sherlock and you are Watson, since he was the bumbling one. The new look doesn't suit you by the way.

My eyes shoot towards the curtained window. Just like the police station, I wonder; is he looking at me, right now?

No, you idiot. He saw you at the apartment.

Sorry if I'm not a swipe right for you, I reply.

Do you really think you two amateur sleuths are going to find me before I find you?

I confidently smile as I type. *Buddy, she'll find you. She's got the network and the resources. You have no idea how good she is.*

Oh, Clay. There's one thing you have to understand …

There's a pause.

Ping.

I stare at the message on the screen and breathe, "No …"

It's a staff photo of Genevieve from the *Herald*.

Ping.

The next message is her bio.

Ping.

Her phone number and email.

Ping.

Her home address.

Ping.

A picture of a smiling Genevieve holding a black cat pressed against her cheek.

Ping.

Snoozy.

Ping.

I know everything.

The sound of a key in the door causes me to spring to my feet and drop the phone.

Genevieve opens the door and walks in, her arms loaded with plastic bags.

"Okay, since we don't have a fridge, I got us—" She stops cold when she registers the expression on my face. "What happened?"

"I …"

She spots the phone, lying on the floor. She quickly wheels around and shuts the door, drops the bags, and picks up the phone. Her eyes widen as she scrolls through the messages, shaking her head in disbelief.

"No … no, no, no, no, no, no!" she mumbles, scrolling through the texts and then looking at me. "What did you do?"

"Nothing. He texted me. I answered."

"Why?! Why would you do that?!"

"Why not?"

"Because it's exactly what he wanted you to do."

"He was just trying to taunt me."

"You—?!" She turns away in frustration as if she's going to scream before exhaling and facing me, again. "No. No, you idiot. This is what he wanted. This right here." She points to the message where I said that we were on to him.

"So?"

"He wanted to know what we were up to, and you told him."

"Yeah, but he knows who you are, so he probably already knew that."

"But if we're 'on to him', then he knows for sure that we're still somewhere in Avalon."

My mouth opens but there's no defense I can offer because once again, I've screwed up.

"And who told him everything about me?" she asks, eyes blazing.

"How should I know?" I helplessly shrug.

She stares at me, scanning my face for any sign that I might be lying.

"Genevieve, I didn't tell him. I swear to you."

She glares a moment longer, then slightly relaxes.

"Thank you." I sigh. "Can I have the phone back now?"

"You're never touching this phone again."

Chapter 16

Genevieve narrows her eyes at me from across the table.

"I think you're lying."

"Genevieve, why would I lie to you, right now? About this?"

"I don't know. Just a hunch that you're not telling me the truth."

"Well, I am."

"Prove it."

"How am I supposed to do that?"

"Show me."

"Genevieve, I'm telling you; I don't have any fours. Go fish."

She reaches for the cards that are spread out on the small table, but doesn't relinquish me from her accusatory gaze. She selects a card and tucks it into her hand, only briefly glancing down to see what it is before resuming her stare.

She bought this deck of cards along with the clothes she purchased for me at the mall. Since then, we've been playing War, Crazy 8s, and now, Go Fish.

It's been a couple of hours and there have been no more texts.

I study my hand. "Do you have any sev— No. This can't be how it works. We just sit here until Greg calls?"

135

"A lot of the time, this is exactly how it works," she calmly replies. "That's why I bought the deck of cards."

"That's what reporters do? Wait?"

"Sometimes. Look, a reporter doesn't do everything by themselves. We'll use contacts who have specialties in certain areas, and they'll track down the information we can't get to. That's what Greg is doing. I want to see that lease."

"Why? What are you hoping to find?"

"That my hunch is right."

"And what is that?"

"… a hunch."

"And until then?"

"You were going to ask me if I had any sevens." She looks at her hand. "Go fish."

I drop my cards onto the table. "Nope. I give up. You win."

"Fine," she says and tosses her hand onto the table.

She gets up and goes to her laptop, which is lying on the bed. She sets her notebook next to it and begins typing.

She's forgotten the burner phone, which is sitting on the table in front of me.

"Working on the story?"

"Yup."

She rapidly types something, mulls it over, quickly hits the delete key a few times, and goes back to typing.

I scoop up the cards into a stack, shuffle, and deal myself a hand of solitaire. I distractedly make my columns, alternating the reds and blacks. I can't stop looking over at Genevieve, typing on the bed.

"Have you ever done this before?"

"Done what?"

"Tried to track down a killer."

"Mmm hmmm." She continues typing. "Back in San Francisco. A hiker found the remains of a woman and a child up in the mountains. They had been dissolved in a plastic drum filled with acid. The police were trying to hush it up, but one of the forensic guys got hold of me. I was on the police beat at the time. He told me that the police had found four other bodies hidden deep in the woods, disposed of in the same way. We teamed up to try to find who did it."

"Did you?"

She stops typing. "Sort of."

"What does that mean?"

She sits up, sets her laptop off to the side, and faces me with her legs hanging off the side of the bed. "The detectives on the case learned that the forensic guy was working with me, sharing information about the case that was not supposed to be shared. He was fired. The *Herald* almost fired me. After that, SFPD wouldn't work with the press on anything. No one on the force wanted to be a source for any stories. It was an all-around shit show."

"But they eventually caught him?"

"Like I said; sort of."

"Who was it?"

Genevieve gets quiet and gently swings her dangling feet before answering. "It was the forensics guy."

"Seriously?"

She nods.

"How did they catch him?" I ask.

"He kind of wanted to get caught. He had been in forensics for over twenty years. Apparently, his first kill had been an accident and he hid the body using what he knew about police procedures, so no one found it. After that, he had a taste for it. He started doing it for the thrill of getting away with it, but then that wasn't enough. He got mad when the police kept hiding the discovery of new bodies. The police thought that there was no way to identify the killer, so they buried it. The forensic guy was too good at it. That's when he contacted me."

"You're saying he wanted you to catch him?"

"Not exactly. He wanted to make the murders public. He wanted everyone to know what he had done and thought there was no way that a beat cop reporter would find out he was the killer ..." She shrugs. "Turns out, he was right ... Anyway, he tried to share too much with me about the case, which is what got the police interested in him. Once the police saw him as a suspect, everything fell into place. They busted him about a year later. He so badly wanted to be recognized for what he had done, he started sending letters to the *Herald* about how he was planning his next kill. The *Herald* was eager to get back in good graces with the SFPD. So, they showed them the letters instead of printing them. They linked him to the letters through his handwriting and that was that."

"But you had the story. Why hasn't anyone heard of this?"

"Because no one wanted them to. SFPD didn't want the world knowing one of their own was dissolving people in acid. The *Herald* didn't want to burn the SFPD again, and they didn't want everyone to know that one of their reporters couldn't figure out that they were working with a serial killer."

"That's ... That's insane."

She shrugs again.

"I hope you don't mind me asking, but why didn't the *Herald* fire you?" I ask.

"They will, eventually. I'm under an NDA with any story I've worked on while at the *Herald*. It extends for eighteen months after I quit or get fired. The guy was sentenced last year. I figure they'll wait another three months and then fire me or until the NDA runs out. They're hoping by then that the story will be long-forgotten. Then, I'll—"

A realization hits me.

"Wait ... Wait, wait, wait, wait. If they're going to fire you, and you're such a black eye to them, why would they let you go after this story?"

She draws a breath to speak but stops. Guilt and embarrassment swirl across her face.

"Are you—? ... No way ..." I shake my head and snort derisively. "They didn't tell you to cover this story, did they?"

"Look, it doesn't matter. I'm still employed by them. I'm still a reporter for the *Herald*, and that carries a lot of weight."

"Until it gets back to the *Herald* that you're telling people you're doing this on their behalf."

"I'm still a reporter, okay?"

"Sure. Technically."

She shakes her head in disgust.

"I mean, that's why you live in Avalon but say you work for the *Herald*. They want nothing to do with you."

Her inability to look me in the eye confirms it.

"I needed to get out, okay? I was burned and needed to get away from San Francisco. So, I took the money the *Herald* was offering me, even if I wasn't working, and came here to clear my head and get back on my feet."

"And this is you 'getting back in the game'?"

"Call it what you want."

"And who is Greg? Is he really your editor or have you been lying about that, too?"

"He is my editor. He still had faith in me after the forensics fiasco. That's why he's been helping us."

"Until he gets fired for it."

"Which isn't going to happen. He's careful."

I can't believe this. Up until now, there's been some comfort in the fact that Genevieve has been helping me. Now, that help is hanging by a thread. No wonder she would so easily give me up to save herself.

"This isn't happening." I sigh, pinching the bridge of my nose.

"Clay—"

"You told me you wanted to get this guy because you knew Emily."

"Yes. I did."

"Did you really know her, or was that a lie too?"

Her jaw drops. "I can't believe that you would—"

"No. No, no, no, no. You don't get to be offended when I ask you if you lied about one thing when two minutes ago, you told me you've been lying about everything else."

"Yes, I knew her," she snaps. "Did I know her well? No. We didn't share the deeply held bond of 'fuck-buddies' like you did, but yes, I knew her. A couple of years ago, I got my start doing puff pieces for the *Herald*. She and her husband were in town for some big financial convention and the paper had me interview the spouses of the mega-hedge-fund managers." She shakes her head. "It was so stupid. The questions were insulting, but it was the job. I conducted the interviews in the bar of one of the hotels. Everyone was giving the standard, canned answers, which is what the *Herald* wanted, but she … Something broke in her during our interview, and we started talking. She told me about the dreams she had when she was my age and how she gave them up when Henry Parker came along. She told me at first she convinced herself that she was going to use his influence and connections to achieve her own goals, but ended up settling for the big house, and the clothes, and the miserable marriage, and told herself that that was okay, because lots of people settled for a lot less … She also told me about the affairs. Believe me, Clay, you weren't the first," she adds pointedly.

Somehow, I've always known that, but to hear it has an effect on me that I'm not prepared for. My ego had always made me feel like I was somehow special to her. How could I not be? But to have the truth held up to my face makes me feel hollow and insignificant. It's not Emily's fault. It's mine. My vanity's. And in this moment, I realize that no matter what she felt for me, I cared for her more than I would allow myself to admit.

"Anyway," Genevieve continues. "She told me never to fall into the same trap that she did. She told me that I was the only one who could make me truly happy. That's when I decided that I wanted that police beat, and I don't care how it ended. I'm proud of the work I did. I'm a damn good reporter ... That's also why I'm in Avalon. She told me about this place in our interview. After the whole forensics thing, I decided to come here as a reminder of what she said to me. I didn't come here to see her, but one night, I ran into her at The Gryphon. She didn't remember or even recognize me, but I never forgot her. So, yeah. I knew her, and I want to get this guy ... Yes, I lied to you. Sorry. But if that really pisses you off"—she motions with her hand—"there's the door."

We stare at one another.

Her phone begins to chime. She checks the ID and shows me the screen.

"It's Greg. If you're leaving, go now so I can tell him to keep his mouth shut and not share anything with me that could get him into trouble."

I glance down at the cards. There aren't many plays on the table.

"Make up your mind, Clay."

"... Tell him I said 'hi'."

"I'll tell him you said, 'thank you'. It's a little more appropriate." She answers the phone. "Greg. You got something for me?"

I go back to playing solitaire, pretending that I'm not really listening, but of course I am. Genevieve is scribbling in her notebook, using her shoulder to press her phone to her ear. Occasionally, she'll mutter stuff like, "Yeah ... uh-huh ... okay ... yeah ..."

Her story was very touching but it doesn't change the fact that she lied. She lied to me, and now I'm forced to keep relying on her, because it's all the help I've got and I still want to catch this guy.

"... Yeah ... Okay ... No ... Not yet ..."

Her voice is grating in my ears and I can't concentrate on the cards.

I need to get away, even if it's for a moment. Since I can't go outside, there's only one option.

As I stand, I pick up the burner phone. It's an old habit of mine. Even though I set my phone to give me alerts whenever I get texts or emails, I'll still check it, even if I didn't get an alert, which is like opening your front door, even if you didn't hear the doorbell, just to see if someone is standing there. There are no new messages and I toss the phone onto the bed as I pass Genevieve, who is too engrossed in her discussion with Greg to notice.

I go into the bathroom, shut the door, and sit on the toilet with the lid down and my hands over my ears, trying to block out her muffled mumblings.

How does my situation keep getting worse?

Genevieve has saved us once or twice, but how long can our luck hold up? And when it runs out, which I'm convinced it will, she's going to turn me over to the cops. She said that she would still work on the story, but she won't be able to.

I'll stick with her for now and work with her as best as I can, but at the first sign that she's going to give me up, I'm running. I don't know what comes after that, but I'm convinced, after what she just told me about her standing at the *Herald*, that I'm going to have to make a run for it. She can keep trying to catch this guy, but if she gives me up, they're never going to find him. I'll be convicted and the story will go away.

So, that's that.

"Clay! Get your ass out here!" she calls from the bedroom.

I stand up, flush the toilet to keep up appearances, and leave my temporary sanctuary.

Chapter 17

Genevieve's laptop is open on the table and she's bounding around the room like a kid who just woke up on Christmas morning.

"What's going on?"

"Sit down and look at this," she insists, pulling out the chair.

As instructed, I sit in the chair, in front of the laptop. The screen displays the image of a scanned document with an official stamp. Genevieve hovers over my shoulder.

"So," she begins. "As I said, we could have gotten this on our own, but it would have taken weeks. But with the name of the holding company, Greg knocked it out of the park! He was able to get hold of a scanned copy of the lease from the city's digital records archive."

"Legally?" I ask, turning to her but she puts her hands on the sides of my head and keeps me facing the screen.

"Now, the apartment was set up to be paid with automatic withdrawals from her account. In other words, she wouldn't have to do anything."

"Okay ..."

"You said that she never mentioned the apartment?"

"No."

"Good. Now, look ..."

My eyes drift over the scanned image.

"Genevieve, it's a lease. I'm not sure—"

"Down at the bottom!"

There are two signature lines at the bottom of the page. One is signed by a representative of the company that owns the building, Casper Holdings. My heart sinks as I read the other signature: Emily Parker.

"So, she did rent the apartment."

Genevieve quickly reaches around, pulls two pieces of paper from behind the laptop, and sets one on either side of the keyboard. One is the slip of register paper that Emily wrote on to tell me she would be in room number 37 at the Seaside Motel. The other is the blood-stained paper I pulled from Mr. Parker's blazer that reads 'PERKIEST'.

"What are you doing? What is this?" I ask.

"Clay, look at the signature on the lease."

I bring my nose closer to the screen. The image is clear enough. There's Emily's signature. Neat. Orderly. Firm.

"Now, look at the writing on those pieces of paper."

Emily's note is written in a flowing hand. It was after she had four vodka tonics, but there's not a hint of the pen slipping or shaking.

Then, there's Mr. Parker's.

The strokes are firm, bold, written by a hand that has signed his name so many times, it has become his trademark. I've seen thousands and thousands of signatures on credit card receipts. You can tell a lot by someone just by the way they sign their names. Rich, self-important people treat their signature as if it carries real weight. It's their name on the line, and it's important, even if it is only a promise to pay for that one scotch and soda.

"Now," Genevieve says. "Look at the lease again."

I put my focus back on the screen. As I stare, I start to see it. Maybe it's the power of Genevieve's suggestion and I'm making

144

things up that aren't there, but the more I take in of the upper and lower case e's, p's, r's, the i, the lines connecting the letters, and the firmness of the strokes of the pen, the more I start to doubt if the hand that signed the lease is the same one that wrote me this playful message on the register paper.

I apply the same overly amateurish analysis to Mr. Parker's one-word note, and I think my theory still holds. The word is written in sharp strokes, upright, confident, considered. Even the blood and dip in the ocean can't change that. The more I study it, the more I think I start to see the similarities in the signature on the lease to the hand that wrote 'PERKIEST', but there's no way to be sure.

I compare the signature on the lease with Emily's message again. Maybe they could pass as being from the same person, but the more I look at it, the more it feels off.

"You think Henry Parker was the one who signed the lease?" I ask, going from the papers to the screen.

"Do I think we could prove it in court based off this? I have no idea. I don't think anyone could ever be one-hundred-percent sure that he signed the lease, but look at her writing. After the whole forensics thing, where the guy was nailed because of his handwriting on the letters, I learned a thing or two about handwriting analysis and I don't think she signed that. I think someone tried really hard to copy her writing. But think about it. It makes sense. You said that she never mentioned the apartment."

"Never."

"Then why, if she had gone to all that trouble to never leave any sort of paper trail, would she sign a lease for an apartment that you guys could use as a … 'sex den', and never tell you about it?"

"'Sex den'?"

"'Sex den'. 'Bouncy-castle'. Whatever. I need you to focus. You also said that he had access to all her accounts, right?"

"Yeah."

"So, how hard do you think it would be for him to set this up?"

"Set this up?" I'm finally starting to put this together. "You're saying that Mr. Parker set it up to look like Emily and I had an apartment so that we could keep sleeping together?"

Genevieve confidently nods. "Yep. Then, you were tricked into planting your fingerprints there, which is where this all gets really interesting."

"Hold on. Mr. Parker wasn't the one who told me to go to the apartment. It was …"

Genevieve beams.

"There it is," she says, thoroughly enjoying this.

"It was the killer. So … how would the killer know about the apartment unless Mr. Parker told him?"

"Right. And, that's not the only thing that both the killer and Mr. Parker knew about, is it … 'my sweet little cupcake'?"

"They both knew … So … you think that Mr. Parker and the killer were connected somehow before he killed him?"

Genevieve's smile goes wall-to-wall. "That is what we're going to find out."

I can't share her optimism.

"You think it'll be that easy?"

"No, but this is a start! This is good. It's a lead!"

Her phone pings. She darts across the room and picks it up off the nightstand.

"Is it Greg?" I ask. "Did he forget to tell you something?"

The blood drains from her face.

"Shit …" she whispers.

"What's wrong?"

Genevieve glances around, panic setting in. Then, she looks over at the table.

"Where's the burner phone?"

"It's on the bed."

"What is it doing on the bed? I left it on the table."

"Yeah, but I—"

"Did you have it in the bathroom?" she snaps.

"What? No, I—"

"Did you text him where we are?!" she asks.

"Who? No. Genevieve, I didn't text anyone. When Greg called, I just checked it for any more messages and I tossed it on the bed on my way to the bathroom."

Her eyes burn and her jaw clenches.

"Genevieve, what's going on?"

She rushes to the window and throws open the curtain. My first instinct is to dive behind the bed to stay out of sight.

"They're coming," she says, furtively glancing left and right out to the parking lot and the street beyond.

"Who's coming?"

"The cops!"

She turns back to the room, slings the suitcase onto the bed, and starts grabbing her things. I'm having déjà vu from yesterday when we fled her apartment.

"Wait … how?!"

She glares at me. "I don't know, but that was Greg. He got a message from his contact at the Avalon PD. Someone sent them an anonymous tip that included a list of motels we might be hiding at. This place is on that list."

"That's— That's impossible."

"It's possible and it's happening."

Genevieve grabs her laptop while I throw the clothes she's purchased for me into her suitcase on top of her clothes.

I can't believe this is happening again, and more importantly, how can this guy know?!

Instantly, the words that he told me I had to understand flash through my mind: "I know everything".

Less than five minutes later, Genevieve opens the door as I carry the suitcase behind her. Thankfully, the rental car is only a few steps from our room. We quickly move to the car and climb inside as the husky woman with the cigarette-scarred voice steps out of the check-in office, waving her hands for us to stop.

"Maybe she wants you to check out," I say.

"She'll figure it out," Genevieve says, pulling out of the parking lot.

We drive down the road in the direction of Avalon.

Once The Gold Coast Suites Motel becomes a speck in the distance, Genevieve pulls into a run-down gas station and parks in one of the handful of spots next to the defunct tire pump/ water station.

She kills the ignition and watches the road.

"What are we doing?" I ask.

"I have to know if this is real."

"The message from Greg's contact at Avalon PD wasn't enough?"

"I need to know," she says.

We stare out at the road, watching the sporadic passing of cars, coming from and going to Avalon.

"What exactly did your contact say?"

She takes out her phone, unlocks it, pulls up the messages, and hands it to me. "See for yourself."

It's a forwarded text that reads;

Forwarded: M
Anonymous tip – Told us to check the following:
1. Starry Night Inn
2. Sandcastle Motel
3. Surfside Inn
4. Gold Coast Suites
5. Triple 7 Motel
6. The Cove
7. Turner Motel

"You have got to be shitting me."

"Do you know those places?" Genevieve asks.

"Of course I do." I hand the phone back to her. "They're the places Emily and I would stay when … How could he possibly know that?"

"Yeah," she says, putting the phone back in her purse. "How could he possibly know that?"

"Genevieve—"

Something catches her eye.

"Keep your head down."

I slouch down but still keep the road in view just above the dashboard.

Two police cruisers go flying by the gas station.

They advance towards The Gold Coast Suites Motel. The other cars dutifully move to the side to allow them to pass. Their brake lights glow and they turn into the parking lot of the motel.

"Look at me," Genevieve says.

I turn.

The intensity of her eyes pins me to the seat.

"I need you to tell me right here, right now: are you working with this guy? And if I think you're lying, I will drive us right back to that motel and turn you in."

"Genevieve, I'm not working with this guy. I didn't kill the Parkers, and I didn't tip off the cops to where we were staying. I swear to god."

She searches my expression.

She has to believe me. She has to.

Finally, she sits back and starts the car.

"Okay. I'm trusting you for now, because we've got problems. We can't stay at any motels and we have to get off the road. The lady at the check-in may be able to describe the car. Hell, she might have even gotten the license plate. Do you have any friends in Avalon that you trust one-hundred-and-ten percent?"

There's only one name that comes to mind.

149

"Yeah," I reply. "But I don't think she can help us."

"That's where the extra ten percent comes in; the police might be watching them, so it has to be a friend of theirs we can hide out at. Do you still trust them enough?"

"… yeah."

"Why are you wincing?"

"Hello?"

"Katie. It's me."

"Clay?"

"Yeah."

"I— Clay. Oh my god. What is going on?"

"It's a long story and I'd love to explain it to you, but right now, I need your help."

"What do you mean?"

"I need a place to hide out."

There's a gap in the conversation filled by the sound of passing cars.

"I don't think it's a good idea. Everyone is looking for you, Clay."

"It's not just me. I'm with someone; a reporter. You'll recognize her from the bar. She's helping me find who killed the Parkers."

"How?"

"Again, a long story and I can't wait to tell you all about it, but we need a place to lie low for a day or two."

"It might be more than that," Genevieve whispers from the driver's seat.

'Shut up,' I mouth back at her.

"… I don't know, Clay … I told them about you and Emily Parker."

"I know, and that's fine. I told you, I should never have asked you to lie to the police."

"But you want me to lie to them now? They told me to call them if you tried to contact me."

150

"Well, like before, it's not really lying. It's just not telling anyone."

Genevieve's eyes go wide in disbelief. I turn away from her.

"Katie, you know I didn't do it."

"... I thought I did, but, Clay, don't you think it would be better if you just turned yourself in?"

"I can't do that."

"Why not?"

I don't want to tell her that it's because the mountain of evidence against me has grown bigger.

"Katie, I'll make you a deal, okay?"

"Okay."

"Let us come in. We'll tell you everything and if you think I'm lying, you can kick us out."

Genevieve grabs my shoulder and frantically tries to turn me around.

"And you can call the cops," I add.

"Are you out of your mind?!" Genevieve whispers.

"Whatever you feel you need to do," I say to Katie.

Genevieve is pounding her fists on my back.

I slightly turn to her, hold up my index finger, and mouth, "STOP IT!"

She folds her arms across her chest and stares out the windshield.

"Katie?" I ask.

"Yeah. I'm here."

"Please ..."

"Okay," she says, like she's just agreed to cut off her own arm.

I give Genevieve a thumbs up. She's not sold.

"I guess you can park your car in my spot in the lot. It'll be off the street."

"Katie?"

"What?"

"This is where it's going to get really awkward, but we can't stay at your place. The cops might look for us there."

"So ... I don't understand. If you don't want to stay at my place, where are you going to stay?"

I draw a breath and tightly close my eyes.

"Are they still on a break?"

Chapter 18

The heavy wooden door slowly opens to reveal a worried Katie.

Genevieve and I are standing on the porch, anxious to get inside but not wanting to be rude to our new, reluctant host, who is standing behind Katie, with his lean-muscled body and chiseled jaw.

"Hi, Katie." I nod. "Mr. McDermitt."

"Oh, for god's sake. Just call me Nick."

"Okay … Nick …"

After that, I don't know what to say. Neither do Genevieve or Katie.

"Well, don't just stand there," Nick grumbles. "Get inside."

Mr. McDermitt's home – I mean, Nick's home – is everything you would expect an ex-MLB ballplayer's house to be. It's not freakishly opulent like the Parkers', but it's still stylish and expensive. He leads us through the living room, which opens to the second floor. There's a fireplace in the far wall and plush couches situated in front of an insanely massive flatscreen television mounted to the adjacent wall. The rest of the wall space in the room is occupied by baseball memorabilia. Nick wasn't an all-star, but he was a respectable journeyman who could hold down a position until the front office worked a trade for someone younger they could mold. He played sixteen years with seven teams and finally landed with the Giants. After four solid but unremarkable seasons, he retired. No one really noticed. He was smart with his money and now handles investments. If you're wondering how I know all of this, it's because I looked him up when he and Katie had their parking lot fling. I wouldn't say that I was jealous at the time, but I wouldn't say that I wasn't jealous either.

Genevieve is bringing up the rear of our little train as he takes us into the kitchen. I told her about the history of Katie and Nick on the way over and the current state of Nick's marriage. She's taking in the house and gives me an impressed glance.

'Nice,' she mouths. She then points at Nick and mouths, '*Very* nice.'

I give her a shake of my head. We're not in the clear yet. This isn't a done deal.

We step into the kitchen, which fits with the rest of the house. The floor is covered in shiny black tiles. The counters are black-and-gray-flecked marble. The fridge and sink are huge. There's a small, flatscreen TV mounted on the wall next to the sink. In the middle of the kitchen is a massive island counter. A spacious, glass-topped table surrounded by chairs sits next to a large, sliding glass door, that looks out onto a deck with a firepit, built-in grill, jacuzzi, and the immaculate backyard which is bordered by towering hedges that keep out the prying eyes of any neighbors.

Nick nods to the table. "Have a seat."

Genevieve and I oblige. Katie sits in one of the high-top chairs at the island counter.

"Anyone want a drink? Beer? Something stronger?" Nick offers.

"Water's fine, thanks," I answer.

"I'll take a water, too," Genevieve says.

"Can I get a water, as well?" Katie asks.

"I hope no one minds, but I'm having a beer," Nick says.

It's obvious he doesn't care if anyone really minds as he pulls a beer from the fridge.

He gets the glasses out of the cabinet, fills them from the dispenser in the door of the fridge, and passes them around.

"Your house is gorgeous," Genevieve says, taking the glass from him.

"Thanks."

This information is not new to him.

He hands me a glass of water.

"Thank you," I say as he offers me a glass.

He hands Katie the last glass, and sits in the chair next to her.

"Thanks, babe," she says.

"And thank you for letting us stay here for a little bit," Genevieve adds.

"Wasn't really my idea," he says, setting his beer on the counter. He's not being rude, just honest. "I was against it, but Katie asked me to reconsider."

Katie slides her hand across the counter to cover his.

No doubt about it. This is not just a fling in a parking lot behind The Gryphon. From that little gesture, it's obvious that he cares for her and she for him.

"But I do have some ground rules," Nick says.

"Of course," Genevieve replies.

It's best to let her do the talking as I'm still pretty sure he doesn't think too highly of me.

"You have to tell us everything that happened. No lies. I want to know what kind of trouble you're in, in case it follows you to my door. If I don't like something, anything, or even if I just feel like it, you have to go."

"Understood," Genevieve answers.

Nick looks at me.

"Understood."

He pops the cap off the beer with his thumb. It lands on the counter and he settles back into his chair. "Okay. Let's hear it."

155

We lay it out, starting with the affair.

Katie squirms uneasily, maybe feeling that my recounting of an affair with an older, married, wealthy regular at the bar is hitting a bit too close to home.

Once Genevieve enters the story, I let her take over because 1. It's better for Nick to hear it from her, and 2. I'm waiting to see if she will be as open and honest as Nick demanded. Sure enough, she leaves out the fact that the *Herald* didn't send her. I sort of get it. For this to work, Nick needs to find her as credible as possible, but when she says, "The *Herald* sent me because of my past work with stories involving serial killers," I can't help slightly flinching.

He said he wanted the whole truth and it only took fifteen minutes for our first lie. Genevieve also skipped over the details about the last time she tried to cover a story about a serial killer. There's also no mention of "my sweet little cupcake".

Nick is listening intently to Genevieve, but Katie saw my reaction. I take a drink of water to break our eye contact and put the focus back on Genevieve.

She continues, but Katie and I occasionally steal glances at one another.

"... and that's when Clay called Katie," Genevieve says, wrapping up her narrative.

Nick doesn't say a word as he quietly digests what he's been told. He also hasn't touched his beer since opening it. He turns to me. "All of this true?"

"Yes," I reply, carefully avoiding Katie's gaze.

"You didn't kill the Parkers?"

"Absolutely not."

"And you have no idea who did?"

"No."

"But you were at the motel on the night Emily Parker was killed?"

"Yes."

"And you were at the Parkers' house the night Henry Parker was killed and also managed to get his blood all over you before escaping the cops?"

I glance at Genevieve for some sort of help, but she's not offering.

"Yep," I reply.

It sounded crazy in my own head, but hearing it from someone else bumps it up to laughable.

Nick turns to Genevieve.

"And you seriously believe him?"

"Yes," Genevieve answers.

Even though she told me only an hour ago that she believed me, I can't help but think her true thoughts on the matter don't match with the answer she just gave Nick.

He huffs in disbelief.

"And you believe him, too?" he asks Katie.

"Yes," she replies in a tone that is more hopeful than certain.

Nick and Katie hold each other's eyes. Then, he nods.

I wondered before, but now there's no mistaking it. This isn't a fling. There's real trust between them.

"Okay," Nick says. "If Katie says she believes you, that's enough for me. You can stay here for a few days. My wife and I are on a little bit of a … sabbatical, and she won't be back until next week."

"Thank you," Genevieve says.

"But I want to be clear," Nick quickly adds. "My rule still applies. If for any reason I want you gone, you're gone."

"We understand," I say.

He glares at me.

"And thank you," I add.

The final terms accepted, Nick relaxes with a sigh. "I'm getting hungry. Everyone okay with steaks for dinner?"

Chapter 19

"Okay. I have to know; did you really jump off a balcony into the ocean to get away from the cops?" Nick asks from across the table.

"Yep."

"That's insane." He laughs and downs some of his Cabernet.

"Yes, it is," I concede.

"It's going to make one hell of a podcast," Katie says, taking a sip from her own glass.

It's surreal to be sitting around a table, enjoying a perfectly cooked steak (Nick knows his way around a grill) and talking about the events of the last few days like we were catching up with the neighbors.

Genevieve has stayed reserved, but I've let my guard down. It's the first time I've felt safe since I read that text message in the police station while sitting across from Detective Mendez. I know that all of this is far from over, but I'm enjoying a breather.

Nick cooked the steaks on the massive grill out on the deck, next to the jacuzzi. I stepped outside to join him for a few minutes, secure in the knowledge that the tall hedges would block the view of any nosy neighbors. After the cramped quarters of The Gold

Coast Suites Motel, it was a luxury to be outside without the fear of someone spotting me and calling the police. I offered Nick my services as a chef's assistant. To do something so mundane as run into the kitchen, grab some peppers and onions from the fridge, and slice them up to throw on the grill was like a breath of fresh air. He even warmed up to me to the point that he put me in charge of picking out the wine for dinner. I scanned over the options in the rack next to the fridge and was sufficiently impressed. I'm a "turn-and-burn" bartender. My forte is cranking out drinks, but I've learned a thing or two about wine, and every bottle in his collection was easily a couple hundred bucks each. I made my selection, opened the bottle, poured everyone a glass, and brought Nick's out to the deck.

"Which one is it?" he asked, holding the glass up to catch the rays of the setting sun in the rich, red liquid.

"Try it."

He took a sip, savored it with his eyes closed, and announced a verdict of, "Nice."

We toasted and he tossed the sliced veggies onto the grill.

So, that's how Nick and I had warmed to each other, or so I thought.

Over dinner, we gradually eased into conversation about the murders. We had been able to uncomfortably avoid it during the first part of the meal, but it was the eight-hundred-pound, knife-wielding gorilla in the corner of the room, and a second bottle of Cabernet had loosened our tongues.

"So, I have to know," Nick says, leaning forward towards Genevieve. "Any theories about the case?"

"Well, nothing concrete. Speculation, really," is her uncomfortable reply.

"Okay." Nick shrugs. "Then speculate."

I'm pretty confident in saying that I've gotten to know Genevieve in the three days we've known each other, and I can guess what she's thinking. She wants to keep her cards close to her vest, but she doesn't want to appear rude to someone who is literally saving our ass at the moment.

"Well, obviously, Henry Parker knew the killer in some way. He was paying for the apartment, and the killer knew about it."

"Okay," Nick says. "But why would he then kill Henry Parker?"

Genevieve shifts in her seat, attempting to delay her answer.

"It's obvious, isn't it?" Katie asks, looking around the table. The wine is clearly having an effect on her.

Nick is enthralled and Genevieve wishes she was anywhere else before Katie continues.

"He came to The Gryphon to tell Clay who the killer was. That's why he was there."

In all of the mayhem, I've never put together a theory about what Henry Parker was going to tell me, but it makes sense.

Genevieve stares down at the table.

"Look at you, Nancy Drew." Nick playfully smiles at Katie. "But you're leaving out an obvious possibility."

Katie leans into him. "Oh yeah, Hardy Boy? What's that?"

They're in their own little world. This is a game to them.

Nick tilts his glass in my direction. "We're only taking Clay's word in all of this. We're taking his word that he was never in the room with Emily Parker at the Seaside Motel. And it's only Clay's word that he was never in that apartment until the killer told him to go there, even though his fingerprints were all over it. What if Henry Parker came to the bar to tell Clay that he knew that Clay was the killer and that he was going to tell the police?" Then, he really has an idea. "Or! What if Clay is the killer and they were working together and Henry Parker was coming to tell him that the deal was off and Clay told him to wait, only so that he could kill him later that night at his house?"

The steak and the wine are not sitting well in my stomach.

"What about the note Clay found in his coat?" Katie asks. "The one that said 'perkiest'?"

"Again, we're only taking Clay's word that he pulled it out of Henry Parker's jacket at the house. He could have written it himself."

"But then why make up the note at all?" Katie asks, reveling in this wine-fueled sleuthing.

"To throw everyone off, of course, and have them chasing their tails with 'perkiest'. It could be a red herring."

Katie stares at me with a wide, gaping smile.

Nick raises an eyebrow in my direction. "Am I right, Clay?"

The conversation around the table comes to a screeching halt.

Nick winks at me and starts laughing. "Clay! I'm messing with you. I totally believe you. I one-hundred-percent believe you. I'm just having some fun."

Genevieve is still staring down at the table.

Until this moment, I've never considered the fact that almost everything has been based off my own word and I have nearly nothing to back up any of it. I thought I had enough evidence to make my story at least plausible, but I don't. Even the stuff about the handwriting on the lease is nothing more than speculation. To someone looking at it from the outside, it's more likely that Emily did sign the lease and we were using that apartment to carry on our affair. The simple answer, the most logical answer, the Occam's Razor answer to all of this, is that I'm part of it.

One look at Genevieve confirms it. Nick may have just come up with this theory sitting here at this table, but Genevieve has been considering it for some time. I was hoping that she was beginning to see that I'm innocent, but her expression is indicative of just how far she is from that conclusion.

"Jumped off a balcony into the ocean." Nick whistles and takes another healthy sip of wine. "That's crazy."

I force a smile and toast my glass but don't bring it anywhere near my lips.

I've had enough wine for tonight.

Genevieve and I will be occupying the guest room, which has two queen beds, which means we won't have to share. We were both gracious to Nick for dinner and showing us to our room, but Genevieve and I haven't said a word to each other since loading our plates into the dishwasher.

She takes to the bathroom first. Listening to the shower through the door, I stare at her notebook, which is lying on her bed.

She still thinks I may have something to do with it. How could she not? She said that until we had the guy, it was always going to be a possibility, but how shaky is my footing with her? Am I going to have to make a break for it sooner rather than later? Maybe Nick's "playful" theorizing has rattled me and I'm overthinking things. Maybe not. The answer of what Genevieve really thinks is in that notebook. All I have to do is take a quick peek, but if she found out, she would never trust me again.

Before I make a decision, the bathroom door opens. She steps out in a long-sleeved T-shirt and pajama pants to find me staring at the notebook.

We're both frozen.

"Don't worry," I say. "I didn't touch it."

"The bathroom is all yours," she replies.

When I step out of the bathroom after showering and brushing my teeth, the notebook and laptop are gone. I assume they're in her suitcase, which is tightly closed at the foot of her bed.

I climb into my own unbelievably comfortable bed. The mattress is firm but welcoming. The comforter is cool and pins

162

me down. I reach over and hit the button on the bedside lamp, casting the room into unsettling darkness.

"You awake?" I whisper after a few minutes of staring into the blank space above.

"Yeah."

"I keep thinking about what Nick said at dinner."

"And?"

"He wasn't wrong. I know I'm asking everyone to take my word on everything, but, Genevieve, I'm not a part of this. I'm not working with anyone. I had nothing to do with the death of the Parkers."

"You've told me."

"But … You're not sure?"

"I'm sure enough to be in a pitch-black room with you, if that makes you feel any better." She lightly laughs in disbelief. "And why am I the one trying to reassure you, right now?"

"Genevieve, I swear—"

I hear her sit up.

"Look, Clay, I told you, until we catch this guy, I have to consider it. 'Pretty sure' is the best that I can do, okay?"

"Genevieve, I didn't—"

"Yes. I know. You told me. Right now, we need to get some sleep."

The silence drags on.

Leaving it there would be the best course of action, but I can't help myself.

"I'm not the forensics guy," I say.

"Neither was he … until he was," she says and lies back down. "And don't worry; if you are a part of this, I have an insurance plan that I'm hoping will keep me safe."

"'Insurance plan'? What do you mean you have 'an insurance plan'?"

"It means you and the psycho shouldn't try anything."

"Genevieve—"

"Go to sleep, Clay."

I should have kept my mouth shut and just tried to fall asleep, but now, I'm lying here in one of the most comfortable beds I've ever been in and I'm only sure of one thing: I'm not sleeping.

Chapter 20

The Gryphon is slammed.

Katie and I are trying to keep up behind the bar.

Someone orders a beer and I make my way over to the taps, find the corresponding handle, hold the pint glass under the spout, and use my index finger to pull open the tap.

I take the moment to relax against the noise and flood of people ordering drinks.

My phone vibrates in my pocket.

Using my free hand, I grab it and check the messages.

Can I get a Bloody Mary, please? 😊

Somehow, I know exactly where to look.

Sitting at the end of the bar is a man wearing a black bowler hat, long, black frock coat, and a red tie. He's smiling at me. I know he is. I can feel it, but I can't see it, because his face is nothing but blank skin. There are no eyes, nose, or mouth. Just a featureless canvas of flesh. While the people around him are talking and bustling, he is perfectly still.

The sound of the bar fades to silence. The people slowly come to a stop, as if frozen in time. Even Katie comes to a standstill, mid-pour on the drink in her hand.

It's just me and this faceless man, staring at each other across the distance of the bar.

Suddenly, the throat of every person in the place opens. Blood runs down their chests and they collapse onto the floor. Only Katie is still standing, untouched.

She turns to me. Terrified tears spill down her cheeks.

"Clay?" she whispers.

A thin read streak suddenly appears across her throat. He eyes widen and she drops the drink from her hand. Blood begins pouring from her neck and down her chest. Katie falls to the floor.

I turn back to the faceless man.

Though he doesn't have a mouth, I sense his smile widening.

Then, I feel something slide across my throat.

My hand goes to my neck. A warm, sticky liquid seeps through my fingers and down my shirt. I try to scream but can't. I can't breathe. I clutch at my wound, trying to stop the blood, but it continues to gush from my throat.

My vision fades as I begin to fall.

It's pitch-black. Total oblivion.

Is this death? Why does death have the sound of someone snoring in it?

Then I remember; this is the guestroom of Nick McDermitt's house. The snoring is compliments of Genevieve.

Sliding off the bed as softly as I can, I shuffle across the thick carpet to the door. My toe connects with one of the legs of the bed as I pass and I bite my lip to keep from swearing. I finally find the door and step into the hall.

The house is unnaturally silent.

The stairs don't give me away as I descend to the living room, which is faintly illuminated by the solar cell lights in the backyard, glowing through the French doors. I walk through the living room and into the kitchen. The interior light of the fridge nearly

166

blinds me as I pull out a beer and shut the door. I hope Nick won't mind.

The smooth tiles are freezing on my feet as I cross the kitchen to the glass sliding door that leads to the deck. I unlock it, pull it open, and step outside.

The night is cool, but not cold. Socks would still be nice, but I'll live. I just want to sit out here, sip this beer, and think for a bit.

The deck chair by the jacuzzi creaks as I ease myself in, twist the cap off my beer, and take a healthy pull on the bottle while glancing up at the stars.

I don't know how this ends.

I don't know how we catch this psycho, or if we even can catch this psycho.

Ever since our pleasant dinner conversation, there's been something that's nagging me; something I'm missing that's so obvious about this guy. I'm no Columbo, but I feel like there's something staring me right in the face that I—

The glass door slides open.

Katie steps onto the deck wearing a hoodie, pajama pants, and slippers.

"Can't sleep?"

"Needed to unwind a little." I hold up my beer. "Should I put this on the waste log for Nick's inventory?"

"I don't think he cares."

She sits in the deck chair next to me and joins me in looking up at the night sky.

"I'm sorry for what Nick said at dinner. He was a little carried away."

"No need to apologize. He wasn't wrong. A lot of this is just my word against … everything else."

"But he knows you didn't do it."

"Even so, I don't think he's a fan of mine."

She grows quiet.

167

"That's because I told him about you and me."

For a long couple of moments, I don't say a word.

See, here's the thing: Katie and I hooked up a while ago. At first, it was for fun. Then, we thought it might be something more, but quickly realized it would never be. After that, we moved on. It was awkward for a while, but then we got over it. Working together kind of forces you to do that. It's happened a few other times with coworkers of mine, and it has always ended in disaster, but somehow, for Katie and I, it made us closer friends; like we had gone down that road, pulled a quick u-turn, and focused on being friends. I'm stunned because she didn't have to tell him. She could have asked me never to bring it up and I would have been more than happy to oblige, but instead, she had opened herself up to Nick. It explains his initial reluctance towards me.

"You did?"

She nods in the faint glow from the lights.

"What did you tell him?"

"I told him the truth; that it didn't go anywhere and that it was a long time ago."

"Well …" I shrug. "It wasn't *that* long ago."

"Clay, please don't joke. Not right now."

"Sorry. What made you tell him?"

"Because we're being honest with each other. We're trying to trust one another."

This is a different Katie from the one I thought I knew last week.

"You two really are serious, aren't you?"

"Yeah. We want to be. I haven't felt like this about someone in a long time."

"What about his marriage?"

"It's over. His wife really wants to work it out, but he's done."

"Obviously," I say, taking another sip of beer.

"What makes you say that?"

"Because you're here. And he's only letting us stay here because of you. He trusts you, which means that you mean a lot to him."

"He means a lot to me."

"You guys have come a long way since the days of the parking lot behind The Gryphon."

She tries to be mad, but smiles. "His marriage was over way before that."

"You two are good together. I mean, I can't remember the last time I saw you this happy."

She sighs and looks back up at the sky. "I am happy."

"I guess that means no more 'stacking numbers'."

She rolls her eyes. "I've been keeping them the past two nights just out of habit, even though you're not there. It's like none of this is real …" She grows quiet, then asks, "Clay?"

"Yeah?"

"What are you going to do?"

"That's what I'm sitting here, trying to figure out."

"Are you really going to try to catch this guy?"

"Honestly, I don't know if I want to be the one who catches him. I'm not really interested in doing any sort of 'hero' thing." The words are coming out of my mouth before I have time to consider them. "If I can figure out who he is, and then tell the cops so they can catch him, that's what I'll do. The first time I ever want to see this psycho is when he's in a jail cell."

"You think you and this reporter can do that?"

I attempt to mentally calculate the odds but the only answer I can come up with is, "I have no idea."

She takes one last look at the stars and then stands, wrapping her arms around her waist against the chill.

"I'm gonna go back in."

"Is it okay if I stay out here a little longer? Maybe have another beer?"

"Of course, but you should try to get some sleep."

She goes to the door.

"Katie?"

"Yeah?"

"Thank you. Thank you for everything."

She smiles. "You're welcome. Good night, Clay."

"Good night."

She goes inside.

She's right. I do need sleep, but I don't want to tell her that the last time I was asleep, I watched her die.

Chapter 21

I have no idea what time it is, but that wasn't nearly enough sleep. With my brain already in overdrive, the two beers stacked on top of the wine at dinner may have been a mistake.

My aching body causes me to groan as I flip over. Genevieve's bed is empty and her suitcase lies open on the floor. The notebook is gone.

There's the sound of the television in the kitchen as I walk down the stairs and the glorious smell of coffee and bacon greets my nostrils. In the kitchen, I find Katie and Nick sitting at the island counter, drinking coffee, and watching the news on the small television mounted to the wall.

"Good morning," Katie says.

"Good morning." I yawn. "Any updates?"

"Nothing new."

"You want coffee?" Nick offers. "Some breakfast?" He moves to get up but I wave him off.

"Thank you, but please, relax and enjoy your coffee. I can take care of it."

He points. "The pods are in the cabinet above the coffee maker."

"Thanks."

I select a toffee-flavored, gourmet brand, pop it into the

machine, and hit the button. The machine begins to hiss and gurgle.

"Where's Genevieve?" I ask.

"She's out on the deck."

The machine stops hissing. I grab the cup, add a little creamer from the fridge, and carry it outside.

Genevieve is sitting in one of the deck chairs, laptop open, her notebook off to the side.

"How'd you sleep?" she asks.

"Not great. Any word from Greg?"

"Nothing yet. I'm trying to find out more about the apartment, since it's still our only lead. You think of anything else that might help us?"

I shake my head.

The door slides open and Nick and Katie join us.

"So, my little fugitives," Nick says. "What's the plan?"

I was just about to ask Genevieve the same question.

She stops typing. "Well, I plan to be working my phone most of the day to track down leads."

"What do you want me to do?" I ask.

"Keep an eye on the news."

That's going to do wonders for my nerves, but I nod.

"We'll make ourselves as unobtrusive as possible. We promise," Genevieve says to Nick.

He shrugs. "I'm working out of my office all day and then driving Katie to work later, so it's all fine by me."

"I'll help you keep an eye on the news," Katie chimes.

Our battle stations selected, Nick heads to his office and closes the door. Genevieve retreats upstairs. Katie and I settle onto the couch and begin flipping through the channels. We also keep our phones handy, scrolling through local and national news sites, while also doing a Google search from time to time.

After a while, the stories start blending together. There's an initial shock that the Avalon PD has now set up a hotline that people can call if they have any information on my whereabouts, but by the time two o'clock rolls around, I've grown numb. All the stations and websites are recycling the same information. There's nothing new. That is until we flip to a local channel, which is broadcasting their *News in the Afternoon.* An anchor wearing a serious expression sits at a broad desk and looks directly into the camera.

"And now, more on the murders that have rocked the coastal town of Avalon. Channel 7's own Shawna Hayworth has the latest developments. Shawna?"

The image on the screen cuts to a woman standing on the sea road. The wind whips her hair and the Parker house is over her shoulder in the distance.

"Thanks, Dan. Police are asking the public to keep their eyes out for this man, Franklin Davis, who goes by the nickname 'Clay'. He's wanted for questioning by the police, and has been named as a 'Person of Interest'."

There I am. It's the picture that they used in the paper with my full beard and head of hair.

"Now, the police think that he may have changed his appearance and have just released these sketches to help the public recognize him." The picture shrinks to the top left corner. The other three corners of the screen are filled with variations of a police sketch of my face. The one in the top right is of me with hair but no beard. The one in the bottom left is of me with a beard and no hair. The one in the bottom right is of me without my hair or beard, and it is freakishly spot-on. The pictures remain on the screen as the reporter continues talking. "I've also been told that authorities have begun questioning Mr. Davis' friends and acquaintances in the hopes of ascertaining his whereabouts." I can feel Katie tense from across the couch. "In the meantime, if anyone has any information about the murders or if they think they've seen Mr. Davis, they are urged to call the number you see at the bottom of your screen. We'll be sure to bring you the latest on this story as it develops. Until then, this is Shawna Hayworth, Channel 7 News. Back to you, Dan."

It cuts back to the anchor at his desk. "Thanks, Shawna. And that'll do it for us here at Channel 7's *News in the Afternoon*. *Let's Make a Deal* is up next. We'll see you folks tomorrow."

I've suddenly forgotten how to breathe.

It was one thing to have a photo of my bearded face and full head of hair in the paper, but to have that sketch, which could have been a photo of me in my current appearance, splashed across the television screen is a fresh kick in the chest. Combine that with the fact that they're beginning to question my "friends and acquaintances", and it means that the police are one step closer.

Katie is staring at the television, but it's not the intro to *Let's Make a Deal* that has her speechless.

"Katie? … Katie?"

"Hmm?"

"You okay?"

"Oh, yeah … Yeah. I'm fine."

Needless to say, she is not.

"How did that second interview with the police go? The one that Detective Mendez asked you about when he came to the bar?"

Katie keeps her eyes on the television.

"It, um, it didn't happen. It was canceled after they found Mr. Parker. Detective Mendez said that he would reschedule it."

"Oh."

We sit silently for a few moments as the intro to *Let's Make a Deal* wraps up and people in costumes desperately try to get Wayne Brady's attention.

Katie slowly pushes herself up off the couch. "I'm gonna go check on Nick." She walks out of the living room towards the office. I hear her knock, open the office door, and then close it behind her.

Ten minutes later, she's still not back.

I have to talk to someone too.

The tapping of keys reaches my ears through the slightly open bedroom door as I reach the top of the stairs.

"Trust me; I'm staying safe ..." Genevieve says quietly, behind the door. "I don't know, but I need to—"

My foot lands on a floorboard that lets out a soft creak. I wince. Genevieve suddenly stops talking. I need to act like I didn't hear a thing.

"Genevieve?" I ask, lightly knocking.

"Call you back," she quickly says and then calls out, "Come in."

I push open the door and step into the room.

"What happened?" she asks, reading my expression.

"We might have a slight problem."

"All right," Nick says, grabbing his keys off the wall peg near the microwave while Katie grabs her check presenter from the table. "We're off."

"You're just going to hang out at the bar while Katie works?" I ask.

"Yeah," Nick replies, as if nothing could be more normal.

"It's a pseudo-date night," Katie adds. "Since I'm going to be working more shifts thanks to your little absenteeism, we're not going to get many of those in the foreseeable future."

I've seen boyfriends who "just hang out" while their girlfriend works behind the bar. They're worried that some guy will hit on her. It's a very bad look. Normally, it's the sign of a toxic relationship that's lacking trust and going nowhere, but that's not Nick's style, and Katie would never allow something like that. This is different.

175

"So, help yourself to anything in the fridge and we'll be back later tonight," Nick says.

"I've got the early shift, so hopefully, we'll be back around ten," Katie adds.

"What time does the babysitter get here?" Genevieve asks, reading my mind.

Nick smiles. "We're trusting you kids to take care of yourselves, so don't disappoint us."

Great. He played along and killed the joke at the same time.

"Okay. We promise not to drink your vodka and replace it with water," I reply.

Katie and Nick force a smile and head out the door, leaving Genevieve and I alone in the kitchen.

"They're totally going to talk about us all night, aren't they?" Genevieve asks, once the sound of the front door closing dies away.

"Totally."

"Probably try to figure out what they're going to do with us."

"That's not a bad idea."

"Meaning?" she asks.

"Detective Mendez may call Katie at any time to reschedule that second interview and the first question he'll ask is if she's heard from us, and Katie isn't going to lie. We need to figure out what we're going to do next."

Genevieve sighs in agreement.

"You want wine, beer, or something stronger?" I ask.

"Water for both of us."

It's Genevieve's crib.

I don't want to throw her the six and the nine from my hand, but I also want to keep my run intact.

Genevieve's not really paying attention to our game of cribbage. She hasn't been paying attention for hours. She's got her notebook open in front of her and has been studying it, which is why I'm going to skunk her, again.

Ultimately, I decide it doesn't matter and toss the six and the nine into her crib anyway, and wait … and wait …

Her eyes stay glued to her notebook.

I clear my throat.

Frustrated, she looks at the board, back at her hand, and then drops the cards.

"You win."

"Let me take a look at your notes."

"No way."

"Why not?"

"Because you won't be able to read my writing," she lies.

From across the table, I can see the scrawls and hastily scribbled diagrams. Yes, I'd probably have had a hard time reading it, but that's not why she's saying no. If that were the case, she'd let me take a shot and allow me to give up on my own. Whatever her reason, I'm tired of asking.

We found the cribbage board and pack of cards in a drawer in the living room and discovered that we both knew how to play. It was more interesting than "Go Fish", so we decided to play a few games while discussing our strategy. That was hours ago. We initially talked about what we were going to do, but eventually, Genevieve became engrossed in her notebook, leading to her atrocious play.

"Fine," I say, pushing the board aside. "Let's get back to theories."

"Okay."

"Okay … What are they?"

"I'm not sure."

"That's why they're theories, and I know there's Nick's theory from last night that I'm in on it."

"He was joking, but it made a lot of sense," she says, still studying her notebook.

"I admit that it sort of fits, but since I'm not the killer nor am I in on it, can we please pull some other strings? The clock is ticking."

"All right."

"Great."

She finally pulls herself out of the notebook. "Let's look at what we know: the killer knew of the rental apartment and we're pretty sure that Henry Parker was paying for it. That means that they knew each other. They had to be working together."

"So, who is this guy?"

"Well, to answer that, we have to know his relationship with Mr. Parker."

"How do we find out? I mean, we can't really ask Mr. Parker."

"No, we can't," she responds with a slight edge to her tone. "Since they were working together, I'm assuming that Mr. Parker hired him."

"'Hired him'? You mean like a hitman?" The term "hitman" feels so strange in my mouth. It's something you only hear in movies and television shows, conjuring up an image of a guy in a black suit and gloves.

"It fits," Genevieve says. "Especially when you look at the alternative, which is someone coming up to Mr. Parker and asking 'Hey, will you help me kill your wife?' and Mr. Parker saying 'okay'. It only makes sense if Mr. Parker hired him to do it and they were working together."

Now I know why Genevieve was playing some terrible cribbage; she was working this all out in her head, but I don't know if she buys it more than the idea that I'm still involved, somehow.

"Makes sense," I say. "So, why do you think Mr. Parker wanted to kill his wife? Like, maybe a life insurance thing?"

"Nah," Genevieve replies, absent-mindedly tapping her finger on the table.

"Why not?"

"I've seen 'life insurance' murders, and they're never framed as actual murders. They're always made to look like accidents. Besides, he's rich. Why would he need the money?"

"Okay. So, why would he want her dead?"

"If we eliminate the idea that it was about money, what else could it be?"

She's got the answer and is walking me through this.

"I don't know." I helplessly shrug.

"Well, what *do* we know?"

Racking my brain yields nothing and I give up.

"He knew about the affair," Genevieve says. "He told you that he knew about it that night he came to The Gryphon."

"So, you're saying … You're saying that he killed Emily because she was sleeping with me?"

"You'd met him before the night he was killed, right?"

"Yeah."

"What did he seem like?"

The memories, few that there are, begin replaying in my mind; the insecurity, the chip on his shoulder. Then there were Emily's descriptions of him; petty, jealous, given to anger.

"He wanted her dead because he was … an angry little jerk?"

"I've seen people murder for less, and it explains why he was okay with you being framed for it."

That one sends ice down my spine and as crazy as it sounds, she's right.

"Okay, so why did the killer end up murdering Mr. Parker?" I ask.

"That was the one thing I think Nick got absolutely correct. Something must have gone wrong. The killer said as much in his text; he was supposed to kill you at the Seaside Motel. Their plan had fallen apart. Maybe Mr. Parker tried to end their arrangement. Why else would he come to you and try to help you out of the danger he said 'you both were in'? The killer turned on him."

I sit back in my chair. "You just put all this together?"

179

"I've been working on it for a while, but it's only one theory."

"The other theory being that I'm somehow involved and working with a partner?"

"It's something I have to consider."

"I keep telling you; I'm not the forensics guy."

"I can't rule it out."

"Then isn't it really stupid to try to help me?"

"So I've been told."

"By who?"

"It doesn't matter," she says, trying to backtrack.

"Tell me. Who?"

"Can't."

"So, why are you still here, alone, with me?"

"We went over this last night. I'm giving you the benefit of the doubt," she replies without conviction, which I guess is the point.

"How much of a benefit?"

"You're asking me to put a number on it?"

"Sure."

She thinks. "Sixty-Forty."

"You have got to be kidding m—"

Ping.

It wasn't her phone, which is lying on the table in front of us. Genevieve reaches into her pocket and takes out the burner phone. Her face clouds as she reads the screen.

"From him?" I ask.

"Yeah."

"What does it say?"

She turns the phone to me.

I miss you. 😊

"What are we going to write back?" I ask.

"We're not."

"This guy is our only lead. Maybe we can get him to slip up and tell us—"

"*This guy* has been ten steps ahead of us the entire time. He's gotten more out of us than we've gotten out of him. We're not answering."

I guess I deserve that little dig at me for the texting incident at The Gold Coast Suites Motel.

We sit back and stare at the phone.

Ping.

We both sit up and read the text message.

Are we no longer friends?

Genevieve is staring at the phone. I'm sitting on my hands to keep from grabbing it and telling this guy what he can do to himself.

Ping.

Uh, oh. Genevieve, did you take away Clay's phone privileges?

"You think he heard us back at the motel?" I ask.

"No. He's just that smart."

Ping.

Oh well. It's all right. You and I will talk later when she's not around, Clay.

Genevieve's eyes flash at me.

"No. Genevieve, I swear to god. He's just trying to mess with you."

Ping.

And as for you, Genevieve, I can't wait to watch the blood pour out of your throat. It's going to be so EZ. 😜 See you soon!

Genevieve is rattled. So am I.

"Genevieve, you said it yourself; this guy is smart. He's trying to get you to suspect me so that—"

The front door opens.

"Kids! We're home!" Nick calls out.

I break eye contact with Genevieve to look over at Katie and Nick as they enter the kitchen.

"How was pseudo-date night?" Genevieve asks, doing her best to appear relaxed, as though we weren't just texting with a murderer.

"Not bad. Could have been better," Katie says, putting her

check presenter, which is stuffed with cash and slips of paper, on the counter. "I need all the cash I can get for the car repairs. They bumped Tommy up to bartender to cover for you, Clay, and he rocked it. I got to go home early."

"Thanks for not burning down the house," Nick adds.

His cheeks are flushed with the light of a couple of bourbons and Katie's hair is frizzed. I'm betting Nick bought her some drinks during her shift. There's also a good chance they had sex in the car before leaving The Gryphon.

"People were asking about you," Katie says.

"Yeah," Nick says. "We said we'd tell you they said 'hi.'"

He starts laughing. Katie playfully slaps his arm.

"Nick's teasing," she says.

"Hilarious," I reply, but my pulse is in overdrive.

Katie turns to Nick. "Okay, I'm going to go take a shower to clean off the bar funk."

Their ensuing kiss starts out as a quick smooch but grows in passion and stretches into an uncomfortable span of time. I'm pretty sure they've forgotten that Genevieve and I are sitting only a few feet away.

"I'm gonna check my emails," Nick says once they finally break.

They kiss, again, but it's a merciful peck this time. Katie walks out of the kitchen. Nick watches her go. After a moment, he turns his head and appears startled to find us sitting at the kitchen table, as if we haven't been sitting here this whole time.

"So," he says, awkwardly. "How was your night?"

"Good," Genevieve says.

"Good … good," Nick replies. He goes to the fridge and grabs a beer. "Well … I'm gonna … to … um …"

"Emails?" Genevieve offers.

"Right. Emails."

He hesitates, like he can't remember the way to his office, but finds the doorway.

"Hey, Nick?" Genevieve asks, stopping him.

"Yeah?"

"Thank you again, for letting us stay here. We'll be out of your hair as soon as we can."

"Mi casa, su casa," he says with a beaming smile and trying really hard to nail the accent before walking out.

He shuffles down the hall towards the office and announces he's arrived with a loud belch.

"I hate to say it, but he and Katie are good together," I say.

"Why would you 'hate to say it'?" Genevieve asks.

"I didn't mean it like that."

"Your jealousy is none of my business."

"I'm starting not to like you."

"That's something I just don't care about."

Although she's only a few feet away, we've never been further apart.

Suddenly, the front door opens and a woman's voice timidly calls out.

"Nick? … Hello?"

Genevieve and I look at one another.

I'm confused but she's instantly alert.

"Oh, shit," she whispers and stands.

I get up as well, but have no idea what is happening.

"Nick, I just want to talk," the voice says as she approaches the kitchen from the hall.

Now I understand, and Genevieve is right.

Oh, shit.

I motion to the sliding glass door to the backyard where we could hide, but Genevieve shakes her head. She's right. The woman will hear it.

We're both frozen as she rounds the corner into the kitchen. She tosses her keys onto the counter, sees us, and freezes.

It's been a while, but there's no mistaking the woman in her forties with auburn hair and piercing eyes. Meet Tammy McDermitt; Nick McDermitt's estranged wife.

"Who the hell are you?" she asks.

Genevieve and I exchange faltering glances as a panicked Nick runs down the hall and into the kitchen.

"Tammy? I thought you were staying at your mother's until Saturday. What are you doing here?" he nervously asks.

The timid, reconciliatory tone Tammy McDermitt entered the house with turns around and goes back down the hall and out the door.

"What am *I* doing here?" she asks. "What do you mean, what am *I* doing here? This is still my house." She drops the suitcase and motions to us. "Who are they and what are *they* doing here?"

Nick fumbles for something to say. "Well … They are … I mean, you remember—"

NICK! DON'T!

"—Clay, the bartender from The Gryphon?"

"Okay, but what is he doing in our h—?"

She stops as the recognition washes over her. Nick winces at the realization of what he's done.

Tammy's mouth twists and turns before forming the words. "Wait a minute … Are you—? … Isn't everyone looking for you?"

All eyes turn to me.

"… Are they?" I ask.

"You're the one who killed the Parkers!" she cries out.

Nick tries to interject. "Tammy, listen, a lot has happened, and I—"

There's a sound from the kitchen entranceway.

Everyone looks over to see Katie.

"Oh. Shit," I hear Genevieve whisper again with warranted emphasis.

Tammy completely forgets about the suspected murderer in her kitchen. Her face reddens. Her body stiffens and her eyes nearly bug out of her skull at Nick.

"What is *she* doing here?"

Nick tries to calm her. "Tammy, listen—"

"No! What is she doing here? In my house?!"

"Mrs. McDermitt," Katie softly says. "Please. It's not his fault—"

Tammy whips around to face her.

"Don't! Don't you fucking dare talk to me!"

"Tammy—"

She wheels back to her husband. "And you! I can't believe you would bring her into our home. I came back early because I wanted to talk to you to try one last time to see if we could make it work, and she's here? You know what? You want a divorce? Fine. You got it, and you bringing that bitch"—Tammy points a shaking-with-rage finger at Katie—"is going to cost you everything."

"Tammy, calm down," he says, but the Tammy train has left the station.

"Calm down? Calm down?! Are you serious? *Is that a goddamn joke?!*"

Genevieve quickly snatches her notebook and the burner phone from the kitchen table. She grabs my wrist with her other hand and begins pulling me towards the entranceway. "Come on. We have to go. Katie? ... Katie?"

Katie snaps out of her stupor.

"Get your things," Genevieve tells her as we pass, heading for the stairs.

Katie is fighting back tears but nods, following us down the hall, and up the stairs.

"Where do you think you're going?" Tammy explodes as she begins to tail us. "You need to get out of my house, right now!" She attempts to climb the stairs, but Nick quickly moves in front of her, blocking the way.

"Tammy, they're leaving, okay? Let them go and you and I can talk—"

"Oh, I see," Tammy says, mockingly. "That murderer and his friend are with your little sidepiece? That's great."

I glance over my shoulder as we reach the top of the stairs. Tammy is taking out her phone.

"What are you doing?" Nick asks her.

"What do you think I'm doing? I'm calling the police."

Nick reaches for the phone. "Tammy, you don't have to—"

Tammy lashes out and slaps him hard across the face. The sharp sound startles Katie and me. We stop and look back down the stairs.

"Come on!" Genevieve hisses.

Genevieve and I race into the guestroom while Katie continues down the hall. Genevieve hastily starts to throw things into her suitcase, starting with her laptop and then puts the notebook and burner phone in her purse. There's really not much for me to grab, so I help her. The whole thing takes no more than thirty seconds before Genevieve snaps the suitcase closed.

"Hi … Yes, I'd like to report that there are intruders in my house," Tammy says downstairs over Nick's protests and loud enough for our benefit. "One of them is that bartender the police are looking for, the one that killed Emily Parker and her husband."

I grab the suitcase and follow Genevieve into the hall. Katie emerges from the master bedroom with a bag. She's still fighting back tears as we head downstairs.

Tammy eyes us the whole way down, speaking into her phone. "They're trying to leave right now."

Nick is standing by helplessly.

Tammy tries to block the door but Genevieve is having none of it. She body checks her with her shoulder, pushing her aside and goes through the door.

"And she just assaulted me!" Tammy nearly shrieks.

I motion for Katie to go out as I stand in front of Tammy, shielding Katie from her wrath. Katie quickly walks out.

I'm about to head outside but stop.

"Clay, we've got to go," Genevieve insists.

I stare at Katie's devastated face.

This is all my fault. She was trying to help us and it's ended in disaster. She looks crushed, standing there on the grass. I'm seized with this irrational need to do something for her and come up with the only thing I can think of.

I quickly turn back and go down the hallway, into the living room, towards the kitchen.

"Clay!" Genevieve yells.

I hurriedly turn the corner, go through the kitchen entranceway, and grab Katie's cash-stuffed check presenter off the counter. I quickly hustle out of the kitchen and back towards the front door.

"Yes … yes … Clay Davis … That's him. He's here," Tammy continues on the phone.

Nick has given up. His hands are on his hips and he's staring, shell-shocked, at the floor. Genevieve is standing on the porch, urging me out the door.

I move past Tammy and step outside.

The three of us go for the garage, which Katie has opened. Thankfully, Tammy parked her SUV on the other side of the driveway. Had she parked behind us, it would have been game over.

Genevieve throws her suitcase in the back and hops in the driver's seat. I get in the passenger side. Katie gets in the backseat behind me, next to the suitcase. Genevieve starts the car. The tires squeal as she backs out and the car bounces off the driveway curb and into the street.

Tammy is on the porch, still talking adamantly into the phone. Nick is behind her, watching us go.

I turn to look at Katie, who's staring at Nick.

"I grabbed this," I say, sheepishly handing her the check presenter.

"Thanks," she meekly says, and takes it from my hand.

Genevieve throws the car in "drive" and we peel off down the street, away from the marital bliss of the McDermitts.

Chapter 22

We should be formulating plans.

Genevieve should be calculating our next move and I should be feebly questioning every turn, but instead, no one has said a word since we left the house.

We're halfway back to Katie's place before I work up the grit to speak.

"We can't take her back to her apartment," I say to Genevieve.

"Why not?" Katie asks.

"Because if Mrs. McDermitt gave the cops your name, they might be waiting for us there."

Katie looks between Genevieve and I in disbelief.

I know what she's thinking. She trusted me, and now, it's become a total train wreck. Who knows what happened to Nick back there? The cops had to have arrived by now. He could very well be under arrest for helping us and, as I said, if Tammy gave them Katie's name, the cops could already be at her apartment.

"Is there some other place you can go?" Genevieve asks.

"No," Katie replies, incredulously.

This is my fault, all of it, and there's nothing I can do to fix it.

"How much money do you have?" I ask.

"Why?"

"There are some motels around Avalon that will take cash if you offer enough. It's what Genevieve and I have been doing."

Katie looks at me with eyes glistening with tears.

"Before, you wanted me to lie to the police. Now, you're telling me that I should hide from them?"

I don't have an answer for her.

In a daze, Katie begins to go through her purse. "I've got, like, eighty-six dollars."

"What about your shift money?" I ask, nodding to the faux-leather check presenter I handed to her when we got in the car, which is sitting on the seat next to her.

She picks it up and opens it in her lap. She sorts through the scraps and slips of paper, and occasional hotel keycard, to pick out the cash.

"So, um, I've got about a two hundred and fifty-two dollars," she says.

"Okay. That should get you through at least two nights somewhere," I offer, trying to sound hopeful.

"Then what?" Katie asks.

I look at Genevieve for help, but she's got none to give.

"I don't know," I finally have to say.

Katie arranges the slips of paper in the check presenter so she can close it. As she does, I see that most of them have phone numbers and requests for her to call written on them.

"You still 'stacked numbers' tonight? Even with Nick there?" I ask, attempting a joke.

"I told you, it's out of habit."

"Any weirdos?" I ask, still trying to pick her up, but all I'm doing is annoying her.

"Plenty. Even a few room keys. You can have them," she says out of spite.

She opens the presenter and holds up a handful of swipe cards with hotel logos on them.

189

I'm instantly drawn to the one that has a physical key dangling from a keyring that pierces the corner of the card. The logo freezes me in place.

Katie notices my reaction.

"Clay? What's wrong?"

"Can I see that one?" I ask, pointing.

She hesitantly hands it to me.

There's a number engraved on the key: 317.

"What's going on?" Genevieve asks.

I hold up the swipe card so she can see the logo as she's driving.

EZ

"Clay, please tell me what's happening," Katie pleads, growing more worried.

"Katie, who gave this to you?" I ask.

"Why?"

"Who was it?"

"I don't know."

"You didn't see who left it?"

"Clay, come on. You know how it is. I could have been talking to him all night and not remember. I don't even remember picking it up."

I do know how it is. I've had times where I've held phone numbers and hotel keycards in my hand and had no idea who left them, even after Katie told me that I was talking to that person all night. If it happens to me from time to time, I can only imagine how often it happens to Katie.

"Clay, what is going on?" Katie asks.

"We need to keep this," I say, clutching the card.

"Why?"

"It could just be a coincidence," Genevieve says.

"Do you think it's a coincidence?" I ask.

She doesn't answer because she knows it's not.

"Clay! Please tell me what's goi—" Katie stops, the full realization hitting her. "Oh my god … It was him?"

I don't want to freak her out, but I don't want to lie, either.

"Maybe," I offer, half-heartedly.

"Holy shit … holy shit … How?" Katie asks. "How could he know?"

"We don't know," Genevieve says. "This guy seems to know a lot of things."

"If he knew that I knew where you were, then he has to know everything about me." Katie's breathing increases as panic takes over.

"Katie, listen to me."

She begins frantically looking around.

"Katie, listen to me," I forcefully say, finally getting her attention. "We're going to drop you off close to your place. When we get there, if the cops aren't already at your place, you call them, okay? You call them and you tell them what happened and you stay with them. You'll be safe."

There's no pushback from Genevieve on my advice.

Katie regains a little control and nods her head. "Okay. What are you going to do?"

"Keep going. Try to find him."

"But … Clay—?"

"It'll be okay. I promise."

It's a promise I have no business making.

We're in Katie's neighborhood and Genevieve nods to an intersection up ahead that's bathed in the glow of the streetlamps overhead.

"Her apartment is about two blocks up," I tell Genevieve.

"Katie, we're going to leave you right here," Genevieve says.

Katie nods.

"If the cops aren't there, you call them, okay?" I ask.

Katie nods again.

I glance at Genevieve, but she refuses to look at me.

We pull up to the curb at the intersection and stop under the streetlamp.

Katie grabs her bag and gets out.

I open my door.

Genevieve grabs my arm.

"Where are you going?"

"I'm going to say goodbye."

"Someone might see you."

"Two minutes. I want two minutes."

Genevieve sighs in resignation as I get out to join Katie on the sidewalk.

"Okay. Once we drive away, call the cops."

"Clay, turn yourself in. You'll be safe. Don't go after this guy."

"The cops think I did it. The moment I turn myself in, this guy will disappear, and it'll be my word against a ghost."

"But doesn't the key prove—?"

"It doesn't prove anything and it might not even be from him."

Genevieve rolls down her window. "Clay, we have to keep moving—"

"One second," I hiss and turn back to Katie. "All right. Gotta go. Stay safe."

"You too."

There's an uncertain hesitation, then we hug. It's awkward at first, but then becomes fierce with the realization that this might be the last time I ever see her.

"Bye, Katie."

"Bye, Clay."

She knows it, too.

"Let's go," Genevieve insists.

Katie and I let go and take one last look at one another before I turn and hustle back to the car. Once I close the door, Genevieve takes her foot off the brake and hits gas fast enough for a quick getaway but taking care not to squeal the tires. I turn and watch Katie through the rear windshield, standing under the streetlamp. She reaches for her phone just as she disappears into the distance. Once she's out of sight, I face forward.

"All I wanted was two minutes to say goodbye to my friend."

"Thanks to the lovely Tammy McDermitt, we don't have two minutes. The cops could be waiting for us just one block over."

I hold up the EZ swipe card and key.

"All right. We both agree that this isn't a coincidence, right? It has to be him."

"Okay. Yes."

"I don't know of any 'EZ Motel'. I can't think of any motel that would call itself that unless it was trying to attract a specific clientele."

"So, what is this? The key says 317. That's gotta be a room, right?"

"I guess. I mean, I have no idea what it else it could be."

She keeps looking back and forth between the road and the keycard and finally nods to the floor at my feet. "Get my phone. It's in my purse."

I grab her purse from the floor near my feet. I set it on my lap and rummage around until I locate it.

"One-one-one-two," she says.

"Really?"

"Just unlock it."

Tapping the numbers unlocks the phone.

"Do a search for the 'EZ motel'."

I open the web browser, pull up Google, and enter "EZ motel" into the search bar.

The results are immediate.

At the top of the page, there's that implied exasperated sigh that Google gives you when you're so close but oh, so far.

Did you mean "EZ STORAGE"?

Chapter 23

EZ Storage, which sits in what would be considered the "industrial" part of Avalon, is the most nondescript block of a building you could imagine. The gray exterior walls are dotted with rows of windows. It's surrounded by other nondescript industrial buildings and warehouses.

Genevieve and I stare up at the building through the windshield while sitting in the car. I'm gripping the key so tightly that the metal teeth are digging into the palm of my hand. We're the only car in the parking lot which is surrounded by a chain-link fence, topped with barbed wire. Genevieve has been quiet for most of the drive over.

I reach for the door handle. "Come on."

"This is a trap," she says. "And we're walking right into it."

"There's two of us. We'll be careful and watch each other's back."

"You think that's going to keep us safe? You think he's not counting on both of us showing up?"

"Genevieve, we have to know what's in there before Katie calls the cops. She'll tell them about the key and that will bring them here, so we don't have a lot of time."

"Fine. You go in. I'll wait here."

"I don't want us to split up. We'll be safer together."

She's still reluctant, but I have to get in there and I meant what I said about not splitting up.

"Genevieve, come on. This is the story. This is how we catch this guy."

She doesn't budge.

I decide to go for broke.

"You're right; it might be some sort of trap. This guy wants people to know what's in here. Our only way to get an advantage is to see what it is and then get out of here. We have to move. If Katie is telling the cops about this key, they're probably on their way. Our only option to figure out what's coming is to check it out. Let's just see what's in there and then get the hell out of here, okay?"

Genevieve stays put.

This is a risk, a horrible, horrible risk, I know, but I have to see what's in here. What other options do I have? I need to see whatever is in here as quickly as possible so we can get away. I don't want us to split up.

"I know you think I might have something to do with this. I get it. I do. So, here's the deal: you keep your knife and pepper spray pointed directly at me, and if there is any sign of trouble, and I mean *anything*, you stab and spray away. Deal?"

Yes, I'm that desperate.

Genevieve lightly laughs while shaking her head. "Okay."

"Great. Let's go."

She finally gets out of the car.

I get why she's being so hesitant, but she's the intrepid reporter who convinced me to risk everything to get the lease. She's been the one putting the pieces together. I want to get this guy. She said she wants to get him, too, and I've basically just given her permission to stab me. Why stop now?

We walk across the parking lot to the tinted glass door under the sign with the logo that matches the keycard. I search the alleys and shadows beyond the fencing for any signs that someone might be watching us, but there are too many alleys, and too many shadows. Genevieve seems resigned to whatever is going to happen and keeps her eyes on the door as she retrieves the knife and pepper spray from her purse.

I go to the card reader that's mounted next to the door. Genevieve hangs a few feet back, knife in one hand, pepper spray in the other. They're for me and I'm going to have to live with that if I want to see what's in unit #317.

I run the magnetic strip through the reader. There's a chirp. The little light next to the panel blinks green and there's a harsh buzzing from the lock. I grab the handle of the door and pull it open, not bothering to hold it for Genevieve. She's not going to let me get behind her.

She follows me inside.

We're in the corner of the building. There are two heavy doors on opposite sides of the cinderblock room. Next to one door is a small plastic plaque that reads '101-140'. The plaque next to the other door reads '141-180'. There's another door leading to the stairwell and the elevator is tucked around the corner.

"Floor three," I say, moving towards the elevator.

"Let's take the stairs. I don't want to be trapped in the elevator."

"Okay."

She doesn't want to be in an elevator with me, but it's not a bad call to stay mobile.

I open the stairwell door and step inside. Like the rest of the building, it's nothing but cinderblock, concrete, and steel.

Genevieve keeps her distance and we ascend in silence, save for our footsteps on the stairs.

We arrive at the landing to the third floor. There are two doors leading in opposite directions. I go to the one marked "301–340", open it, and go through. Genevieve follows, continuing to keep her distance.

The hallway stretches out before us. The row of lights overhead cast a sickly glow that's interrupted here and there by burned-out tubes. We start making our way past the orange roll-up doors in the wall to our right, which are spaced at regular intervals and marked with numbers.

As we near #317, my anticipation grows, as does my frustration with Genevieve's suspicions.

I'm doing everything I can to assuage her fears, but how can she still think I have something to do with this? When exactly does she think I snuck off to leave the key for Katie at The Gryphon? Or for that matter, when did I leave her side to rent a unit here?

311 ... 312 ...

Shake it off. I need to stay sharp for whatever is behind the door up ahead.

I finally come to a stop outside the segmented roll-up door marked "#317".

"This is it."

Genevieve stops a few feet away. She's still got the knife and pepper spray in hand.

"Can I have one of those?" I ask.

I know the answer, but I want to hear it from her.

"I've got your back," she says.

"Right."

I slide the sleeves of my shirt to cover my hands and grab the padlock.

"What are you doing?" she asks.

"I learned from the apartment that I don't want to leave fingerprints."

I insert the key and twist. The lock pops open. I remove the padlock, undo the latch, and pull the bolt back. Crouching down, I grab the handle, sleeve still covering my hand, and fling it open. The door rattles upwards.

I quickly step out of the way, like I'm worried that it's

booby-trapped. Genevieve also steps back so that we're on opposite sides of the door.

The only sound is the low buzz of the halogen tubes overhead.

We peek our heads around the corners and look through the open door into the unit.

It's dark inside, but the light from the hall illuminates enough to see a large rectangular object against the back wall.

Genevieve cautiously reaches in and feels the wall next to the door, searching for a light switch, but comes up empty.

I do the same on my side but there's no light switch.

She stares at me, waiting.

Waiting for what? What does she want me to do?

I give her a shrug that tells her as much and she nods to let me know that I should enter.

I step around the corner and ease myself two paces into the unit. Suddenly, a light mounted to the ceiling springs to life, causing me to leap backwards.

Genevieve raises the pepper spray and knife in my direction.

"It's okay! It's okay! It's okay!" I sputter, holding up my hands towards her and trying to get my heartbeat under control.

There's a large refrigerator against the far wall, the kind some people have in their garage that's more like an ice chest, lying on the floor.

I advance slowly towards the refrigerator.

I arrive at the refrigerator and glance over my shoulder to Genevieve, who has the knife and pepper spray at the ready.

I take a breath, place my hands on the lid, and lift it open.

A face stares back at me through a large, heavy plastic bag. The body is curled into a fetal position to fit into the chest. The eyes are open behind the thick, tortoise-shell glasses, which rest on his long, freckled nose. A shock of wiry red hair sits on its head.

I recoil, stagger backwards, and stumble to the concrete floor.

Genevieve quickly steps over to the refrigerator and looks inside. She draws a sharp inhalation of breath and backs away.

The smell of rot and decay begins to fill the unit.

The initial shock is overtaken by the flash of recognition and the need to be sure. I stand up and go back to the ice chest.

It can't be him, but it is.

The bruises around his neck from where he was strangled are clearly visible. Other than that, he looks exactly as I remember him from a few nights ago.

"You have got to be kidding me …" I whisper.

"Clay, who is that? Why do I feel like I've seen this guy before?" Genevieve asks behind me.

"It's Sydney Loomis."

"Who?"

"Sydney Loomis."

"Who's Sydney Loomis?"

"He was one of my regulars at The Gryphon. He—"

No. Oh, shit. No.

Genevieve was right.

This is a trap, but not for the two of us.

This is a trap for me.

If Katie told the cops about the key, then they are on their way, and they are going to find one more dead body whose only connection to the other dead bodies goes right through me.

"We have to get out of here," I say and begin turning towards the open door. "We have to get away from h—"

I stop.

Genevieve is pointing the knife and pepper spray at my face.

"That's it. I'm done. It's over, Clay."

"Genevieve, what are you—?"

"Stay right there."

"Genevieve, we have to go. We have to—!"

"Don't come any closer!"

199

She no longer *thinks* I have something to do with all of this. She is absolutely convinced of it.

"Genevieve, I was with you the whole night. There's no way I could have—"

"Stop it, Clay! You were at both murder scenes. Your fingerprints at the apartment. How could the killer know everything about me? How could he know my cat's name? How could he know which motels you and Emily Parker stayed at? How could he know that we were at the McDermitt's? And now, this?!"

"I have no idea! But how could I have left the key at The Gryphon for Katie? I was with you the whole time!"

"Katie doesn't remember picking up the key! You could have slipped it in there when you went back into the house to make sure she had her check thing!"

"I went back into the house to get the check thing because I felt bad for her! I wanted to do something for her and it was the only thing I could think of!" I plead, but she's having none of it. "Genevieve, please, put down the knife and pepper spray! The cops might be on their way!"

"Well, thank god, because this is done."

"Damnit, Genevieve, listen to me! I didn't do this. Whoever did, wants you to think I did!"

"Then they've done a hell of a job."

"It's not me! How could I have text messaged you while I was taped to a chair or sitting next to you over at Nick's place?!"

"You have to be working with him! It's the only explanation!"

I hold up my hands. "Genevieve, look at me. I'm telling you, I'm not the forensics guy."

I take a hesitant step towards her. I don't like her pointing the pepper spray or the knife towards my face.

"Stay right there!"

"Genevieve, the police will be here any minute. We have to go!"

I glance back at the ice chest and the horror of Sydney Loomis's face causes me to involuntarily stagger forward.

"STOP!!!"

I flail my arms in frustration.

"DAMNIT, GENEVIEVE!!!"

HSSSSSSSST.

In the fraction of a second before the spray hits me, I dodge to the left.

I drop like a ton of bricks onto the cold, smooth, concrete floor. My eyes are suddenly on fire. My lungs are vacuum sealed. My ears work fine, and above my hacking and retching, there's the sound of Genevieve's footsteps running away, down the hall. My attempt to call after her is cut short by my vomiting across the floor. I try to wipe away the searing hot coals that are embedded in my eyes, which I can only keep open for seconds at a time.

I didn't take the full hit, but it was more than enough. I have to get out of the noxious cloud that's filling the storage unit.

I open my eyes for a split second to get my bearings and begin dragging myself towards the open door. As soon as my head emerges into the hallway, the effect is immediate. My lungs are still in agony, but I can taste clean air, allowing me to breathe.

I pull myself down the hall a few feet to distance myself from the poisoned fumes, all the while trying to keep my eyes open, but the sensation of red-hot pokers being rammed through them makes it impossible.

My flashes of vision reveal a window in the wall above me.

I hoist myself to my feet and look down into the parking lot just as Genevieve emerges below. In the brief moments that I can keep my eyes open, I watch as she races to the car, before I have to close my eyes and wipe away the stinging tears. When I can finally look, again, she's opening the driver's side door. There's movement in the parking lot behind her. I can't keep my eyes open anymore and press the palms of my hands against them, trying to smother the burning sensation. It's unsuccessful, but I have to see what's happening and force myself to keep them open.

A figure, clad in black and wearing a ski mask, runs towards Genevieve. He crashes into her, slamming her against the car. Her purse falls to the pavement.

"Genev—!"

My scream is cut short by a fit of ragged coughing.

Genevieve struggles against the figure, who presses something against her neck and she goes limp.

I scream in rage and frustration as I'm forced to rub my eyes again.

Moments later, when I can open them, I see the figure putting Genevieve's limp body into the back seat.

I begin slamming my hands against the window.

"NO!" is all I can manage before my lungs surrender to another fit of coughing.

The black-clad figure stops and looks up.

Through my gasoline tears, we stare at one another.

This is the guy. This is the guy who has killed three people and has tried to frame me for those murders. This is the psycho I've been chasing. This guy is pure evil and now, he has Genevieve.

We continue to stare at each other.

Then, he cheerily waves and gets in the driver's seat.

I lurch to my left and begin frantically pinballing down the hall to the stairwell.

The stairwell door makes a sound like thunder in the stairwell as I crash into it and stumble down the stairs faster than my impaired senses can calculate. Finally, on the last landing, my momentum overtakes my balance. My ankle rolls, sending me tumbling down the last flight of stairs.

I pick myself up with a pathetic groan. I have no idea if I've really hurt myself. The pepper spray is masking any pain, but everything seems to be in working order.

The cold night air fills my lungs as I stagger out of the lobby and into the parking lot.

Genevieve's car is gone. In its place is her purse, lying on the ground. In the struggle, she must have kicked it under the car.

I stagger over and pick it up.

Inside are her wallet, notebook, her phone, and the burner phone.

Sinking down to the ground, I begin pulling in ragged breaths, but before I can even begin to calm myself, I hear them. It's a sound I've become very familiar with.

Police sirens.

My head drops between my shoulders.

"GODDAMNIT!" I scream.

There's a decision to make.

I can finally turn myself in. That way, the cops won't waste their time and resources looking for me. They can focus on finding Genevieve, but that's only if they believe me, and it might take days to convince them. That's also assuming that I *can* actually convince them.

The burner phone pings with a text.

We're not done playing. Go to the police and your friend is dead and I disappear.

And like that, my choice is made.

The only way to save Genevieve is to keep running.

The sirens are growing louder. I can't tell from which direction they're coming, but I can tell that there are a lot of them.

I stuff the burner phone into my pocket, turn to leave, but stop.

On second thought, I reach back into the purse, pull out Genevieve's wallet, extract the cash, and add it to the pocket with the burner phone. I also grab Genevieve's phone and cram it into the other hip pocket. Finally, I take her notebook, tuck it into the waistband of my pants, and toss the purse away.

I dart across the lot towards the street to get an idea of where the sirens are coming from.

No wonder I couldn't tell which way they were coming. There are flashing lights approaching from both directions, but it sounds like they're closer than they look.

On cue, a cop car bursts from a side street, two blocks down, and swerves in the direction of EZ Storage.

I pivot and run towards the far side of the parking lot, towards the chain-link fence, topped by barbed wire.

I throw myself against the fence, reach up, and begin climbing. I take a second to try to gauge the safest spot, grab the top strand of barbed wire, and pull myself over. Searing pain rips through my thigh, side, and shoulder, causing me to cry out in pain as I go over the top. I drop down into the alley behind EZ Storage, next to a warehouse as police cars swarm into the parking lot.

I don't know if they saw me, but I stay low, trying to make my way to the edge of the warehouse.

More cop cars continue to arrive. There are shouted orders and screeching tires that echo off the surrounding buildings. The only available cover is a dumpster, which I duck behind as the police cars surround EZ Storage. The nearest car comes to a stop ten yards away. An officer gets out. The only thing between me and her is the fence and this dumpster.

My eyes are still stinging and my lungs are tight. The glare of the parking lot lamps provides enough light to see that my ripped jeans took most of the damage to my thighs. I don't know about my side or shoulder but there's no time to deal with that.

It's a twenty-yard sprint to the alley at the side of the warehouse. I don't care where it leads, so long as it's away from the police, who are focusing their attention on EZ Storage.

Crouched by the edge of the dumpster, I steady myself, inhale, hold it in my chest, keep my eyes on the nearest cop, and when she sweeps her light through the fence, satisfied that no one's there …

Now.

I start running, doing my best to stay low and quiet. The shouting of the cops masks the sound of my footsteps, but these twenty yards feel like a mile. I'm waiting for someone to scream, "There he is!"

Ten yards …

I start making the turn …

Five yards …

I round the corner …

MADE IT!

Suddenly, I'm wrapped in a blinding glow.

I've activated a motion-sensor flood light that's mounted to the side of the warehouse.

I keep pumping my arms and legs. My one saving grace is that the alley is out of direct view from the parking lot of EZ Storage, but they're sure to notice the light.

I hurtle towards the opening at the end of the alley and emerge onto an empty street, which is lined with more office parks and warehouses, illuminated by the occasional streetlamp.

They had to have seen the motion-sensor lamp turn on in the alley and someone is going to check it out.

I have to take whatever twists and turns to get away.

I spot another alley down the street next to a one-story, brick building whose sign announces that it deals with air-conditioning. I only hope they're not doing well enough to afford motion-sensor lights.

My wish is granted as I duck into the alley and it remains dark. I continue on to the back of the building.

The alley behind the building stretches out in both directions, offering multiple options for escape.

I head to the left, taking the third (or maybe fourth) turn and enter the darkness as a cop car sweeps a spotlight down the alley two buildings away.

A few minutes later, once I'm confident I've lost them, I begin making my way back towards Avalon, alone, with nothing more than two burner phones, some cash, and Genevieve's notebook.

Chapter 24

Pressing down on the knob releases a pulse of water that falls from the faucet to the dented, stainless steel sink below.

I cup my hands under the stream and bring the water to my side to wipe away the dried, crusted blood.

It stings but I really dodged a bullet with that barbed-wire fence. The cuts are more like deep scratches, but I would feel safer with a tetanus shot and some antibiotic ointment. I press down on the knob again for another pulse of water, which I use to clean the scratches on my shoulder.

It took almost all night to get back to Avalon. I went slowly, making sure the roads were clear. As I got closer to the residential and business areas, I occasionally encountered people on the street, but no matter what town you live in, people walking around outside at four in the morning are going to mind their own business.

The only place I figured I could wash up without anyone asking questions were the bathrooms at this public park. There were three options available when I arrived; one had the sink busted out of the wall. The next bathroom appeared to be occupied for the night. Thankfully, the last bathroom had a functional sink and a metal panel mounted in the wall above that was pretending to be a mirror.

I'll spare you the details of the toilet.

I've done my best to clean myself up, but I need new clothes, and fast.

After doing the best to wash my wounds, I put my slashed shirt back on. It's damp and cold against my skin from my attempts to rinse the blood out of it. I take out the burner phone and text Emily Parker's burner phone.

Where is she? I type and hit send.

It's the umpteenth text I've sent since walking back into Avalon and like all the other texts I've sent, I'm not expecting an answer. Eventually, I'll have to stop because I need to conserve the power on this phone. I have no idea when I might be able to charge it again, but I'm not waiting long. I have to know that she's alive or I'm going to the police. The only reason that I haven't, yet, is because of his threat.

I return the phone to my pocket, alongside Genevieve's phone and the cash I took from her wallet, which turned out to be a smart move. I've already assembled a plan to put it to good use.

Time to disturb the neighbors.

I step out of the restroom into the cool, hazy morning. The sun isn't up yet, but there's plenty of light.

I knock on the door of the adjoining bathroom, hoping the occupant is still there from the night before.

"Hey, buddy? You in there?"

There's grumbling from inside.

I knock again. "Hey? You hear me?"

"Go away!" a voice calls out.

"You got a shirt?"

There's more grumbling.

"Do you have a shirt?" I ask again.

"Yes! I have a shirt! Fuck off!"

"I'll give you twenty bucks to trade me shirts."

208

There's silence and then some scuffling. The bolt clicks and the door opens.

The face that greets me is grizzled, the eyes frenzied, and the mouth sparsely populated by teeth. All of that is nothing compared to the rank whiff of body odor. Thankfully, we're about the same size and his shirt, while dirty, isn't shredded and blood-stained, like mine.

"Why you want my shirt?"

"Who cares?" I ask, holding up a twenty-dollar bill.

I never would have guessed that one day, after watching someone be abducted by a murderer and running from the police, I would purchase a dirty shirt from a meth-head in the bathroom of a public park so that I could buy a cheap, clean shirt from a thrift store, but here we are.

I took the shirt back into my bathroom and washed it in the sink with the pink hand soap in the dispenser. It's damp and clings to my skin, but most of the smell is gone. At least I look more "down-on-his-luck" than "on-the-run-from-the-cops".

The woman at the Goodwill store barely blinked when she saw me waiting at the door for them to open. After browsing the shelves and racks, I buy a hoodie, a T-shirt, pants, socks, and an old duffel bag.

Moments after walking out the door, I'm around back, changing into my new purchases. I throw the smelly, meth-head-hand-me-down T-shirt and barbed-wire-shredded pants into the dumpster.

The burner phone is back on and I'm constantly texting Emily's burner phone at least once every five minutes. I'm no longer worried about the battery. I need to know what this guy wants me to do.

I emerge from the alley and look for anyplace nearby that might sell a charger for the phone, when it lights up with a message.

I hope you are behaving yourself, Clay, and not inviting other people to play our little game.

I instantly begin typing my response.

I need proof that she's alive, right now, or I'm turning myself in.

I wait for a reply.

I don't have to wait long.

Ping.

You don't want to do that. It would be game over for your friend and we are so close to the end.

Proof. Now.

It's taking so long, I begin to wonder if he's going to answer, but the phone finally pings with a picture.

Genevieve.

There's tape over her mouth and her hair falls in front of her face. Her eyes are wide with terror. It's a tight shot, but it looks like her arms are suspended over her head, as though she's hanging from something. Next to her face is a copy of today's newspaper. Behind her, there are only shadows. There's nothing to give away where she's being kept.

Ping.

Clay, you've played the game so well. Don't blow it now and cost Genevieve her life. It'll be the last turn soon.

No. That's it.

Game Over.

The image of Genevieve, the fear and pain in her eyes seals it. I'm doing what I should have done a long time ago. I'm turning myself in. Detective Mendez has to believe me. I'll make him believe me.

This phone has almost no charge left. I'll use Genevieve's phone to call Detective Mendez so that I don't have to worry about the burner phone dying in the middle of the conversation, but I need to send him this photo before the burner phone dies. I can't waste a second.

I take out Genevieve's phone, say a quick, mental "thank you" that she told me her PIN last night, and pull up the web browser. Detective Mendez's number is on the Avalon PD site. I tap the number and the phone automatically dials.

"Calling: M" the top of the screen reads.

Wait. What?

I quickly hit "End Call".

How is that possible?

The only way Genevieve's phone would say "Calling: M" is if the phone contact had already been created in her contact list.

Genevieve's phone waits, letting me know that the call I just made to "M" lasted 00:01.

I pull up Genevieve's contact list and scroll through the numbers. I stop on the entries for "M".

Laura A

M

Matthew S

Meredith L

Mom

I tap on "M".

Detective Mendez's phone number fills the top of the screen. Underneath is a list of the incoming and outgoing calls to his number. There's a handful of entries. One call was as recent as yesterday and I remember her talking to someone as I approached the guestroom at Nick's place.

The phone begins to vibrate in my hand. The screen lights up. *Incoming Call: M*

I tap the answer button.

Detective Mendez's eager voice fills my ear. "Ms. Winters? Where are you? You need to get away from Clay Davis, right now. I don't give a damn about the deal with the *Herald*. Get away from him and tell me where you are. Do you understand me?"

I stare blankly ahead, my mouth stupidly hanging open.

"Ms. Winters? … Ms. Winters, are you there?" When there's no answer, his detective instincts kick in. "Clay? … Is that you?"

"… um … yeah."

"Clay, where is she?"

All sense of order has flown out the window and my mind reels.

"You're her insurance plan," I say.

"What?"

"You were talking to her."

"Clay, what have you d——"

"Detective Mendez, please, you've got to hear me out; Genevieve is in trouble. He's got her."

"Clay, what have you done with her?"

The words tumble out of me in a sputtering mess. "Nothing. It's not me, but last night, at EZ Storage, he took her. We went inside and found Sydney Loomis. The killer was there. She ran away from me and I saw it through the window. He attacked her, threw her in the backseat of the car and drove off!"

"Clay. Stop. You need to tell me where she is, right now. It only gets worse for you every second you don't tell us."

"No! Please! Listen to me: he's got her! I can prove it. Hold on!" I quickly take the burner phone and pull up the photo. There's three percent left in the battery. I tap the photo, which brings up the "share" option. Genevieve's phone displays Detective Mendez's number and I enter it into the burner phone. I hit send and a moment later, it displays a notification that it was successful.

"I just got this a few minutes ago and decided to call you," I say into Genevieve's phone and wait.

The notification alert on the other end of the line dings and is followed by the sound of a deep breath.

"Detective?"

"Clay." His voice is hardened and angry. "If you harm her——"

"I didn't do this!!! Why won't you believe me?!!"

"Because no one believes you! How could they?! Three people are dead and you're the only person who connects them. Now Ms. Winters is gone and you're calling me from her phone!"

"But … I … the photo …"

"That *you* sent me. Why would I believe that anyone else took it?"

"… because they did … I mean, Genevieve—"

"Even Genevieve thought you might have something to do with it. She was almost certain of it."

"How do you know that?"

"She told me."

"You spoke to her?"

"I was working with her editor. We traced her plates when you were at the apartment complex and I called her paper to find out what was going on. I spoke to her editor, a guy named 'Greg'. He lied to me and said that she wasn't working for the *Herald* and told me about her past. He said they were going to send another reporter and we could work together. He promised to share anything the paper found out about the killings if I would share tips with him."

"But … but you sent the tip about the motels you were checking on so we could get away," I reply, still trying to make sense of all of this.

"I sent it to her editor. We had already dispatched officers to check the motels, so I thought I really wasn't giving him anything important. If I had known he was going to send it to Genevieve and that you were with her, and hiding in that motel, I never would have shared that, we would have arrested you, and right now, Genevieve would be safe."

He's right that Genevieve would be safe but for the wrong reasons.

"Then, her editor got back in touch with me later that day and came clean. Genevieve was worried that you really were in on it. Who else would know about the motels? I didn't believe

213

him until he sent me a photo that Genevieve had taken of you duct-taped to a chair."

"But, I— I didn't do it."

"Stop, Clay. Just stop. I spoke to Henry Parker after we found Emily Parker's body and before I talked to you. He was suspicious that you and Emily Parker were having an affair. You were a suspect before you even set foot in the police department. Why do you think I showed you the photo of her dead body in the motel room? I wanted to see your reaction and it told me everything I needed to know."

The phone almost drops from my hand.

"Ms. Winters got in touch with me after you ran from The Gold Coast Suites Motel. I pleaded with her to tell me where you two were. Instead, she wanted to make a deal. She was going to stick with you and try to get the story, but if she became convinced you did it, she was going to give you up. I told her that I wasn't going to give her or her editor any more information. We would still try to apprehend you, but I told her to keep in touch in case something happened."

My legs can't take it anymore and I sit right down on the sidewalk, unable to speak.

"Clay, there's no way out of this. You have to tell us where she is. You're in a bad spot, but the only way to stop it from getting worse is to turn yourself in. You've killed three people and are holding a fourth hostage, if you haven't already killed her yet. The police will not hesitate to shoot you if they feel it's necessary. You have to end this, right now."

I'm staring blindly at the pavement. I'll never be able to convince them. They'll lock me up and question me for days, trying to get me to tell them where Genevieve is, and in that time, this guy is going to kill her and then quietly disappear.

The situation from last night hasn't changed. If I turn myself in, Genevieve's dead.

"Clay, answer me."

I don't care if she doubted my innocence. If I was in her shoes, I would, too, and in spite of that, she gave me every chance to prove myself. She saved my ass more than once. Detective Mendez was right. She should have been suspicious, but if I turn myself in or if I try to escape Avalon, he'll kill her and they'll find me anyway.

Genevieve's terrified face stares back at me from the burner phone.

There's literally nothing left for me to lose.

"Clay?"

"Detective Mendez, I can't turn myself—"

"Damnit, Clay! Stop! Tell me where you are so we can come get you, and you can turn yourself in."

"I can't."

"And why the hell not?"

"I have to finish a game," I reply and hang up the phone.

The image of Genevieve goes dark as the battery in the burner phone dies.

Chapter 25

The waves crash and roil onto the sand, where a smattering of people have arrived to get some early morning rays before the rest of the beach-goers arrive.

I can't stay here for long. I've already seen more cop cars prowling the streets than I'd like, but that could also be my paranoia. I don't know if the discovery of Sydney Loomis has gotten out yet, but it's only a matter of time. Then, there'll really be no place to hide. I've got the cash and Genevieve's notebook in the duffel bag, along with the phones and the charger I purchased for the burner phone. All I need is an outlet.

That's what brought me here to the beach. No, not an outlet. I'm not gonna try to plug this thing into the sand. I need to get to the library, which is still about three miles away. I've come this far, but as Avalon awakens, I need to get off the roads in case someone recognizes me. I'm here because I know those cars that are parked on the street with drivers waiting inside are most likely rideshare drivers who will take cash. Just like at The Gryphon, they'll sit outside and wait. They're everywhere; bars, sports stadiums, any public gathering places, like this beach. I'm going to take my chances that this one driver won't recognize me instead of risking the hundreds of people who would see me if I tried walking the rest of the way to the library. Once I get to the library, my plan is to grab one of those study cubicles, which I figure is the best place to hide while the phone charges and I wait for instructions.

I select the red Chevy Spark with the younger guy behind the wheel.

"Hey, man," I say, stepping up to the open driver-side window. "You doing rides?"

He doesn't look up from the game he's playing on his phone. "Yup."

"You take cash?"

"Sure."

"Need to get to the library over on Vista Way."

He tosses the phone onto the passenger seat. "Hop in."

Simple as that, I climb into the back seat.

He barely glances at me in the rearview mirror as he starts the car. It's exactly what I was hoping for; youthful indifference.

Outside the window, the residents of Avalon are blissfully unaware of the alleged serial killer cruising by as they stroll along the sidewalks. The kid flicks on the radio. I'm worried that he may tune in to the local news but instead, he hits one of the preset buttons, and hip-hop music floods the car.

"Cool with you?" he asks, not bothering to glance at me in the rearview mirror.

"Perfect."

We've passed four cop cars on our way to the library. Is that more than usual? I have no idea but it feels like way more than usual.

He pulls over to the curb across from the steps leading up to the library.

"How much?" I ask.

"Let's call it ten bucks."

I pull a twenty from my pocket and hand it to him.

"Keep it."

"For real?"

"Yeah."

That may not have been the best move. I don't want this kid to remember me and my generous tip has caused him to really check me out for the first time.

"Cool. Thanks, man."

I open my door to get out. "Don't mention it."

"Hey, listen," he says as I step onto the curb.

"I gotta go," I protest.

"No. I know but let me give you my card." He opens the glove box, pulls out a cheap, flimsy business card, and reaches back to hand it to me. "You ever need a ride that you don't want the missus to know about, or whatever, you give me a call."

"You have cards?" I ask, taking the card and momentarily forgetting my haste.

"Sure. I've got my regulars. Love the cash. I mean, fuck the app and fuck Uncle Sam. Why should I have to split anything with them? Am I right?"

"Right." I stuff the card into my pocket. "Well, thanks for the ride."

"Thank *you*," he says, nodding to the twenty in his hand.

I shut the door and begin walking up the steps as he pulls away.

The Avalon Library is an old art deco building with white, stucco walls and a red-tiled roof. Instead of modern sliding doors, it has a brass, glass-paned revolving door. I've been here one time. It was a couple of years ago when I thought I wanted out of the bartending game and decided to "improve myself" by reading more books to become "educated". I spent twenty minutes breathing in the musty air and browsing the dusty shelves before saying to hell with it and buying a Kindle I've never used.

Thankfully, this place is massive. There are plenty of corners and crannies to hide. The librarian behind the large help-desk in the middle of the ground floor is too busy with a stack of books to look up as I enter and there are only a handful of people browsing the shelves.

I climb the thread-bare carpeted steps to the second floor, half of which is taken up with shelves. The other half is filled with cubicles that have raised partitions to help people concentrate, or to hide the faces of suspected serial killers, like me.

Taking my pick, I walk down the aisle, inspecting the floor underneath.

Here we go. This one, about halfway down, has an outlet in the floor below. I lightly set my thrift-store duffel bag, containing the notebook, phones, and charger, on the desk. I pull out the chair and sit down. I extract the burner phone, along with the new charger, and plug it in. The little lightning icon begins flashing red, which means it's charging, but there's not enough juice to turn it on.

I tuck my chair into the desk as close as possible to bury myself behind the wooden partitions.

While the phone charges, I'm going to try to find out who this guy is and if there is anything else Genevieve was hiding.

Setting the notebook on the desk in front of me, I flip open the cover.

Good lord. Her writing is almost unintelligible, but after staring at it like some sort of Magic-Eye image, it becomes a little clearer.

The first couple of pages of notes are an overview of Emily's murder. There's a brief summary of her life. There are some things I didn't even know, like where she went to school, her maiden name, and her wedding anniversary. There's also a write-up about Henry Parker with roughly the same information; school, birthday, employment history, etc.

Then comes three pages with the details of her murder; The Seaside Motel, naked, throat cut. Under that are hastily scribbled notes, like "kidnapped?" but it's crossed out. Then there's the word "affair". It's circled, underlined, and has arrows pointing to it. Next is a timeline of the day leading up to Emily's death. She had lunch with someone named Patricia Crawford at a restaurant called Brick & Mortar. Yoga at her preferred studio. Dinner at Noble's, 8pm. Then, at 10pm, The Gryphon. There are more scribbled notes: "Husband out of town. Went to bar alone. Meeting someone?"

It's unbelievable. Was it that easy to put all of this together from the beginning?

Below, there's a column of names marked "friends". I recognize some of the names as regulars at The Gryphon.

Yes, apparently it was that easy.

All Genevieve had to do was call these people and ask a few questions, which would have pointed her in my direction.

"Yes, I knew Emily Parker ... Her marriage? It wasn't going well ... I would catch a drink with her sometimes at The Gryphon. Her and the bartender were *very* friendly."

That would be all Genevieve needed.

Sure enough, at the very bottom of the page, there's my name with a big, old circle around it and the word "affair".

I know Emily and I weren't exactly being covert, but this makes it appear as though we were walking around with signs that read "WE'RE HAVING SEX!" taped to our backs. I don't know. Maybe we were.

I flip the page and it's a wash of more scribbled notes. This has to be from the night Genevieve was at The Gryphon and Henry Parker came to talk to me because here's his name and mine with a bold line connecting them. There are written questions like, "Did he know about the affair?", "Working together???". The question marks are almost carved into the page. I can just imagine her writing this at her table as she watched Henry Parker speak to me at the bar.

I flip the page. More notes. This time, they're about me. She's traced my entire life up until the moment she hounded me on the street corner outside The Gryphon. It's eerie to see the general timeline of your existence in a stranger's handwriting. I stop. "Emily Parker Dead. Murdered. Throat Cut". "Henry Parker Dead. Murdered. Throat Cut". There's a line from each to a name in the middle of the page; my name.

I flip through some more pages.

Now, I'm really in the picture.

There are a series of questions written down to ask me. Then, the notes that she took while I was duct-taped to the chair. It's all here; everything about the affair, how Emily and I met, where we would meet, Emily's attempt to keep it a secret by changing up motels, her use of the burner phone, and paying cash to rideshare drivers. Here's my accounting of the night at the Seaside Motel and my trip to the apartment where I touched everything. Here's my narrative of what happened at the Parker house when I found Henry Parker's dead body in the chair. Here's the word "perkiest" with a bunch of question marks and "my sweet little cupcake". I can only assume that she didn't believe me at the time, because she's jokingly drawn a frowny face next to it. The only thing that saved me was the text message from the psycho.

Here's her notes about the apartment, where her suspicions really started to grow. It was when she came back to The Gold Coast Suites Motel and found that I had been texting with him, and someone tipped off the cops to where we might be. She's written a series of questions: "How would the killer know that Emily would be at Seaside?", "Who knew where Henry Parker would be that night?", "Who would know the motels where C & E stayed?", "The fingerprints in the apartment?", "The blood in the car?", "Murder for hire?" After all of this is written one word: Clay. Underneath, she's written, "Cons: Why would he take the risk of contacting me? Who sent the text while taped to chair? Seems sincere."

There's nothing else because from that point on, we were on the run.

How could she possibly think it was anyone else?

Any rational person would have to think that—

The chirps and chimes of the ringing of the burner phone pierce the silence of the library.

I hastily pick it up as someone shushes me.

The caller ID displays the number of Emily's burner phone.

I hit the answer button and whisper, "Hello?"

The voice is garbled, like it's being run through one of those things you see in spy movies that masks the identity of the caller. "Are you ready to finish the game?"

"Is she still alive?"

"Yes."

"Let me talk to her."

There's the sound of the phone being moved around, and I faintly hear him instruct someone, "Say 'hi'."

"... Clay?"

It's Genevieve. Her voice is about to break.

"Genevieve?!"

Someone shushes me, again.

"That's enough," the voice says. Genevieve is still talking, but the killer walks away from her.

"You have to let her go," I say, fighting to keep my voice low.

"That's up to you."

"How? How is that up to me? You've been—"

"If you want to save her life, all you have to do is find me."

"How am I supposed to do that?"

"You've played the game so well. You'll figure it out."

"I can't! I'm not a detective. I'm not a reporter. I have nothing."

"Don't say that, Clay. You've gotten further than I ever thought you would. It was going to be over so quickly, but you escaped every snare I set by being decisive and resourceful. You've managed to survive when everything was stacked against you. It should be easy for you to ..."

As he drones on, my mind is racing through everything I know about him. I know he's smart. I know he's crazy. I know that

222

Henry Parker hired him to kill me and Emily, but he changed his mind, and Henry Parker tried to give me a clue—

"Perkiest," I blurt out.

He stops ranting.

"What did you say?" he asks.

"Perkiest. What does 'perkiest' mean?"

The silence on the other end of the phone stretches from seconds into what feels like hours.

"What does 'perkiest' mean?" I ask, again.

"Who told you that?"

The voice-masking thing he's using can't hide his surprise. He's rattled.

Did I just make a mistake?

By asking him what it means, I just showed him the only trump card he didn't know I had, but since I've already played it, I ask again, "Tell me what 'perkiest' means."

He laughs lightly.

"It means that you know everything, Clay. It also means we have to speed up our game."

"Wait! Wait, wait, wait. Why does that mean we have to—?"

"Tonight, I'll be where it all started. You can find me there, which means that you only have a few hours to figure it out. Find me, and you'll find your friend. If I see, or think the cops are with you, you'll never see your friend, or myself, again."

"Wait. No. I don't know what you—"

"Good luck, Clay."

The line goes dead.

There's less than an hour before the library closes.

I haven't eaten anything all day. The only time I've gotten out of this cubicle was to go to the bathroom. More people have come to the library, but there's been no danger of someone spotting me. Only about half of the other cubicles are in use, and no one's come near me. I've been left alone to stare at

Genevieve's notebook. I still don't understand what I'm missing. She was formulating theories and connecting dots that I never considered. How am I supposed to figure out something that she missed?

She knew about "perkiest" and she had researched way more information than I did, so what didn't she think of? Is "perkiest" code for something? Maybe it was this guy's codename.

"That's stupid," I whisper out loud.

It's not this guy's codename, and even if it were, what good would it do me? Who do I ask, "Hey, do you know a killer lurking in the underworld of Avalon who goes by the name of 'Perkiest'?" Ridiculous.

But he told me I had "everything". So, it has to be in this notebook. Why else would he initially freak out when I asked him?

I've texted Emily's burner phone, asking for more time, but they've all gone unanswered. This really is the last turn in our little "game".

Okay. I really can't start talking like him.

I start at the beginning of the notebook and work my way through for what has to be the fifth time. I've been doing this for hours and nothing in Genevieve's notebook has changed. It starts as the picture of a killer that quickly morphs into a picture of me, but the real answer has to be here. There must be something that Genevieve wrote down that can help me, something buried in these scribbled notes and pages of information.

The one thought my mind keeps coming back to is, what if she got something wrong? What if she got something wrong and that's what's keeping it all from falling into place?

That's not really fair. A lot of what's in here is what I told her, and I can't spot anything I said that's wrong or was misinterpreted. So, I don't think that's the issue. I told her everything that happened; at least everything I knew.

Did I get something wrong?

I don't think so. Everything I told her was accurate, as far as I know.

"The library will be closing in twenty minutes," a voice calls from downstairs.

I'm pretty sure I know where he's going to be, tonight, and I need to get there. I'm going to have to call that kid for a ride to—

My hand slides into my pocket. As soon as I feel the corner of the flimsy business card against my thumb, it's like a bucket of ice water has been dumped over me.

Genevieve wasn't wrong.

It was me.

I got something wrong. It was something I had just assumed. Genevieve and I had been mystified as to how this person seemed to know everything about Emily and me; first and foremost, how they knew where Emily would be the night of her murder, and the motels that she and I had used. How could anyone know that?

It was so simple and I had been the one to cloud it up, because I assumed something, something that the card in my pocket has now blown clear.

Of course, there was someone who would know that she would be at the Seaside Motel that night. Of course, there was someone who would know the motels we used.

I had assumed that she used different drivers, but what if she used the same driver?

What if, like the kid who dropped me off here at the library, she was someone's "regular" and she was using the same damn driver every time?

Suddenly, everything fits.

That's how he knew who I was. That's how he knew all the places we stayed. It's so damn simple. To put this all together, he had to have studied us. He had to have been parked outside The Gryphon, like all those other cash-accepting drivers, watching us through those big windows, present but invisible. That's how he knew who Katie was. That's how he knew Sydney Loomis. It's how he knew everything. How many times had I walked the street outside The Gryphon, seen the drivers waiting, and never given them a second thought? Hell, I've probably laid eyes on this guy a hundred times and never noticed.

There's no way to prove this, but I'm right. There's no other explanation, no other person this could be. I still don't know what "perkiest" means, but I know where to look tonight—

"Excuse me, sir?"

The librarian is standing next to the cubicle.

"The library is closing."

Without a word, I cram the phones, the charger, and Genevieve's notebook into the duffel bag. I quickly get up and breeze past him to the stairs.

I nearly run across the ground floor and shove my way through the revolving door on my way to where it all began.

Chapter 26

"Seriously, man, whenever you need a ride, you call me," the kid in the red Chevy Spark says as I hand him another twenty.

"Sure," I reply, stepping out of the car and onto the curb.

"Call me if you need a ride later tonight."

"Yeah. Okay."

There's no reason to tell him that one way or another, we'll never do business, again.

He drives off down the street, passing the entrance to The Gryphon.

Even at this distance, I can see through the large windows that the bar is packed. I guess the murder of two, well, now three regulars by their bartender is good for business. It makes a strange, morbid sense.

Every parking spot on the street is occupied. Some have the silhouette of the driver sitting in the front seat. One of these cars is my psycho. The problem is that I still don't know how I'll be able to tell which one, but I'm trusting that I'll know it when I see it.

A knot of people passes me on their way to The Gryphon. Only a week ago, I was one of them; blissfully unaware of the danger around me, of the plans that had been set in motion. Tonight, it will all come to an end.

I flip up the hood of my thrift-store jacket, bury my hands in my pocket, and begin walking slowly down the street. I was worried about being recognized, which is why I had the kid drop me off a safe distance from The Gryphon, but looking around, through this new lens on life which I've acquired in the last few days, it's obvious that no one is going to notice me. No one notices anything. Doing a quick scan of the street, there are three other guys who are walking by themselves, hands in their pockets, their faces to the pavement. No one is keeping an eye out for anything. They're only thinking about themselves. That's how this guy was able to hide in plain sight, but he's here now, and I have to find him.

The sun has set. There's a faint glow off the low hanging clouds but almost all of the light is being provided by the streetlamps overhead.

I continue my leisurely pace, eyes furtively darting back and forth, trying to mark every parked car, especially the ones with drivers in them.

Maybe he'll recognize me and wave me down.

Despite my revelation about how everyone minds their own business, I still don't want to get too close to the front door of The Gryphon. I'm not too worried about a stranger seeing me. I'm worried about one of the regulars stepping out for a smoke, or that I might catch Alex or Tommy on a break.

There's a flood of relief when, through the windows, I catch a flash of blonde hair as Katie comes around the bar. Normally, she'd be rocking out with a smile on her face and holding court. Instead, she looks frazzled. She's deep in the weeds and it's easy to see why; Tommy and Alex are behind the bar, trying to keep up with the drink orders. Two inexperienced bartenders and a crowd like that is a recipe for disaster. I don't know what happened after we dropped her off last night, but I'm just thankful that she's at work.

Man, what I wouldn't give to be behind the bar right now; to be cranking out drinks and slapping ass with Katie while flirting with the customers, pretending as though there was no such thing as "tomorrow", but I have to focus on the cars.

I pass one that has a driver inside. It's a woman talking on her phone. There are three rideshare company decals on her windshield, so she's got her bases covered.

There's another car across the street with the driver's face hidden in shadow. He takes a hit on a vape pen and turns his head in my direction when he senses me looking at him. He blows the billowy white fumes from his nostrils as he watches me. The fumes pour out of the open window and take on a luminescence from the streetlamp overhead.

Is that him?

He doesn't take any special interest or seem to recognize me. Also, for some reason, I don't think my psycho vapes. From our text conversations, he strikes me as someone who thinks too highly of himself to pollute his body in that way.

I'm close enough to The Gryphon that when a guy opens the door for his girlfriend, I can hear the commotion from inside; the loud music, the shouted conversations, the laughter.

I keep my head down, continuing to check out the cars on the side of the—

He's here.

That's him, about five cars up; the Toyota Prius. There's no doubt. That's "Perkiest". I can see the silhouette of the driver's head in the front seat. I don't know if he's seen me.

I quickly duck into the darkened alley between two buildings on my left. I stand motionless, my back against the wall, and take deep breaths, preparing myself for what I'm about to do.

Moments later, I step out from the alley and begin walking towards the Prius.

In the sideview mirror, I barely catch a glimpse of his face, which is shrouded in darkness. He's seen me. There's no going back.

I step over to his open window.

The faint light coming through the windshield casts a sharp shadow over the top half of his face, like he's wearing a cowl.

"How you doing this evening?" I ask.

"Good man. You?"

"Good. I'm good. You giving rides?"

"Yep."

"Cool." I glance around. "Listen, I've got a suspicious wife who's gonna take a look at the credit card bill and ask me where I went. You take cash?"

The corners of his mouth lift in the slightest of smiles. "Sure. I take cash. Go ahead and hop in."

"Great."

I climb in behind the passenger seat, keeping him in sight. I hesitate before closing the door so that the cabin light stays on a split second longer.

I want to catch a glimpse of what the Devil looks like.

His profile is unremarkable in every way. Thin frame. Short dark hair and a weak chin. Late thirties, maybe early forties. About average height, I would guess since he's sitting down. In fact, everything about him is average. If you saw him on the street, you'd never guess that there was anything interesting about him.

The inside of the Prius is like the inside of every other Prius I've been in. There's no strange smell or spots of suspicious blood on the gray cloth seats. Like its owner, it seems normal, boring, and routine. Nothing would tell you that this man has slit people's throats, strangled others, and stayed ahead of me and the police at every turn.

Once I close the door a second later, he pulls away from the curb.

"Where we heading?" he asks me in the rearview mirror.

I thought everything was normal about him, but I was wrong. Now that we're looking at each other, albeit through the mirror, those eyes are anything but normal. The confidence. The curiosity.

They're like two intense dark marbles that shine as we pass under each streetlamp.

"You know the big white house out on the sea road?" I ask.

He smiles. "I sure do."

"That's where we're heading."

"What's going on out there?"

"I'm looking for someone."

"Yeah?"

"Yeah."

There's a silence while he stares at me in the mirror, waiting for me to speak while he suppresses a smile.

"That's an interesting license plate you've got," I say. "'Perkiest'? What does it mean?"

"Wasn't mine. Got the car used. Too broke to change the plates. I should probably get new ones, though."

"Nah. It's cool."

I need to keep him talking.

"So, how's your night going?" I ask. "Been doing a lot of rides?"

"A few." He studies me in the mirror. "You look like you've had a rough couple of days."

"You have no idea."

"I'm pretty sure I do."

We cut through town. Instead of staying straight onto Sea Cliff Road, he turns onto Cheston, taking us away from the coast.

I turn and look at the intersection as it disappears into the distance. "Hey. Why are you heading north? The house is back that way."

"You don't want to go to the house."

"Why not?"

"Because the person you're looking for isn't there."

"What are you talking ab—?"

"Clay, you can stop pretending now. You've played a great game. Really, you have. You gave me a run for my money, better than anyone else, but you were never going to win."

I sit back. Well, at least the ice is broken. He's so confident and at ease. It's like we're going for a pleasant ride.

"Where are you taking me?" I ask.

"To her. That's what you want, right? Either you want to trade yourself for her, or you think that you can come up with some way to save her and yourself. It's really admirable. Maybe you're not such a bad guy after all."

"Will you let her go?"

"That's up to you."

Outside the window, the buildings are becoming more industrial as we reach the edge of Avalon.

"We going back to EZ Storage where you hid Sydney Loomis?"

"I didn't hide him. I left him there for you to find. Well, I should say 'to frame' and you have to admit, it worked better than I could have hoped."

"Except for the part where you grabbed Genevieve."

"What are you talking about? It worked perfectly. That's who I needed to get. I had to silence her. She was a much bigger risk to me than you were and I couldn't take a chance on grabbing you both at the same time. So, I used Sydney's body to divide and conquer. Of course, she would think you had something to do with it. It was one coincidence too many. Once I got her alone, I took her."

The car gently bounces and rocks.

"How did you know that we were at Nick McDermitt's house?"

"I didn't. I had no idea where you were, but I was outside The Gryphon, watching your coworker and her boyfriend the whole night. I couldn't understand the way that they were talking, like they were afraid of someone hearing them. Then, I figured it out. They were talking about you, and I knew they were seeing each other and his wife was away. Then, it was so simple. You couldn't be hiding at her place, so if they were talking about it, where else could you be?" My expression in the rearview mirror is giving him the ultimate satisfaction. "Yes, Clay. I know everything. I've been studying you and everyone around you for weeks. So, I slipped inside and left the key and keycard for her, knowing it would make its way to you, and then texted my little hint."

Genevieve was right. He's that smart.

"But how did you know we'd go there?" I ask.

"See, that's the beauty of it, Clay. Either you would show up at EZ Storage and the discovery of Sydney Loomis would further drive a wedge between you and Genevieve, or you would call the cops and they would find another dead body that was connected to you. Either way, I would win."

"Okay, but you have to give me some credit. I found you."

"You sure did, buddy, after I told you where I would be, and here you are, all alone, sitting in my car, as I drive you to … oh, I forgot, you have no idea where we're going, do you? Good job."

"My guess is somewhere northeast of town. Probably some place where—"

Anger flashes through those intense brown eyes. "Clay. The only reason you are in this car is because it is exactly where I wanted you to be."

There it is. There's the guy who could cut someone's throat. Those eyes were probably the last thing that Emily saw.

I settle back in my seat.

"Why?" I ask. "Why all of this?"

He's calm again, confident that he's in total control of the situation.

"Why should I tell you?"

It clicks. That question: "What can I get you?"

What do you want from me that will get me what I want? He's talking about playing a game. This guy outwitted the cops, outwitted Henry Parker, outwitted Genevieve, and outwitted me. He thinks he's brilliant. He might not be wrong, but here he is, forced to give rides for cash, under the table. How would that make this brilliant guy feel? Ashamed? Embarrassed? Cheated? It was right there in his text messages. After I escaped the house, he congratulated me. He said, "I guess like me, you're more than what people give you credit for."

What does he want?

The answer is obvious.

He wants to be recognized for his genius. He wants to gloat.

"Because I want to know how you did it," I say, trying to inject a subtle hint of admiration. "You outplayed everyone. I want to know how and why you did it."

His eyes narrow slightly in the rearview mirror.

Ohhhhhh, man, did I just hit the mark.

He so badly wants someone to know and acknowledge how clever he is, so I keep pushing.

"I *need* to know how you did it. Because let's face it; once you take me to where ever we're going, which looks to be in the middle of nowhere, even if I somehow convince you to let Genevieve go, this is probably my last car ride. If I played such a good game, the least you can do is to tell me." I glance out the window. "I want to know, even if I can never tell anyone else."

That smile, the relaxed confidence, like we've just shaken hands over a chessboard after I've laid down my king, is perfect.

"You've got nothing to be ashamed of, Clay. You also have to know that it wasn't personal. I really do have the utmost respect for you. I meant it when I said that you were like me. No one really looks at us. No one takes notice. We're only here to serve drinks and give rides. We are people without lives. No one thinks we're capable of doing anything else, until we're shoved into a corner and have to prove to them that we can do a lot more." He smiles warmly at me. "So, I respect you. And out of that respect, when the time comes, I will make it quick and painless. Okay?"

"Thanks," I reply, my skin crawling from his "noble" gesture. "So … Why? … Why all of this?"

He marshals his thoughts. After all, I might be the only person that will ever hear the details of his masterpiece. "Like you, I was stuck in a dead-end life. I moved here from Seattle. I had a number of jobs up there, jobs that had some future in them, but I let my emotions get the better of me. I was hot-headed, frustrated because I was being bossed around by idiots. It got me into trouble. I had to get away."

"You killed someone in Seattle?"

He lightly laughs. "No, no, no. I kept getting fired because of my intelligence. I was always the smartest person around, which people didn't like. I also had a temper. I punched one of my bosses. That led to problems getting a job. Well, a job that I was suited for, anyway. So, I had to get menial jobs, which was worse. I was so bored. I still hated my bosses. Then, I found that it was so much more edifying to mess with them. I didn't have to physically beat them. I could mess with their heads. And I'll tell you something, Clay; there's never a need to physically outmatch anyone you can outwit. Anyway, it got to the point that I needed a fresh start. And by that, I mean a complete fresh start, which is why I moved here. So, the answer to your question is, no, I didn't kill anyone in Seattle, but I had those tendencies. Those urges. I recognized them very early in my life."

Of course you did. You're so intelligent that you diagnosed yourself, didn't you, you freak?

"You know how serial killers start with animals as a kid and work their way up?" he asks.

"Yeah. I think I've heard something like that," I reply, keeping my voice as steady as possible. I need him to keep talking while I try to figure out where we're going, or hopefully get him to blurt it out.

"Well, that was me. When I was young, I wondered what it would be like to kill someone. I thought about going into the military to find out, but I couldn't deal with being disciplined by mental inferiors in order to explore my psyche."

"Is that all Emily Parker was? You were just acting out a curiosity?"

"No. Not at all. I have more restraint than that. I moved to Avalon and I was doing this rideshare thing for a little money. I had to create an entirely new identity for myself to try to get a job because no one would hire me due to my past. So, I was doing it under the table for cash. The Gryphon was a good place to set up shop. Lots of rich people coming and going. Not wanting their spouses to know. You and Emily Parker weren't the only ones sneaking around. There was your friend. The other bartender. What's her name?"

I glare at him in the mirror. "I hope you don't mind if I'd rather not tell you."

He smiles. "Clay, I already know her name. Katie Watson. She lives at 314 Kenniworth Avenue, apartment B. I wanted to see if even now, when all hope is lost, you would still try to protect your friends, and you did. You're an all right guy."

I think I'm going to be sick.

"Anyway," he continues, "one night, I was sitting outside The Gryphon and out comes Emily Parker. She asks if I'll give her a ride and says she only has cash. I told her it wasn't a problem. I drove her to some dive hotel and she gives me five times what I normally would make. After that, it became a regular thing. I'd wait outside The Gryphon and give her rides. She trusted me. It wasn't a bad little setup."

We approach an intersection with a four-way stop. He pulls through.

I glance out the window, again. "You might want to be more careful. You just rolled through that stop sign and I think I saw a cop car in the parking lot of that Seven-Eleven."

"Thanks," he says, confused but eager to get back to his story.

"So, I was her little driver. This went on for a while. I got curious as to why this woman, who obviously had plenty of money, kept going to crappy motels. So, one night, out of pure curiosity after I dropped her off, I hung around and there you were. I found out everything about you and that was that. I didn't really care. I only wanted to know who you were. It's in my nature. That's all. I knew she was married to that hot-headed asshole. Then, a few weeks after that, I had just dropped her off at a motel and this guy walks up to my window, all pissed off."

"Henry Parker?"

"Yep. He said he had been watching his wife and he wanted to know where she had been going and with whom."

"Did you tell him?"

"For a price. I needed the money."

"Did you tell him about me?"

"Kind of came with the package. Sorry," he says with a guilty shrug. "He was enraged. He said he couldn't call his wife on it because he had had affairs, too. She would divorce him and take half his money and he wouldn't allow that to happen. Can you believe that? It was fine for him to have affairs, but not her, and he was upset because if they divorced, he might only have ten million dollars instead of twenty million. You and I could live happily for the rest of our lives with that, but not this guy." His eyes light up. "Then, I had an idea. I had a way that solved so many problems. He could keep his money, I could make a lot of money, and I could indulge something that I had always wondered if I was capable of doing my whole life. And he would provide unlimited funds. I'd have every resource to carry out my experiment at my fingertips. It was a fledgling killer's dream. Something that was more than a once-in-a-lifetime chance."

"And he agreed to let you kill his wife?"

"Not right away. It took some convincing. I had to explain to him in exacting detail how I was going to do it."

"Which was?"

"Easy. I was going to frame you. A simple murder-suicide. It was my plan to get you at a motel. It was simple. Elegant."

"… How did you know about 'my sweet little cupcake'?"

"Oh, that was easy," he says, those dark gleaming eyes locked on me in the mirror. "You told me. Henry Parker had known about the affair for weeks. She had affairs before and this time, he bugged the house. He wanted proof. He recorded you saying it. I was trying to come up with a way to convince him to let me kill her. I asked him to tell me everything he knew about the affair and he played me the recording. Clay, it was too perfect. Not only were you the guy to frame, but you gave us the way to do it. That's what sold him. So, congratulations, Clay. You chose how she was going to die."

I've been holding it together, but now, my stomach is churning. I fight down a gag, sit back, and wait for it to pass as we approach a railroad crossing.

"You okay?" he asks.

"You can drop me off at these railroad tracks. I'll hobo it out of here and you'll never see me again."

He laughs. "I admire your sense of humor."

"Thanks."

We continue over the tracks and into the night.

"So, where did you screw up?" I ask.

Annoyance sweeps across his face, but it's quickly replaced by bemused acceptance. "It was something I've been meaning to ask you about and now seems to be the perfect time. I had studied you for weeks; noting what time you left on which nights, memorizing your schedule. That night, at the bar, you were supposed to be the first one off, weren't you?"

"Yes, I was … but I—"

"You switched with Katie?"

"… yeah."

He shakes his head. "That's all it took. After dropping off Emily Parker, I left to give you a few minutes to arrive. When I came back, there was a gray Honda Civic in the parking lot. I thought it was your car, and that you were already in the room. I was too anxious, too eager. It was my one screwup. I was going to come into the room and catch you two unaware, kill the both of you, and make it look like a murder-suicide. I had your suicide note all ready to go." He looks at me again. "You were very sad but passionate. You were heartbroken that she was going to leave you and you couldn't take it. You killed her and then killed yourself ... Imagine my surprise when I walked into the room and you weren't there. But in my defense, did you know that the gray Honda Civic is the most common car on the road in America?"

"You screwed up."

"Fine. Yes. I screwed up. I was over-excited. I should have checked the license plate, but ... oh well."

"'Oh well'?"

"No plan survives first contact with the enemy. You know who said that?"

"No."

"A man named Helmuth Karl Berhhard Graf von Moltke. He was a Prussian general from the eighteen-hundreds. Ever heard of him?"

Keep trying to impress me with your knowledge, buddy.

"Nope."

"Brilliant man."

We pass a sign that reads "San Francisco – 186 miles".

"We getting close or are we taking this all the way to San Francisco?"

"Maybe."

I need to get him back to his story.

"Tell me something: when I knocked on the door at the Seaside Motel, was she still alive?"

"No. She was dead. When I got to the door, I thought I was going to have to pick the lock but it was slightly open. I couldn't believe my luck."

My heart sinks. Emily liked to be waiting for me in bed, nude, with the door slightly ajar so that she wouldn't have to get up. Why would anyone think a killer was coming to their room? I can't let the guilt overwhelm me. I've got to stay sharp.

"I pushed it open and as soon as I saw her alone on the bed,

239

I knew what had happened. I screwed up and had to retake control of the situation, right away."

His description causes me to visualize the scene. I really am going to be sick. I don't want to hear any more, but I need to keep him talking.

"Why didn't she scream?" I ask.

He leans over, opens the glove box, and takes out a pistol.

"I wasn't going to fire it. It would have woken up every person in the motel but more importantly, it would have cheated me of the thrill. I wanted to see the life run out of someone. I needed to see the exact moment they weren't there anymore. I craved that sensation, but sadly I couldn't take my time. I had to kill her before you got there. So, I used the gun to intimidate her into silence, and then I cut her throat as soon as I could."

He sets the pistol on the passenger seat.

"Why didn't you kill me when I knocked on the door?" I ask.

"There was no way to make it look like a suicide at that point. I was going to use the gun for that, but once I realized you weren't there, I had to adapt. I could still pin the murder on you. I collected some of her blood and once I was done, I went to your place, broke into the trunk of your car, and smeared the blood in it."

"Wait. 'Once you were done'? She was already dead."

"There was more work to do."

"Like what?"

He smiles. "You know how I got your fingerprints in that apartment, right?"

"Yeah. You tricked me. Well done."

"Thank you, but how do you think I got hers in the apartment?"

"What are you talking about?"

"After you left, I went and got some boxes from my car. They were full of things like a toothbrush, coffee mugs, toiletries, silverware. I put her fingers on them and then after I put the blood in your car, I went and put the things in her apartment. I originally intended to put both of your fingerprints on them, but I adapted and got you to do it for me."

"But … Why do the apartment at all?"

"It was Henry Parker's idea. I told him I didn't think it was necessary. Frankly, I thought it was stupid, but he wanted to totally humiliate her, even in death. That's how petty he was. He wanted everyone to know that she was sleeping around, like it would make him look better. Like he was a victim. I tried to convince him that it was unnecessary, but he insisted on it. So, I made it work."

I'm too stunned to say anything.

"You have to appreciate the brilliance of it, Clay; adapting on the fly, keeping a cool head?"

I'm still incapable of answering, which causes his frustration to grow.

"Oh, come on, Clay. You're smarter than that. Don't be like them. Don't be ordinary. You can be appalled but still recognize that it was genius."

He's genuinely pissed off that I'm not congratulating him, that I'm not telling him how masterfully he's handled himself.

"Don't be like *them*?" I ask.

"Yes! Like them! The people who freak out. The people who think they want something, but when they're confronted with what it will take to get it, they run for cover, like Henry Parker."

"What happened to him?"

He shakes his head. "Exactly what I just told you. He was all for my plan until the night got nearer. Then, he started getting cold feet. Then there was the whole thing with Sydney Loomis."

"What was 'the whole thing' with Sydney Loomis?"

For the first time, I see something resembling disgust in his expression.

"The night after I killed Emily Parker, I decided to do a couple of rides for some extra cash. Mr. Parker hadn't paid me yet, because he was freaking out about what happened at the motel. So, I was in my old prowling grounds near The Gryphon, which was closed, and who should get in my car but Sydney Loomis. Did you ever talk to him?"

"Yeah. Whenever The Gryphon was closed, Sydney drank at the bar down the street."

He nods. "So, you knew him. He didn't say much but the man saw everything, and he recognized me from outside The Gryphon and he had seen Emily Parker get in my car on multiple occasions. Well, I couldn't have that. I had planned everything almost perfectly, except for taking into account some savant who watched and noted everything. I took him back to my place and strangled him. He didn't even put up a fight, really. I'm not sure he was capable of processing what was happening. Very unsatisfying. When I told Henry Parker about it, that's when he really lost it. He didn't understand that I had it under control."

"So, that's all Sydney Loomis was? Collateral damage?"

"You're still not seeing it. I was able to get control of the situation, overcome an obstacle, and even use it to my advantage. The only thing connecting Sydney Loomis to the Parkers was you." He looks at me in the rearview mirror. "Clay, I promise you; none of this was personal."

It's getting harder and harder to listen to this guy casually brag about how he wrecked my life before he finally takes it.

"Henry Parker was already freaking about you getting away from the motel. When I told him about Sydney Loomis, he lost it. That's when he tried to talk to you."

I'm still trying to wrap my head around it, now that everything has been pieced together. Knowing exactly what happened and picturing it in my head is almost worse than being clueless.

"Can you pull over at this rest station?" I ask. "I think I'm going to be sick."

He laughs as we drive past it.

"I was there, you know? That night Henry Parker came to the

bar to talk to you? I was outside, parked on the street outside The Gryphon. I saw the whole thing through the window."

"Of course you did. You were always there, weren't you?"

He eagerly takes up the bone I just threw him. "I was about to tail him when I saw the reporter go after him. That's when I realized that she was involved. So, I followed them both to his house. It was tough, but I waited her out. I guessed that he was waiting for you. He was trying to tell you something at the bar and you told him to wait until you were in private. You really are smarter than anyone gives you credit for."

"... Thanks."

"When I went inside their house, I tied him to that chair. I tried to get him to tell me what he wanted to tell you, but he wouldn't say. I knew he was trying to give me up. He couldn't handle the fact that I had gotten the better of him. Tell me; what did you two talk about?"

"He was trying to tell me who you were."

A menacing smile plays on his lips. "How did that go?"

"It didn't."

His smile widens. "That's because he didn't know my name. I gave him the fake one that I created. He thought he knew everything about me. Imagine how terrified he was when he realized he knew nothing."

"He gave me your license plate."

"That was all he had." His smile widens further. "And how did *that* go?"

"It's not a real license plate, is it?"

"It's easier to do what you want when you're no one. You have so much more power over people who have something to lose."

"Then you killed him?"

"It was perfect," he says with a contented grin. "It tied up every loose end. You were delivering yourself to the house, in your car, with her blood in the trunk. The police would find you there, and you had been at the motel, your fingerprints were all over

243

the apartment, and everyone at the bar had seen you talking to him. There was no way they would believe anything you said. It had all worked out better than I had planned." He gives me a look of mock disapproval. "Then you had to get all clever and escape … I'm kidding. I was incredibly impressed. It's amazing what you can do with your back against the wall, isn't it?"

"How did you find out so much about Genevieve?"

"Please tell me you weren't blown away by that. I know it looked remarkable but it was so mundane. It was boring. All of the stuff I sent to shock you is public information."

"What about the name of her cat?"

"She posted the cat's name and that photo on Instagram."

Now that he says it, he's right; it doesn't sound impressive at all.

"Why didn't you just leave?" I ask.

"What do you mean?"

"You had everything set in motion, all this evidence against me. Why stick around at all? You could have left Avalon at any time and I still probably would have been caught."

"If you had been caught at their house after you found Henry Parker, I would have. That would have been the end of it, but you just kept getting away, and I didn't want any loose ends. That would have been sloppy. Once you got the reporter involved, I began to worry. Then you went back to the apartment and when I saw you carrying a copy of the lease to the car, I knew you two were on the right track and I really couldn't leave until I had silenced you. Plus, I still wanted to see the visceral part of my experiment through."

"The part where you kill people? Your 'thrill'?" I ask.

He answers with a confident smile. "Guilty."

That's it. I can't think of any more questions. I now know everything that happened and what he intends to happen.

"Where is she?" I finally ask, glaring at him from the back seat.

"Not far."

We turn onto a two-lane road that winds away into the fields. There's a rusted signpost that reads "Orchard Lane". I can see the ocean in the distance.

"Well, we better hurry, because looking at the ocean is making me have to pee," I reply.

He contemplates me in the mirror. "That wasn't as good as your last joke."

"Sorry."

"It's okay. It's a common defense mechanism."

"What is?"

"Humor."

"Defense mechanism? Wouldn't that be a coping mechanism?"

"No. A coping mechanism is used for problem solving. Defense mechanisms are techniques used to avoid dealing with a situation. I've read a lot about it."

"I'm sure you have," I say, fighting the urge to add "you educated psycho".

Up ahead, there's a light in the darkness of the lonely road. It's faint, but grows as we approach.

"That it?" I ask.

"No more talking."

He turns off the road and into the driveway. The headlights sweep over a rusted mailbox, a small, squat, abandoned house, and a detached garage at the end of the drive. The windows and doors of the house are long gone. It's like the owners left sometime in the nineteen-thirties and never came back. There's a car under a tarp parked to the side of the driveway. I assume it's Genevieve's rental.

He stops the Prius in front of the garage.

"What is this?" I ask. "Are you squatting at your childhood home in the middle of nowhere or something? Going back to where it all began?"

"That would be poetic, but no. Just squatting." He frowns. "You'd make a terrible psychologist."

He grabs the pistol from the passenger seat, gets out, and makes his way around to my side, leaving me alone in the car for the briefest of seconds before he opens the door.

"Let's go," he says.

I don't move.

"Clay?"

"If you're going to kill me, why not just do it now?" I ask, while mentally pleading for him not to kill me now.

"I just told you why I'm not going to kill you out here."

He needs his fix. He wants to see the life run out of me. He needs to get the satisfaction he didn't get from Emily Parker or Henry Parker or Sydney Loomis.

"I do like what you're trying to do, though," he says.

"Yeah? What am I doing?"

"Playing for time. You're still trying to figure out if there's some way you can win this thing. You're not freaking out. Not cowering. You're not giving up until it's finally over. I admire that, Clay, I really do, but now, it is *finally* over. For both of you."

"Is she still alive?"

"She might still be. I hope so. Let's go into the garage and find out."

I refuse to move. I need more time.

He points the gun at me.

"Clay, don't make me do this."

"Don't make you do what? Shoot me? Why not? Because you won't get your thrill?" I really hope it's dark enough in this backseat that he can't see how much I'm sweating or how badly I'm shaking.

He points the gun at my knee. "Maybe I'll just wound you."

"You're gonna shoot me in the leg? You'll have to carry me into the garage."

He rolls his eyes. "Fine."

He adjusts his aim and fires.

My left arm erupts in blinding, searing pain.

.I scream and thrash across the backseat. I try to move my arm but it's useless. I press my right hand against the wound. Blood pours out through my fingers and the pressure of touching it brings a shockwave of pain throughout my body. I continue screaming until my lungs can't scream anymore.

"No one can hear you, Clay. That's why I chose this place," he says, growing impatient, "but we do have to get going."

He points the gun at my other arm.

"Okay! Okay! Please," I plead, holding out my blood-soaked hand.

He backs away and allows me to pull myself out of the car with my good arm. My left arm hangs limply at my side. He doesn't seem to care about how badly I'm bleeding. It's not a good sign for how much time he thinks I've got left.

"This way," he says with a nod towards the side of the garage.

I shuffle up the drive and approach a door in the side of the garage.

"Here. Let me get that for you," he says with a mocking smirk and pulls it open.

I step inside.

In the dimness, I can see that the floor is covered with a plastic tarp. The smell of urine and feces assaults my nostrils. He steps behind me and closes the door, plunging the room into total darkness. There's a click and a work light illuminates the garage.

It's a "kill room".

Plastic tarps cover not only the floor but the walls. There's a table off to the side, upon which rests an array of knives and other cutting tools. There's a chain with a hook suspended from the ceiling. Hanging from the hook by her bound wrists is Genevieve. She's gagged and there are bruises about her face. She's wearing the same clothes as when I last saw her. Next to her is a wooden chair. She blinks as her eyes attempt to focus.

She sees me and those eyes fill with fear and hopelessness.

"Genevieve ..." I whisper.

247

The blow to the back of my head sends me staggering forward and I fall to the ground. Out of instinct, I try to stop myself, but only one of my arms works. My face slams into the tarp-covered, concrete floor. He's instantly on top of me, pulling my arms back, which causes me to scream in agony. It's like shards of broken glass are scraping against one another in my shattered arm. He binds my wrists together with some sort of cord while keeping a knee squarely on my back. Once completed, he hauls me up, thankfully by my good arm, drags me to the center of the room, spins me around, and pushes me into the chair, next to Genevieve.

I can't stop screaming. I can't see.

"Clay?"

He's barely audible over my cries.

He slaps me across the face.

As the entire side of my face goes numb, he winds up and slaps the other side.

My ears are ringing. I've stopped screaming. I'm trying to work my jaw. My arm is still in anguish, but for the moment, I'm focusing on the pain in my face.

My vision settles.

He's standing over me, smiling.

I turn my head and lock eyes with Genevieve.

It's over. She knows it.

"I really do admire you," he says, turning to the table of knives and selecting a gleaming, razor-sharp scalpel. "You had to have known that this was probably how it was going to end, and you took the chance anyway, trusting in yourself, that maybe you could make it work. That maybe, you could find a way out. That really is admirable." He slowly walks back towards the chair and looms over me. "And against anyone else, you would have won." He holds the scalpel inches from my face. "But unfortunately, you got dealt a superior opponent. And now, as you said earlier, 'I'm going to get my thrill'. I'm going to cut you open and watch the life run out of you. I want you to scream. I want you to beg. I want you

248

to tell me how much it hurts. I want to record in my mind the moment you are no longer here. And I want her," he says with a flick of the scalpel in Genevieve's direction, "to watch. I want her to see because I want her to know that she's next, and as I watch you die, I'll know what I need to do differently with her to make it more pleasurable for me." He lets it sink in. "See how well I've planned this?" He leans back and lovingly runs a finger over the scalpel, applying the lightest touch. Then, he shows me the trickle of blood it's drawn, demonstrating the sharpness of the blade.

"Now," he says, drawing a deep breath. "Shall we begin?"

He brings the scalpel closer to my neck.

I lean backwards, trying to put as much distance between me and the scalpel as possible.

In one last monumental effort, I focus my mind, steady my voice, and start speaking as loudly and rapidly as I can.

"Okay! Okay, that's it. Do it now. Whatever you're going to do, do it now. You have to do it now. Hurry, hurry, hurry, hurry. Let's go! Let's go! Let's go!"

Confused, the psycho stops, the scalpel almost touching my skin.

"I'm … I'm about to cut you open. I said I wanted to hear you beg and scream, and you're telling me to hurry up?" He shakes his head with a *tsk-tsk-tsk*. "Clay, I've already told you that I respect you. You don't have to keep up this show of being br—"

"Oh, would you please *shut the fuck up!!!*" I spit at him.

He stares at me, completely baffled.

I keep my eyes fixed on his.

"I'm not talking to *you*."

One last time, allow me to back this up.

He's here.

That's him, about five cars up; the Toyota Prius. There's no doubt. That's 'PERKIEST'. I can see the silhouette of the driver's head in the front seat. I don't know if he's seen me.

I quickly duck into the darkened alley between two buildings on my left. I stand motionless, my back against the wall, and take deep breaths, preparing myself for what I'm about to do.

But first, I take out Genevieve's phone and call Detective Mendez's number.

"Clay?" Detective Mendez asks.

"Yeah."

"Where are you?"

"Outside The Gryphon, but I need you to listen to me. He's here."

"Who?"

"The killer. The one who killed the Parkers and Sydney Loomis and he's got Genevieve."

There's a pause.

"Clay, you need to stay right there."

"I can't. If you send cops, they're going to arrest me, he's going to drive off, and Genevieve is dead."

"He's in a car?"

"Yeah."

"Okay," he says, satirically. "Can you see the license plate?"

"PERKIEST. P-E-R-K-I-E-S-T."

"Seriously?"

"Yes! Damnit, hurry up."

There's the sound of typing through the phone and then, another pause.

"Clay, what are you trying to pull?"

"What do you mean?"

"It's not a real plate."

My heart falls into my stomach.

I now know what I have to do. I wish there was some other way, but it's the only chance to save Genevieve. It's the only chance to save us both.

"Clay? You still there?"

"Okay. Okay. I'm going to get in the car with him."

250

"What? Clay, I don't know what's going on but—"

"No. Shut up and listen. He's in a green Prius. I'm going to keep talking. Do not hang up this phone! I'm going to try to tell you what's going on and hopefully, he'll take me to Genevieve. I'll try to let you know where we're going, okay?"

"Clay ... What are you doing?"

"Essentially, I'm butt-dialing you."

Back in the garage, the realization slowly overtakes the psycho.

With his free hand, he furiously digs into my pocket. He picks the wrong one first, tries the other, and finds Genevieve's phone.

He holds it up.

The call is still going.

His eyes go back to me and I see it; he's replaying the drive to this place in his mind. There's the recognition, the fear, and finally, the understanding that I outplayed him, even if it all may be in vain. He's remembering everything I said.

"Why are we heading north?"

"I think I saw a cop car at that Seven-Eleven."

"Are we taking this all the way to San Francisco?"

"You can drop me off at these railroad tracks."

"Can we stop at this rest station?"

"Looking at the ocean is making me have to pee."

"Are you squatting at your childhood home in the middle of nowhere or something?"

And, of course, in those brief moments he left me alone in the car outside, he didn't hear me say "One-four-one-seven Orchard Lane", which is a combination of the road sign I saw, plus the numbers on the mailbox I witnessed at the end of the drive as we pulled in.

For the first time, there's fear in his eyes.

He looks at me and a single thought passes between us.

He's killed three innocent people.

He meticulously planned it out and adapted every step of the

251

way to make sure I would be blamed, but in this final round, even if he kills me right now, and this is the last thing I'll ever see on this Earth, at least I have the satisfaction of knowing I've robbed him of his thrill and totally fucked his plan.

He looks back at the garage door and listens.

It's quiet, but who knows for how long.

His calm, collected demeanor is gone.

Enraged, he hurls the phone away and lunges for me, scalpel in hand.

I press my chin to my chest, trying to protect my throat.

Genevieve tries to scream through her gag.

He steps behind me and wraps his arm around my head.

With no hair to grab, he's forced to pull against my forehead.

I struggle, trying to curl myself into a ball to protect my neck. I no longer feel the pain in my arm. Everything I have is being put into keeping my chin against my chest, but his frenzy is too much. He's able to pull my head back a fraction of an inch.

The scalpel finds its way under my chin.

He slashes.

I don't really feel anything until the blood starts running down my shirt. I try to once again press my chin to my chest, like it will somehow close the wound.

I fall forward, out of the chair, and onto the floor.

He goes for Genevieve.

She's screaming and struggling.

I can't move.

Blood, my blood, is spreading out across the plastic tarp in front of me.

My vision begins to fade.

Genevieve is still screaming and fighting.

She grunts and there's the sound of an impact.

He curses.

At that moment, just as my vision fades to black for the last time, the large garage door explodes inwards.

There's screaming.

Blue and red lights flash across my eyes.

There are loud bangs but they sound like they're on a train, being carried away into the distance.

People are running. There are hands on me.

The last thing I hear is Genevieve's shriek.

"CLAY!"

Everything is nothing.

Chapter 27

Click-click-click-clickety-click-clickety … click-click-click …

Genevieve is sitting next to my hospital bed, furiously typing on the keyboard of her laptop. She's been here every day that I've been awake, and I'm guessing the days before that, too.

I try to turn towards her, but the best I can manage is to look at her out of the corner of my eye. There's a brace around my neck to prevent me from moving. The doctor told me that I really don't want to turn my head. My arm is also immobilized in a cast.

"How's the story coming?" I ask. My voice sounds like sandpaper being scraped across a cheese grater.

She glances up, gives me a quick smile, and goes back to typing.

"Good. I'm at the part where we went to EZ Storage. The *Herald* wants the whole thing by Thursday." Her fingers tap-dance across the keyboard. "How are you feeling?"

"I could use a lozenge."

That gets a chuckle out of her.

She reaches out and hits the button on the side of the bed that delivers a hit of sweet, sweet morphine through the IV in my arm.

"Thanks."

"My pleasure," she says.

It had been extraordinarily close.

Thanks to my struggles, he didn't hit any major arteries in my neck, but he hit enough and he also sliced my windpipe. The surgeon described it as a very barbaric tracheotomy. It would have taken a couple of minutes, but he definitely did enough damage to punch my ticket. The only thing that saved me was the fact that Detective Mendez dispatched an ambulance with the fleet of cop cars as they tried to follow the vague directions from my butt-dial.

They're still trying to ID the guy from his dental records because it's all they have to go on. He had nothing but fake IDs and a stolen car with fake plates. They're also checking rap sheets in Seattle but no luck, yet.

"Who got him?" I asked Detective Mendez when he gave Genevieve and I the rundown after I woke up from surgery.

"I did," Detective Mendez said. "I was the car that busted through the garage door. Had the first shot at him."

"Yeah, about that," Genevieve said. "You could have killed us both."

Detective Mendez shrugs. "It was either ram through the door and take a chance that I would maybe hit one, both, or none of you, or go around and knock, where he definitely would have killed you both. It worked out for the best, so let's not dwell on it."

I tried to point and laugh at Genevieve, but my arm didn't work and my attempt at laughter led to a bout of sputtering and coughing.

"I'll leave you two for now," Detective Mendez says but turns to Genevieve. "However, Ms. Winters, I am going to need to have a long talk with you and your editor."

"I hope you're not too upset with him, Detective. He was covering for me and he wasn't technically lying. The *Herald* didn't send me to work on the story."

"No," Detective Mendez says. "They'll just reap the benefits when you run it."

"And I assure you, in my article, I do nothing but praise the Avalon Police Department and I will particularly highlight your attempts to protect me," Genevieve replies. She sounds sincere.

"Will you allow me to read the article before you go to print?" he asks.

Genevieve gives him a sly smile. "It sounds like you've worked with reporters before."

Detective Mendez smiles back. "Unfortunately, yes."

"You can read it beforehand, but I won't alter it."

"Fair enough."

"It seems the least I can do," she says. "Seeing as you're the one who shot the guy before he put a knife in me."

"Then, I guess we'll call it even."

Every reporter wants the story, but Genevieve is holding all the cards. As I said, she hasn't left my side since I've been awake. From time to time, she'll ask me about details as she writes. I've gone over the ride to the abandoned house and garage at least a dozen times. I know she's working on the story, but her concern is more than that. She's slept in the chair beside my bed more nights than I've been able to count, even when I commanded her to go home and get some real sleep in a real bed, but I'm really glad she's here. More than once, I've woken up with the feeling that there is a blade under my chin and she's talked me down. I've caught her freaking out too. She'll be typing and the sound of the keys will come to a sudden stop. I'll look over and she'll be shaking with tears running down her cheeks. She hasn't gone into detail about the twenty-four hours she spent hanging from that chain in the garage. I don't blame her.

"He got in your head, didn't he?" I asked.

She nodded.

We quietly held hands until it passed.

* * *

256

After another week, and a lot of ice chips later, it's time to go home.

They took off the neck brace this morning. Genevieve stood by and did her best to hide her shock as the nurse removed it.

"How bad is it?" I asked.

I thought I saw smoke coming out of Genevieve's ears as she struggled to come up with something positive to say. The best she could manage was, "Well ... It's like I said; you should probably grow your beard back as soon as possible."

"Good morning," the nurse chimes as she enters the room, accompanied by Detective Mendez.

Genevieve is in her chair, working on her laptop. Ever since the brace came off this morning, I've been pacing around the room, thankful to be out of bed and at the absence of IVs in my good arm.

"Are you excited to be leaving us?" the nurse asks.

"No offense, but you have no idea," I respond. It's getting easier to speak and my voice sounds less and less like an anti-smoking ad.

"I've got a car waiting out back," Detective Mendez says. "I'll drive you home."

"I'll take him," Genevieve offers.

"Is that all right?" I ask.

Detective Mendez shrugs. "I don't see why not. We've got all we need for now. If there's anything else, we'll be in touch."

"Thank you, Detective Mendez," I say, shaking his hand.

"Take care of yourself, Clay."

He leaves and I turn to Genevieve.

"Let's get the fuck out of here."

The morning is gorgeous.

It's the first time I've been outside in over two weeks and the sunlight feels amazing on my skin. There's a faint trace of the ocean on the breeze.

My window is rolled down as we drive through Avalon. Genevieve takes the long way. She's got the streaming music station set to hits of the nineties. I try to sing along but it's too much and the strain hurts my throat.

We approach The Gryphon.

"Fancy a drink?" she asks.

"Absolutely not."

We finally pull up to my apartment building.

We get out and stand on the sidewalk at the start of the path leading up to my door.

"So, what happens for you now?" she asks. "You going to stay in Avalon?"

"I think it might be time to move on."

"Where you gonna go?"

"Don't know, but they need bartenders everywhere."

"Well, don't go too far. I'm going to need your help with the best-seller I'm writing about all of this."

"The profits of which we'll split fifty-fifty, right?"

She gets a pained expression. "More like fifteen-eighty-five."

"My agent may have something to say about that."

"When you get an agent, we'll let our agents fight it out."

I lightly laugh but grimace at the pain. It passes and we share a silent moment on the sidewalk.

"Thank you, Genevieve."

She smiles. "Thank you, Clay."

We shake hands, which feels awkward, until we pull ourselves into a long embrace, which I can only manage with one good arm.

"Take care of yourself," she says as we part. "And get that beard back."

"Will do."

She walks back to her car.

"Thirty-seventy?" I playfully call with my hoarse voice.

"We'll see what the agents say."

I wave as I watch her drive away and then turn and walk to the door of my apartment.

I've forgotten how small this place is.

The screen in the bathroom window hasn't been replaced since the night I crawled in here to get the jar of change.

It's amazing how unlived-in this apartment looks, and I don't mean from these past few days. I mean that there is nothing personal to me on the walls. Not even any art that I might enjoy on the walls. Nothing that really makes this place mine.

What do I do?

What's the first thing you do to get back to a normal life after you've gone through something like this?

Watch television?

Make yourself a snack?

Catch up on emails?

The answer is obvious: there's no going back to a normal life. Not here. Not after this. I was right when I told Genevieve that it might be time to move on. The life I had in this apartment, in Avalon, at The Gryphon, is over.

It's time to go.

I find the box in the closet and take out the map of the United States, along with the single dart.

I mount the map to the living-room wall, which is not an easy task with only one arm.

I take a few steps back and stare at it.

Where to?

Florida? Nah. No one wants to bartend there.

Being overrun by kids ordering drinks on spring break sounds like a nightmare.

The Pacific Northwest? Oh god, no. I have bad memories associated with Seattle and I've never been there.

My eyes drift to the right, eastward, across the country.

I hear Atlanta's nice.

I take a general aim, close my eyes, and throw.

**Gripped by *Deadly Games*? Don't miss *Dark Hollows*,
another unputdownable novel from Steve Frech.
Available now!**

Acknowledgements

I again have to thank everyone in my HQ family.

Less than a year ago, my debut was published, and it's been an amazing ride. One of the biggest things a new author learns is that these stories are nothing without the support, guidance, and contributions of countless people. From the graphic artists who design the eye-catching covers, to the legal department who makes sure everything's in the clear, to the editors who catch the small typos or misplaced commas so the reader won't get pulled out of the story, to the interns who support it all, and to people like Abigail Fenton, who are the teachers, cheerleaders, and captains. I can't say it enough, but I will say it again: thank you.

And finally, I also want to thank each and every person I encountered in the years I worked behind the bar while dreaming and working to become a writer. Thank you for telling me your secrets and providing me with the experiences that make up this book. You are all in these pages.

Keep reading for an excerpt from
Dark Hollows ...

I'm standing in the basement of a run-down, abandoned warehouse, staring at the padlock on a heavy steel door. The walls are coated in grime and there is the sound of dripping water from somewhere in the darkness.

The padlock begins to tremble. It's subtle, at first, but then grows violent, as if some enraged, unseen force is trying to pull it open. The padlock rattles against the door.

"No ... please ... please, hold ..." I whisper, my voice weak in pain and fear.

The shaking intensifies. It begins to infect the door and the walls, filling the basement with a low rumble.

"Don't ... I'm so sorry ... Please ..."

The rumble grows into a deafening roar. It feels like the entire building is going to come down on top of me. Bile rises in my throat.

"No ... no ..."

Everything stops.

I know what's coming. I know what's behind that door.

Oh my god, what have I done?

The lock snaps open.

*   *   *

I sit bolt upright in bed. Sweat pours down my face and my lungs pull in rapid gulps of air.

In the dawning light of morning, I can see Murphy, my black lab mutt, lying in his bed in the corner of the room. He cocks his head at me.

I grip my side and hiss through clenched teeth. Sitting up so fast causes the old injury in my side to flare with pain, but it passes. I steady my breath and wipe the sweat from my eyes. I throw off the covers, hop out of bed, and head to the bathroom. The nightmare is nothing new. I've been having it for years, reliving the panic and shock of that night over and over, but I've learned to quickly put it out of my mind.

After throwing some cold water on my face, I pull on a pair of jeans and a shirt and head downstairs to start a pot of coffee. Murphy joins me in the kitchen, but instead of coming over to the counter, he sits next to his food bowl and gives me those big, dinner-plate eyes.

"What? Are you hungry?" I ask.

His tail thumps against the floor.

I feed him a little dry food from the bag in the pantry, and then go to the window over the sink and glance down the drive, past the pond, to the cottage sitting at the edge of the woods.

The Thelsons' car is gone. No surprise there. They said they were getting an early start back to Manhattan.

Coffee in hand, I walk to the front door and pat my leg as I step out onto the porch.

"Let's go, Murph."

Murphy inhales the last of his breakfast and hustles after me. I don't think I've ever seen him chew, even when he was a puppy. He springs off the porch and down the steps. We walk past the pond, towards the cottage. As we pass the truck in the driveway, I make yet another mental note to fix that damn taillight. Somehow, all the mental notes I make about it go unremembered.

I walk around the fire pit and note the wineglasses sitting next to the chairs. I step over to the front door of the cottage, take out my key, and open the door. Before doing anything, I go to the kitchen table and open the guestbook. I flip through the pages until I find the latest entry. The ink is so dark and sharp, it had to have been written not more than an hour ago.

We were in town from Manhattan to do some leaf-peeping and had a wonderful time. The Hollows is a beautiful little town. We loved the shops on Main Street and strolling through the cemetery at the Old Stone Church. What can we say about Jacob's cottage? So amazing! We began every morning with a walk through the woods to check out the hills and always stopped at 'The Sanctuary'. Jacob is the perfect host. The wine and the s'mores were just the right touch. And then, there's Murphy! Such a sweetie! Can't wait to come back!

~ John & Margaret Thelson

I snap the guestbook closed and look around the cottage. It never fails; whenever someone from Manhattan signs the guestbook, they always have to mention that they're from Manhattan. Hopefully, they'll post the review on Be Our Guest this afternoon, once they get home.

The Thelsons were standard New York City types; taking their yearly fall pilgrimage up north to see some trees. They were a wealthy couple who would call this quaint, one-bedroom cottage 'roughing it', even though it had all the amenities, a couple of bottles of wine, and a fire pit outside. Still, they were pleasant, and they've left the cottage in good shape. The turnaround should be quick, and I've got it down to a science.

Murphy walks through the open front door. He's done scouting the fire pit for any stray graham crackers or marshmallows left by the Thelsons, and goes right for the kitchen to see if there are any scraps lying about.

"Happy hunting, Murphy," I say. He deserves it. He's one of my best selling points.

I clap my hands and rub them together. "All right. Time to get to work."

First thing I do is bring in the wineglasses and wash them in the kitchen sink. Then, I collect the bedsheets and towels, put them in a bag, and carry it to the house. Murphy follows close behind. I take the bag down to the basement and pop the contents into the washing machine. Even though we've done this process hundreds of times, Murphy bolts as soon as I open the lid because to him, the washing machine is still some sort of monster. Once I get that going, I head back upstairs. Murphy's on the porch, waiting for me.

"Coward," I say.

He responds by letting his tongue flop out of his mouth and starts panting.

As we begin walking back to the cottage, Murphy spots the ducks that have settled onto the glassy surface of the pond. He pins his ears back and sprints after them.

"Murphy!" I shout.

He stops at the water's edge and looks at me.

"Nope. Come on."

He stares at the pond and then back at me as if to ask, "But do you not see the ducks?"

"Come," I say, with a forceful slap on my leg.

He runs to catch up, but instead of following me into the cottage, he lies down on the cottage porch to enjoy the cool New England morning.

I restock the complimentary toiletries and clean the bathroom. No disasters there. One time, I had a young couple from Los Angeles stay for a weekend and after drinking too much wine, they destroyed the bathroom. I almost left them a bad review, but they were in the "Elite Class" on Be Our Guest, so I held my fire. Thankfully, they left me a glowing review.

I finish scrubbing the tub and stand up a little too quickly. The pain in my side flares again, but it barely registers.

Time to tackle the kitchen. I clean the plates from the s'mores and refill the basket by the coffee maker with packs of Groundworks coffee. I wipe down the counter and sweep the floor. After that, I retrieve the vacuum cleaner from the hall closet. I have my routine down, working my way from the bedroom, then the bathroom, down the hall, and into the living room/kitchen area.

I push the vacuum around the bookcase, which is filled with some of my favorite books—a few thrillers, some Michael Crichtons, *A Christmas Carol*, et cetera. No one reads them while they're here, but they make for good pictures on the Be Our Guest website. There's also a row of DVDs no one watches: *Casablanca*, *When Harry Met Sally*, *Vertigo*, *Roman Holiday*, and *Dead Again*. As I glide the vacuum cleaner over the rug by the fireplace, my eyes catch the stick doll I made years ago, resting on the mantel. It's a crude figure made of twigs tied together with twine. It adds a nice, rugged touch to the place. In Boy Scouts, they taught us to use pine needles instead of twine, but those don't last long—

"For me?" she asked in mock flattery.
"Just something I learned in Boy Scouts."
She saw right through my bullshit.
"Well, I shall treasure it always," she said, clutching the
    doll to her chest, toying with me …

I'm pulled from my memory by Murphy whining.

He's sitting in the doorway. His expression is a perfect balance of wanting to enter the cottage but respecting the vacuum cleaner.

I flip the switch, and the vacuum engine whirrs to a stop.

"Done," I tell him, and put the vacuum back in the closet.

While in the closet, I rotate the stacks of towels, and accidentally knock over the small dish hidden on the top shelf, which contains a spare key to the house and the coffee shop. I keep a spare key for both out here because I learned the hard way that I should when I locked myself out of the house about a year ago. I put the keys back in the dish, tuck it all the way back on the shelf, and close the door. I pull out my phone and take a series of pictures of the cottage. It's been a while, and I need to change the photos on the Be Our Guest website.

I head back to the house and transfer the sheets and towels to the dryer. Once again, Murphy stays by my side until I get to the basement stairs, because the dryer is the washer's evil twin. That accomplished, I head back down to the cottage to do one last spot check to make sure everything is perfect.

I normally wouldn't do an extra check, but tonight, I'm breaking a rule.

Here's the deal—a few years ago, my parents died. We weren't particularly close. In fact, we weren't close at all, which is strange for an only child, but there was history. They were the successful, wealthy, married couple who had done everything right, while I was nothing but one dumb decision after another. I could never get my feet under me and it was my own fault. I squandered every chance they gave me.

It got so bad that they finally cut me off after I screwed around my sophomore year in college. I had to find another way to pay my tuition, which I did. I told them I got a job, but not the whole story about what the job was. They were pleased that I had finally taken responsibility for myself and tried to reconnect, but for me, the damage had been done. I wanted nothing to do with them. There were obligatory phone calls on Christmas and birthdays, filled with awkward conversations. I was living in Portland, Maine, while they had moved to Hilton Head, South Carolina.

Their passing was quick. Mom became ill. I offered to come down and help out, because that's what an only child does, right, even if we hadn't really spoken in years? Dad declined my offer, claiming he could handle it. Well, he couldn't. The stress got to him and he had a heart attack. It was over before he hit the floor. I got the call from the nurse Dad had hired to look after Mom. On my way down to the funeral, Mom passed away. The nurse said it was from a broken heart. I didn't know how to feel. They hadn't been a part of my life for so long, it felt like they were already gone, but I did wish that I had maybe tried to patch things up.

The dual funeral was surreal. There were a lot of people there, and I didn't know any of them. When they found out who I was, they came up and commented on how painful and sad it must be for me, and what wonderful people my parents had been. I tried to be sympathetic, but I worried that they would be able to tell that I really didn't know my parents. The worst was having to give a speech. I felt like a fraud. No, I *was* a fraud. Thankfully, any question of my sincerity could be chalked up to shock and grief. I felt guilty for not knowing them. All those people were moved by their passing, and I was ashamed of myself. I pictured what my funeral would look like, and it was not a well-attended affair.

Then came the will.

My parents left me everything. There was no personal declaration in it—no directions as to what I was supposed to do with their life's savings. There was only the simple instruction that I was to receive everything. I assumed that it was their way of saying that I had shown myself worthy after making my own way. Maybe they were saying that they were sorry. Maybe they thought that some day, we really would be a family again. I don't know, but that's when I made the decision. I had made so many mistakes—the worst of which were only known to me. I decided then and there—no more messing around. It was time to straighten out my life.

I grew up in Vermont, and since I was looking at this as a

reset, I decided to go back. I did my research, found The Hollows, and bought the property on the outskirts of town. The nearest neighbor was a half a mile away. The property was secluded, but not isolated. I loved the plot of land, which was nestled up against the woods. There was the main house, the pond, and the cottage. The cottage had been the main house when the land had been a farm, but around a hundred and fifty years ago, the land had been sold, the new house built, the pond dug, and the cottage was abandoned. The fact that the main house was old gave it a sense of maturity and responsibility that I now craved.

I also loved The Hollows. It had originally been settled by two French explorers in the early 1600s, who named it "Chavelle's Hollow". Then came the British, and after the French-Indian War, they decided to change the name to "Sommerton's Hollow", in honor of the British General, Edward Sommerton. The problem was that the town was so small and located right on the border between the French and British territories, people called it by both names. Then the American Revolution happened, and Sommerton served in the British Army. After the war, the citizens of the newly formed country didn't want to have a town honoring their recently vanquished enemy, so they changed the name to "Putnam's Hollow", in honor of Rufus Putnam of the Continental Army.

This all happened so fast, relatively speaking, that people were calling the town by all three names at the same time, depending on if they were French, British, or American. When the town finally got a post office, which is what makes a place an official town in the eyes of the government, the surveyor was so fed up with trying to determine the correct name for such a small town, he simply wrote down "The Hollows", and it stuck. The Hollows became one of those towns you see on travel websites—a charming New England town with a Main Street comprised of three-hundred-year-old, colonial-style buildings, a town green, an old stone church, and winding roads, hidden among the rolling hills and forests.

After purchasing the house, I moved on to the next phase of my plan—opening my own business.

I rented a storefront on Main Street and opened a coffee shop. Like the rest of the town, Main Street was a postcard. The centuries-old buildings that line the street each have a plaque identifying the year they were built and for whom. Instead of switching to electric lights, the town kept its old gas lamps. At night, it was a fairy tale.

My shop was a small, single-story structure just down and across from the church, which everyone called the Old Stone Church. My coffee shop's large front window gave the perfect view with the town green across the street, and the old cemetery next to the church, to the south. I named the place "Groundworks" and began my little endeavor. I quickly realized that I had bitten off way more than I could chew, but since there was no Plan B, I had put nearly all of my inheritance into the house and the shop, so I had to stick it out.

Little by little, I got it under control. I started by giving out free samples of Groundworks' signature coffee to the local hotels and B&Bs to put in their guestrooms. They jumped on it as a way to promote local business. That's what the fall tourist season is all about. The Hollows is a cottage industry. It also paid off in that everyone staying at the hotels and B&Bs came to the shop during their exploration of the surrounding hills and countryside. I slowly fought my way out of the red, and while things were looking up financially, it was really hard work.

One downside of moving to a new town and putting in so many hours was that I was lonely. On an impulse, I took a trip to the local animal shelter. Behind the shelter was a pen where they allowed the dogs to run and play. I told myself I was going to adopt the first dog who came up to me. I stepped through the gate and this little black ball of fur with oversized paws broke from the pack and came flying at me, ears and jowls flapping wildly. He charged and didn't stop. He simply plowed into my shins and careened across the ground. He instantly sprang up and repeated the process. After the third time of tumbling over my feet, he was going to try again but was so dizzy, he fell over.

I was laughing so hard, tears poured down my cheeks, and I had to sit down. The mutt leaped at me and attempted to lick my face off. That was that. I named him Murphy, and we've been inseparable ever since. I'm not exaggerating about that. In four years, we've rarely left each other's side. With the long hours I was putting in at the shop, I couldn't leave him at home, alone, so I brought him with me. Before long, Murphy was Groundworks' unofficial mascot.

I remodeled Groundworks to give it an "old-timey" feel and it started to pick up steam. I was there almost fourteen hours a day, seven days a week. Business continued to grow.

One morning two years ago, Maggie Vaughn, who runs the Elmwood Hotel a block away, stopped by to pick up her supply of coffee, and remarked that her hotel was so full, she was turning people away.

That sparked an idea to give myself a side project and make a little extra coin.

By that time, I had hired some staff to lighten the load and had some time for myself.

I had been using the cottage as storage for Groundworks, but I took out some money, and renovated it as a place to stay. I fixed it up into a charming, one-bedroom affair with a remodeled kitchen and bathroom. I even added the fire pit out front. At the time, Airbnb was starting to take off. I thought they might be too crowded, so I went with a rival start-up called "Be Our Guest". It marketed itself as a more selective and upscale version of Airbnb. They weren't going after people looking to save a buck. They were after wealthy people wanting a different experience. These were exactly the tourists who were coming to The Hollows.

Since Be Our Guest was new, they wanted unique properties. I contacted them with photos of the cottage, and they went berserk. A representative from Be Our Guest came out to inspect the cottage and loved it. We went through the formalities. I had to sign a bunch of papers, promising to comply with their policies, one of which was that I wouldn't become involved "physically or otherwise" with a guest during their stay at my property. I had to submit to a background check, which always makes me nervous. I was confident they wouldn't find anything, but still, I worry.

Once that was done, I was cleared for takeoff, and take off, it did. Be Our Guest ran the cottage as a featured property and immediately, the reservations filled up. It was great. I was charging $200 a night in the off-season and $300 a night in the fall. If I wanted to, I could have booked the cottage every night. It's the easiest money I've ever made. I usually only saw my guests once or twice. They were always polite—well, most of the time—and all it took was an hour or two, at most, to clean and reset the place after they left.

Some of the hotel owners in town were upset that I had gotten into the game, but not too upset. They were still operating at capacity. I think they were more worried that other residents with extra bedrooms might try to go the Airbnb route. Anyway, like I said—easiest money I ever made. I could set my own dates, and if I wanted to take a break from keeping up the cottage, I just blocked out a week or two here and there. People enjoyed their stay. I made sure to keep the cottage stocked with wine from local wineries and coffee—only Groundworks, of course. Once I put in the fire pit, I also made sure to have the stuff to make s'mores in the kitchen. Everyone took advantage of it.

And everyone loved Murphy.

I did have some rules, though. I didn't allow anyone to stay at the cottage who hadn't already written at least three reviews on Be Our Guest. That's one of the beauties of the site. Hotels have to let anyone stay at their place, so long as they have a credit card. With Be Our Guest, I get to vet who stays at my place. I can see what they've said about other places, and you can tell who's going to be a problem by their reviews. They're the people who are determined to have a bad time, no matter what. That's my rule—three reviews to prove that you are a reasonable person. It's my most sacred rule.

And tonight, I'm breaking it.

Two months ago, I received a request from a woman named Rebecca Lowden to stay in the cottage for one night only. I was going to reject the reservation request when I saw that she had no previous reviews, but I always check the reservation request to see where they heard about me to stay informed about where Be Our Guest is advertising. I clicked on her request, which took me to her profile page. She was undeniably beautiful, with brown hair and blue eyes, but it was her bio that caught me.

In the bio sections, Be Our Guest encourages you to list things, like your hobbies, favorite books, and favorite movies. As one of her favorite books, she listed *A Christmas Carol*. And in the "favorite movies" section? *Dead Again*, which is in my top five. Also, she had grown up in a town not too far from where I grew up.

So, out of simple curiosity, I broke my rule and accepted the reservation.

Dear Reader,

We hope you enjoyed reading this book. If you did, we'd be so appreciative if you left a review. It really helps us and the author to bring more books like this to you.

Here at HQ Digital we are dedicated to publishing fiction that will keep you turning the pages into the early hours. Don't want to miss a thing? To find out more about our books, promotions, discover exclusive content and enter competitions you can keep in touch in the following ways:

JOIN OUR COMMUNITY:

Sign up to our new email newsletter: hyperurl.co/hqnewsletter

Read our new blog www.hqstories.co.uk

🐦 : https://twitter.com/HQStories

📘 : www.facebook.com/HQStories

BUDDING WRITER?

We're also looking for authors to join the HQ Digital family!

Find out more here:

https://www.hqstories.co.uk/want-to-write-for-us/

Thanks for reading, from the HQ Digital team

ONE PLACE. MANY STORIES

Dear Reader,

We hope you enjoyed reading this book. If you did, we'd love to know. Your feedback is important to us. It helps us and the author create the books that you want to read.

If you enjoyed this book, please consider leaving a review. It will help you return to pages that you want to read, it takes only a minute. To find out more about our books, new titles, and to join our author and reader communities you can find us in the following ways.

JOIN OUR COMMUNITY

Sign up to our newsletter to get all our latest news first

Read our blog www.hqstories.co.uk

https://twitter.com/HQStories

www.facebook.com/HQStories

SHARE YOUR REVIEW

Write and submit your review to join the HQ Digital family
Find it here
https://www.hqstories.co.uk/join-hq-why
Thank you for reading from the HQ Digital team

If you enjoyed *Deadly Games,*
then why not try another gripping
thriller from HQ Digital?

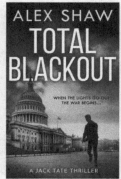